"I had hoped [...] would think of me as a friend."

"That's part of the problem, Emilie. The story of your past seems to keep changing, depending on whom you're talking to. What you told Master Sergeant Fetterman doesn't exactly fit with what you told me, or with what Jerry Maxwell told me about your past. Is there any truth to any of it?"

"A little. Enough. What does it matter?"

"Who are you?" Gerber practically shouted.

"You know who I am. I have told you. I am Brouchard Bien Soo Ta Emilie. I was once a Vietcong. Now I am a Kit Carson scout for you."

"And whose side are you on, ours, or the VC?"

"My own, Captain. There is no other side worth being on."

There was a long moment of silence.

"If you find that I am the traitor you believe me to be, you will then have to kill me, yes?"

Gerber said nothing.

"Suppose I were to walk away right now. Just disappear into the bush and never come back?"

"Then *I* would have to kill you, ma'am, with much regret, of course," said Fetterman, who had come up softly behind her.

VIETNAM: GROUND ZERO
THE KIT CARSON
SCOUT

ERIC HELM

A GOLD EAGLE BOOK FROM
WORLDWIDE

TORONTO • NEW YORK • LONDON • PARIS
AMSTERDAM • STOCKHOLM • HAMBURG
ATHENS • MILAN • TOKYO • SYDNEY

First edition June 1987

ISBN 0-373-62706-8

Printed in Canada

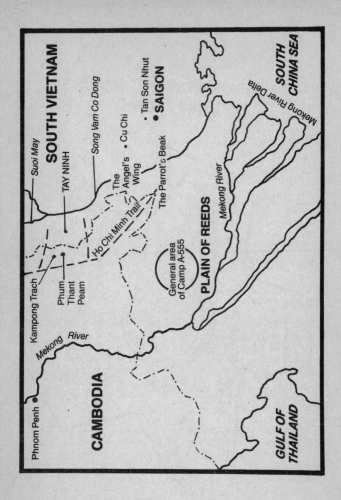

U.S. Special Forces Camp A-555
(Triple Nickel)

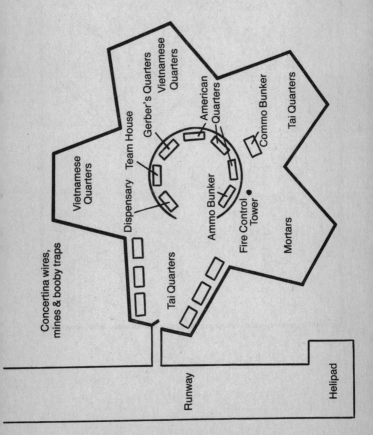

VIETNAM: GROUND ZERO

THE KIT CARSON SCOUT

PROLOGUE

THE HO CHI MINH TRAIL
NEAR PHUM REUL
CAMBODIA

North Vietnamese Army Corporal Tran Minh Ngo sat in the nearly nonexistent shade of the devastated jungle, sweating from the heat and exertion of his march along the trail. In moist hands he held the diary that he had just started. He wanted to record everything that he saw and felt because he believed that the people of the North, the people who lived under the constant threat of American bombing attacks, or the terrorist raids of the Saigon government commandos, would want to know how their soldiers who were sent south lived. Ngo was determined that the North Vietnamese, his people, should hear the real story rather than propaganda speeches given by the political officers who knew no negative words.

He leaned against the rough bark of a palm, wiggling his shoulders to kill an itch in the middle of his back, and read what he had written.

"We march in the forlorn gray of the jungle, along the Ho Chi Minh Trail, moving away from it and following paths that only our guides know. We march across land that has been stripped bare by the American planes raining orange death. Huge trees, their branches all naked, reach into an uncaring sky. We rest for a few minutes, seeking shelter under the few trees that seemed to have escaped, but whose leaves are beginning to shrivel, a sure sign that they will die. It is here we wait for the rain that will soak us and then never dry; for the sun to set so that the land will cool, but never does. It is here we wait for the Americans in their expensive war machines to find us and kill us.''

Ngo studied the paragraph, written in light blue ink on rough paper already yellowed with age. Sadly he lifted his eyes to look at the men of the platoon around him. They were young men, almost all drafted in an effort to keep up with the flow of Americans into the South. These youths, Ngo knew, wanted only to work their father's rice paddies or vegetable gardens or cornfields, to chase and sometimes catch the local girls, and maybe make a pilgrimage into Hanoi. Many of them had never heard of America or the war in the South and cared nothing for the goals of the National Liberation Front or the unification of Vietnam. They only wished to go home and forget about the pain and suffering of the long march into the south.

''We held a big rally before we started,'' Ngo continued to write. ''There were many army officers, village leaders, important men there. They talked of the glorious fight in the South and our duty to the people of the South, caught by the American lackeys. I did not understand all of what the officers said, and I was confused by the number of men who had traveled to our village to speak to us. Each had something to say. There was talk about the great adventure on which we were about to embark. We were reminded of our duty and our courage and our sacrifice. All spoke to us, except one man who wore a strange khaki uniform and said he was a comrade from China. He had fought the Americans in a place called Korea, he told us, where the great might of the Americans had been unable to overwhelm the Chinese comrades.''

Ngo sat back, looked into the gunmetal sky and blinked rapidly, unable to believe all that he had just written. It had an unreal quality, like a photograph that was slightly out of focus, or something remembered from the distant past. But it wasn't the distant past, only a few weeks ago. Still, it now seemed to be an eternity away.

The NVA corporal turned his attention to the young men who had attended the meeting with him. Together, they had marched west, into Laos, and then south into Cambodia. They were armed with AK-47s, the assault rifle that the Russians had invented, then given to the Chinese, who in turn had passed it to the NVA for their war. Some of his fellow soldiers wore dark green fatigues, marking them as members of the NVA. Others wore black shirts and black pants that the Americans called pajamas. All wore large backpacks loaded with spare ammunition, extra food, medical supplies and a few small personal items, like the tiny black notebook that Ngo carried.

The food wasn't much. A couple of small sacks of rice, maybe a few fish heads mixed in, and a biscuit or two. These rations didn't need cooking; smoke from a fire sometimes drew American planes. And the traffic along the main arteries of the Trail ensured that they didn't need to carry much. Their officer could requisition food from the porters moving supplies on their bicycles. Or he could take them from the villages they passed, sometimes giving the headman a worthless receipt for the food.

Ngo looked down at his notebook and added, "They call this a Trail. The men in the North are proud of it. The Americans claim it is a highway to the South. But we march uphill all day, everyday, it seems. Always climbing, through jungle that tries to grab us and hold us. Ten, twelve hours a day, always marching, never talking, never joking, and listening to the buzz of annoying insects and the roar of American planes. Planes that fly over us day and night, searching with their electronic eyes but never seeing us."

He read what he had written and knew that he had to write something more positive. The political officer, if he wanted, could take Ngo's notebook and read it. Ngo didn't want to be punished for his work, so he added, "Around us is the destruction brought by the Americans. Trees scattered to the four winds by the imperialist bombs. Trees with trunks of gray that look like old farmers forced into their fields for one more day of work for the pleasure of the capitalists. A jungle paradise ruined as if we had somehow angered the gods and they had unleashed their fury on us."

The lieutenant left his place of honor, under the largest tree with the heaviest foliage, and told the men it was time to move. As Ngo slipped his notebook into his pack, he was ordered to move forward with the local guide to help clear the Trail. Ngo shrugged and took the machete from the man who held it. He looked at the sharp blade, which caught and reflected a bit of sun that found its way through the overcast sky.

The corporal took his place next to the guide. The man pointed, and Ngo slashed at the vines, bushes and short, skinny trees, clearing them from the path as they moved into thicker, greener growth. This portion of the jungle had escaped the devastation of the Americans.

The work, at first, was simple. The blade was so sharp that it seemed to cut through the thick vegetation on its own. But then the heat began to sap Ngo's strength, and his arms became weary. Sweat poured down his face, staining his already soaked black shirt. He felt wetness under his arms, on his neck and down his back. His feet seemed to be awash in water. The ground was covered with rotting vegetation that absorbed moisture of a hundred monsoons and then released it when disturbed to make the trek harder and more miserable.

It took only a few minutes for Ngo to feel worn out. His breath was ragged in his throat, and his mouth felt as if it was filled with dry leaves. His arms ached with the strain of swinging the machete, and he knew that he would soon collapse. Worse yet, the moment he fell to the ground, unable to move, he would be shot by their lieutenant, who despised them and thought of them all as peasants. Where was the celebrated Trail, Ngo wondered, that the Americans, with all their technological know-how and their great firepower, could not close? Where was the superhighway that would allow them to ride to the South in the trucks given to them by their comrades in the Soviet Union so that they didn't have to struggle through thick jungle in the mountains?

Just when Ngo thought he would drop and be shot by the political officer as a weakling and a coward, the guide stopped. Ngo observed that they were on top of a cliff and could now see down into the surrounding jungle. Portions of the Trail appeared far below them, cut into the virgin vegetation to leave red, gaping wounds that seemed to bleed a sea of mud. It crossed his mind that this was the way it must appear to the American reconnaissance aircraft that roared overhead. The clearly marked, rutted road was so wide that two Soviet ZIL trucks could pass side by side.

And directly in front of him was the edge of a huge stone cliff that descended into the jungle—a steep limestone formation exposed to the sun and the sky. To the right, Ngo noticed crude stairs carved into the face of the cliff. Partially concealed by bushes growing from the rock, the stairs descended into the ocean of the jungle, lost from sight where they passed the top of the trees.

It would be a long, dangerous climb down that could only be completed at night when the enemy planes wouldn't be able to see Ngo and his platoon strung out on the cliff, perfect targets for the automatic cannons on the American fighters.

The lieutenant called a halt and Ngo gratefully fell to the soft jungle floor. For a moment he was too tired to even fight the canvas cover of his canteen, but then thirst won out and he pulled it from his belt. He drank slowly, sloshing the water around his mouth before swallowing it. Having finished his drink, he fell back to the ground, lying there watching the heavy rain-swollen clouds boiling over his head, wishing that he was home, watching his child-swollen wife work the rice paddy.

1

EAST OF THE HO CHI MINH TRAIL NEAR PHUM REUL CAMBODIA

Nearly a klick away from Corporal Tran Minh Ngo's platoon, on the eastern side of the Ho Chi Minh Trail, United States Army Lieutenant Jason Kincaid lay hidden in the thick foliage on the top of a cliff that overlooked part of the Trail. From his perch, he watched the traffic flowing into the South, recording the numbers of vehicles, bicycles and people that he saw. Behind him, six other Americans scanned their back trail, making sure that no one sneaked up the rear of the slope to cut their throats while they did their job. And surrounding them were four Vietnamese who knew the area and who served as scouts and riflemen.

Kincaid was getting sick of it all. He had to lie in virtually the same position all day because the slightest movement could be detected by an alert enemy observer. Then there was the heat that baked him and the humidity that soaked him. On top of all that were the clouds of mosquitoes that came at dusk and left thick black smudges as he brushed them from his body when he could no longer stand the tickling of their tiny feet or the pricks of their snouts on his arms, neck and face. Flies hovered around his head during the day, some of them landing to bite him. Finally there was the chance that someone would make a mistake, which would bring the wrath of the entire army of North Vietnam down on them.

Kincaid wanted to get a drink of water but couldn't shift around far enough to get at his canteen. Actually he didn't want water. He wanted an ice-cold beer, served by a waitress in a skimpy costume at one of the army clubs springing up around South Vietnam. He wished he could take a shower right now so he could get the sticky, smelly scum off his body that caused a bright red rash, which itched almost uncontrollably. In his mind he saw a bed with clean sheets and no insects, in a room that had air-conditioning; air you could breathe without the feeling that your lungs were filling with water. He had heard that there were men who spent their whole tours in such luxurious conditions, claiming to one another that war was hell.

A tap on his foot by one of the other men warned him that someone was coming. Kincaid moved his right hand an inch and touched the black plastic stock of the M-16 that he had been issued before the mission. With his thumb, he snapped off the safety and then waited for the men behind to alert him to more danger.

Far below, on the Ho Chi Minh Trail, the traffic continued to move unabated. There was the rumble of a diesel engine from a ZIL pulling a long-barreled antiaircraft gun that Kincaid thought was a Soviet-made S-60. In the past few days he had witnessed that sight several times: Soviet trucks dragging antiaircraft equipment, ZSU-23s and S-60s, all heading south.

He closed his eyes to concentrate on the sounds around him but could hear no one moving through the jungle close to him. He waited. There was a second tap, telling him that the enemy—an armed patrol—was moving in his direction and that it hadn't spotted the American LRRPs or their South Vietnamese allies yet.

Kincaid realized that he was holding his breath, and he let it out in a long, slow exhalation. Feeling the ache in his muscles, he tried to relax. The tension threatened to make him jumpy, and that was the last thing he needed. The enemy must have turned, because he got no further warnings.

Suddenly there was a ripping sound, as if someone was tearing silk near his ear. Kincaid recognized it as a single AK-47 firing on full-auto. Around him, he heard the leaves being stripped from the trees and bushes as the bullets tore through the vegetation. When the firing stopped, there was a deadly silence throughout the jungle. The diesel engine had quit rumbling, and the roar of jets overhead had vanished. Kincaid heard a quiet rustling as a beetle dragged food across the dead leaves.

A single, quick snap followed as one of the men fired a round from his M-16. A moment later a grenade detonated, showering the nearby vegetation with dirt and debris. A cloud of dust and smoke drifted through the trees.

"To the south," whispered one of the NCOs.

Kincaid rolled to his left and stood up next to the smooth trunk of a teak tree. He saw one of his men kneeling by a bush, a claymore firing control in his hand. Another of his men had dropped back and was crouched behind a log. His weapon was aimed at something in the jungle, but he didn't fire.

For an instant everything remained in stasis. Kincaid could see or hear nothing of the enemy or his men. He waited, his weapon held at the ready, his eyes scanning the jungle. With an effort, he tried to swallow, anticipating return fire. The shooting had to attract attention. In the the past two days he had seen several hundred enemy soldiers pass him. Now they could be running back up the Trail, hoping for a bit of the action while the American soldiers waited for orders from their NCO.

Kincaid turned toward the west. Through a gap in the trees and bushes, he made out a section of the Trail. The activity seemed to have ground to a halt as the VC and NVA scattered at the first sound of firing. Kincaid glanced at the ridge far to the west and thought he could see movement at the top of it, but then his attention was drawn back to his side of the Trail.

One of the NCOs appeared in front of him. "Parker's going to pop the ambush. Viets will cover the rear."

Kincaid nodded and pointed to the rear, to the south. "Get everyone else and go about a hundred yards or so and wait."

On turning back, he heard a series of explosions, loud, sharp bangs, as the claymore mines, which had protected the rear of their formation, were detonated. Firing erupted in the jungle, and muzzle-flashes winked in the half-light of the thick foliage, followed by the sounds of bullets snapping through the jungle around him.

Just then Parker appeared, running in a crouch, his M-16 in his left hand. Kincaid pointed to the south and then turned to run. In a few seconds they found the first NCO.

"Anything in front of us, Davis?"

"No, sir. Jungle's clear."

"Then get a point out and head due east. We'll come to a hill-top that is fairly open. If we can make radio contact with base, we can use it for extraction."

"Yes, sir."

"Near the stream, divert to the south and then back east," added Kincaid.

Davis understood the plan. They had laid a second mechanical ambush, which they could use to slow down their pursuers in case they were followed. He dropped his pack that contained food, clean clothes and a few personal items, then took off, trotting into the trees, leaping over a fallen log and dodging around a rocky outcrop.

As Davis disappeared into the trees, Kincaid threw his back-pack into the pile and followed. Parker added his, directed the rest of the men to do the same and then stuck a WP grenade under them so that the enemy, when they found the packs, would trigger the grenade. Parker hoped that the white phosphorus would kill any VC who happened upon the gear and destroy everything they were forced to leave behind.

For nearly an hour they jogged through the jungle. After only a few minutes at that pace, it felt as hot as the inside of a steam bath. Sweat poured from them, and their lungs screamed for oxygen, the pain in their chests almost unbearable. The men scrambled down the hillside, splashing across a small clear stream and leaving thick muddy stains in it. Finally they made it into dense jungle.

They stopped, and Kincaid tried to arm the mechanical ambush. His hands were slippery with sweat. He rubbed them on his thighs, then continued to work on the grenades and clay-mores while Davis strung the trip wires and Parker kept a look-out for the enemy with the rest of the LRRPs.

They finished quickly. The trip wires would jerk grenades with no pins from C-ration cans and explode in the center of the nar-row weed-choked path. Others would fire claymore mines and rake the most likely hiding places with thousands of tiny steel balls. There were also a couple of special grenades with long-delay fuses that the VC might think were duds and put into their packs to use later. These grenades had chemical-fuse delays of an hour or more.

Without a word to one another, they started running again until they reached the top of a hill that was only two miles from the Cambodian border. They stopped at the edge of the trees and looked out on a clearing sprinkled with stumps, dwarf bushes and other debris. Near them the jungle rose to nearly a hundred feet, but there was no sign that the VC or the NVA had ringed the clearing with bunkers as they sometimes did in South Vietnam.

Kincaid took out the URC-10 UHF radio, extended the antenna and whispered, "Sidewinder, Sidewinder, this is Mamba."

There was a quiet crackle of static and then a voice said, "Mamba, this is Sidewinder. Authenticate."

"Sidewinder, I have whiskey, tango, tango, hotel, Yankee, uniform."

"Roger. Say message."

"Extraction. Code three-one-one-three. Immediate."

"Understood."

Kincaid collapsed the antenna and moved close to his two NCOs. "We'll be extracted about dusk. Let's spread out and see if anyone followed us."

Both men nodded and moved deeper into the jungle. The tiny force fanned out, looking for hiding places while they waited for dusk. Kincaid stopped at the edge of the clearing, settling into a shallow depression at the base of a huge flowering bush where he could watch part of the jungle and all of the clearing.

THE HEAVY BEAT of rotors told Kincaid that rescue was close. He extended the radio antenna and waited. There was a sudden scream of jet engines as two F-4 Phantoms buzzed the clearing, one of them passing so close that the heavy black smoke from the engines settled to the ground and the jet blast shook the trees.

Both climbed suddenly to the west, broke around and came back. Far to the south, as the light was beginning to fade, Kincaid saw a C-130 orbiting. He figured it was probably still over South Vietnam and high enough to be out of effective range of small arms and 12.7 mm machine guns. Kincaid wondered how far south those S-60s and ZSU-23s had gotten, and if they could get them back in time to throw some flak at the aircraft.

Once again he was asked to authenticate and to give the condition of the LZ. Kincaid responded with the proper code and added, "The LZ is cold."

"Roger. Inbound. Will you throw smoke?"

"I will throw smoke," said Kincaid. He jerked the last smoke grenade from his pistol belt, pulled the pin and tossed the grenade into the clearing. A yellow cloud billowed upward, and Kincaid knew it would make a visible smudge against the darkening landscape.

"ID yellow," said the pilot.

"Roger yellow," said Kincaid. He collapsed the antenna and tucked the radio into a pocket. To Davis and Parker, he spoke in a stage whisper. "Chopper's inbound. Let's go."

The men moved to the edge of the clearing but remained hidden in the trees. They could just make out the helicopters, dark shapes in the rapidly blackening sky. Kincaid took his weapon off safe and listened to the jets as they circled the area, waiting for a chance to pounce on the enemy, searching the ground for a suitable target.

As the helicopters crossed the last of the trees and began their final descent into the clearing, a landing light stabbed out, illuminating the ground momentarily, then was quickly extinguished. Kincaid leaped from the trees and jogged across the open field as the helicopter flared, the rotor wash hitting him like the wind from a dying hurricane.

Davis and Parker followed their lieutenant, the rest of the LRRPs spread out behind them, watching for the enemy. As the chopper's skids hit the dirt, there was a single burst of fire from a light machine gun. Green tracers flashed out of the jungle, some of them slamming into the side of a Huey like someone was banging on it with a ball peen hammer. Return fire erupted from the door gun, and a three-foot-long tongue of flame licked at the jungle where the enemy was hidden, the ruby tracers disappearing into the blackness.

Both jets peeled off, dived and then came back, their cannon raking the jungle in sustained bursts. From the south slope of the hill, 50-caliber machine guns returned fire, filling the sky with crisscrossing patterns of emerald tracers.

Kincaid leaped into the cargo compartment of the helicopter as AKs opened up in the tree line. The muzzle-flashes looked like lightning bugs gone mad. He swung his own weapon around but held his fire.

There was a piercing scream, and Davis went down, rolling to his back, one hand clawing at the sky. Parker skidded to a stop and ran back. He snatched at Davis's hand and tried to jerk him to his feet. Another of the LRRPs grabbed at Davis, dragging him upright. The enemy firing increased. Green tracers bounced around them, some spinning into the sky. The door guns began to hammer steadily, the ruby tracers punching into the jungle, aimed at the muzzle-flashes.

Kincaid dropped to the skid, felt a hand on his shirt and saw one of the crewmen grabbing him. The man jumped around Kincaid and ran to Parker and Davis as the enemy found their range. Suddenly the earth around them seemed to explode, and they all went down in a loose-boned fashion that suggested they were dead before they hit the ground.

A bright flash partially lit up the trees, and a moment later a mortar round detonated in front of the chopper. The single burst brightened the ground for an instant. Kincaid heard the shrapnel rattling against the thin skin of the chopper's fuselage.

Two of the Vietnamese LRRPs fell. One got shakily to his feet, staggered two steps forward toward the helicopters and collapsed back into the scrub. Out of the corner of his eye, Kincaid saw another LRRP hit the ground. As he started to run toward the man, a VC, his face blackened by soot, raced from among the trees. He collided with Kincaid, knocking him down. Kincaid's rifle was jarred loose from his hand, and as he scrambled around, trying to regain his feet, he grabbed at his knife.

The VC was hunched over, his AK pointing at Kincaid's stomach. Kincaid stepped inside the arc of the barrel, grabbed it and tried to jerk it from the enemy's hand. The man held the weapon fast, swinging the butt around. Kincaid let go, ducked and came up with his knife. He thrust forward and felt the blade penetrate the soft skin of the man's belly. The knife twisted in Kincaid's hand as it encountered bone. The VC emitted a blood-curdling scream, his foul breath assaulting Kincaid's nostrils. The enemy soldier dropped his weapon and grabbed at his belly, trying to hold himself together. There was a stench as the man's bowels were ripped open.

A burst of M-16 fire erupted to Kincaid's right. Still hunched over the screaming man, he looked up to see three VC drop, riddled by one of the LRRPs. A moment later a machine gun began to yammer, filling the LZ with green tracers that ripped into the LRRP.

Above the noise of firing and the popping of the rotor blades, Kincaid heard someone shout, "We're pulling pitch. We're getting out."

Kincaid spun, stood to grab his weapon and ran back to the helicopter, lighted in the strobelike flashes of the firing door gun. He stepped up on the skid and saw the last of the Americans fall in a hail of bullets. The crew chief was behind him, urging Kincaid to climb aboard. Kincaid could see the dark shapes that were the bodies of his men scattered in the LZ. He hesitated there, wondering if he should stay to help them—if he could help them.

The crew chief hauled Kincaid into the chopper as the skids broke ground and they began a dash for tree cover. Kincaid twisted around so that he could look into the heart of the clearing where his men lay. The enemy's tracers were streaking across the ground, some of them vanishing in the trees on the other side. Muzzle-flashes from enemy weapons winked among the trees. There were hundreds of flashes, as if a battalion of VC was scrambling up the hill toward the clearing. He saw a line of tracers climb into the sky, searching for the helicopters as they made their escape.

The Phantoms rolled in again, this time using something heavier than their cannon. There was a sun-bright flash and then the rumble of an explosion as a small part of the jungle blew up and began to burn rapidly.

Three more explosions followed, and all at once it seemed that the whole jungle was on fire. Hundreds of tracers climbed into the sky, filling it with a deadly green glow. Red ones lanced at the ground as the Phantoms tried to suppress the enemy fire, while the door guns of the choppers added to the assault against the VC.

Kincaid heard someone open up right under them. He knew the rounds found the door gun because it suddenly stopped firing. Kincaid slid across the floor and looked into the crew chief's well. The man lay against the gray soundproofing, his blood-stained hands on his groin. His eyes were tightly shut, and over the whine of the turbine and the popping of the rotors he could hear the man screaming, "My nuts. My nuts."

Kincaid pulled the first-aid kit from the fuselage, ripped it open and then tried to force the crew chief's hands out of the way. As he got one free, there was a spray of blood that covered the man's thighs and stained the soundproofing black in the fading light.

"Sweet Jesus," said Kincaid. He turned his head and felt his stomach convulse several times, but he didn't throw up. When he stopped dry-retching, he looked at the man's face. It had taken on a strange, waxy look, reflecting the red of the navigation light on that side of the chopper, and only the whites of the eyes were showing. Again Kincaid tried to move the hands so that he could bandage the wound. This time there was no spray of blood and no resistance. The man had bled to death, the blood flowing along the floor and out the door to be blown back along the tail boom.

For a moment Kincaid stared at the dead man. It was the first American he had seen die at close range, almost in his arms. It wasn't like seeing his men drop fifteen or twenty feet away, or like sticking his combat knife into the body of the enemy soldier. This was the messy death caused by multiple gunshot wounds that found their way under the chicken plate that was supposed to protect the man.

He crawled forward to the copilot, who had turned in his seat to look at the body of the crew chief. Kincaid followed the gaze. He then looked out the door but could no longer see the Phantoms or hear any firing. In front of him, through the windshield of the aircraft, the twinkling lights of an American base camp appeared.

He stared at his blood-covered hands and tried to wipe them on the front of his fatigue jacket. Someone touched his shoulder, and Kincaid turned back to face the copilot.

"Are you hit?" the man shouted.

Kincaid stared into his face, feeling dumb. The question seemed to make no sense to him, and then he realized what he was being asked. "No. No, I'm not hit," he said, quietly at first and then shouting over the noise in the chopper. He shook his head. "I'm not hit, but the crew chief is dead."

"We're going to land at the hospital at Chu Chi," the copilot shouted. His face was drained of color.

"I have to get to Saigon," said Kincaid. To his own ears it sounded like a boy whining for his mother, but he repeated it. "I have to go to Saigon."

"Yes, sir. But we have to land at Chu Chi first. I'm hit. It won't take long. Then we'll go to Saigon."

"Okay," said Kincaid. "Fine." He sat down on the floor and looked out of the cargo compartment door. He had left his team in the field. Left his two sergeants, a PFC who had been in Vietnam for only a month and all the Vietnamese, one of whom had just saved his life. They were dead, he was sure, but he had left them nonetheless. He had done his best to try to help them, to get them to the choppers, but they hadn't made it. He hoped to hell that the information was worth the cost. He realized that he would never know how important Saigon thought it was. The disastrous end of the mission was just something that he would have to live with.

2

U.S. ARMY SPECIAL FORCES CAMP A-555 SOUTH OF THE PARROT'S BEAK RVN

Tired almost to the point of exhaustion, U.S. Army Special Forces Captain MacKenzie K. Gerber slowly entered the plywood-and-tin structure that served as his quarters and office. One of the first things he noticed was a pile of mail sitting on his desk. He set his M-14 in a corner of the hootch, glanced at the official mail and then sat on the metal cot. He sighed resignedly as he shifted his buttocks on the inch-thick mattress that was covered by a camouflaged poncho liner. Nothing seemed to be going right, he thought, as he pulled off his boots, which were covered with red mud and black peta-prime, and dropped them on the dirty floor.

Gerber reflected on the activities of the past night. It had been a long and trying one. The events of the past few hours seemed to have conspired against him. First there had been a patrol with the ARVN just outside the wire in an ambush that had been more of a training mission than a combat operation. The men had never been in the field at night, and they'd been armed with weapons that they had only had for two weeks. Gerber scowled as he thought of the drizzle that sometimes changed to a downpour, soaking everyone and everything. The results had been less than spectacular. One man had been hurt when he'd slipped in the mud and fallen on the stock of his weapon, cracking a couple of ribs.

Another had been injured by a punji stake, and then had had to be evaced when it had been discovered that the VC had dipped the punji stakes in excrement. And a third had decided that being in the field, away from the camp, meant it was time to go AWOL.

Gerber unhooked his pistol belt and let it fall to the floor. He rubbed at his face with both hands, feeling the stubble that suggested he should shave, but he wasn't sure he could find the energy. He shivered in his wet fatigues and wondered if he was coming down with something. But the clouds had scattered near dawn, and the day was shaping up to be hot and humid.

Forcing himself off the cot, he padded in his stocking feet over to a metal folding chair behind the tiny combat desk that could collapse to form a two-foot cube. When unfolded, it housed an unstable collection of drawers and shelves that was painted a hideous green. He opened the bottom drawer and reached for his ever-present bottle of Beam's Choice, pulled the cap and took a deep drink. He felt the liquor burn its way into his stomach and pool there as liquid fire. He shivered once and then picked up the handful of mail.

It was as he had suspected. Most of it was official. New directives about the operation of the camp, reports on the supply problems, a field maintenance directive about jamming problems with the new M-16, a request for an accounting of the ammunition being used, to be broken down into rounds used for training and rounds used in combat situations, and a warning about a possible Montagnard revolt.

Gerber flipped through the pile quickly and then stopped when he came to an envelope with familiar handwriting. He immediately recognized the light blue ink and neat, feminine hand. It was a handwriting that he had expected never to see again. Maybe hoped never to see again.

He felt a chill along his spine and a cold knot in his stomach. There was no name attached to the return address, but Gerber knew who it was from anyway. He laid it on the desk, then glanced at his metal wall locker, which stood open across from him. His gaze fell on the jungle fatigues, washed and pressed by one of the Vietnamese women. He looked at the ceiling fan that rotated slowly over his head and then at the plywood walls that ended four feet from the floor. The rest of the hootch was enclosed in screen that theoretically kept the insects out and let the cool breeze in, except that the insects got in the door or through holes in the screen and there were never any cool breezes.

Gerber realized he was being childish. He'd seen the hootch and its contents a hundred times. Why the sudden interest? Then it came to him. He was reluctant to open the letter. He picked it up, jammed it into the side pocket of his fatigue shirt, went to his wall locker for an unopened bottle of Beam's and then hurried off in search of Master Sergeant Anthony B. Fetterman.

Gerber found Fetterman in the Tai area nearest the gate, surrounded by a group of fifteen men. All wore U.S. Army issue fatigue shirts, black shorts that might have been VC issue and black combat boots. All held one of the new M-16 rifles. Fetterman, a small man himself, was barely taller than the strikers in the Vietnamese and Tai companies. He had black hair and a dark complexion, like many of the men sitting around him, but his face was Occidental. His cheeks were nearly blue; it was one of the rare instances when he needed a shave. And his eyes were definitely not Oriental, but a sort of blue-black, and they were as cold as the steel of a brand-new pistol.

Fetterman had been with Gerber in the field all night, but his uniform looked fresh except for the sweat stains under the arms and down the back. Somehow he had managed to remain dry. His boots were recently polished and shined, the mud and peta-prime scraped from them. If he had taken time to shave, it would have seemed that Fetterman had stayed in the camp while Gerber had been falling in the mud on the other side of the wire.

Gerber stood on the edge of the group, feeling dirty and uncomfortable, the sweat standing on his face and trickling down his sides. He glanced at the mud-stained front of his uniform and thought that he should have changed before venturing out into the camp.

At last Fetterman spotted him. The master sergeant instructed the men to take a break and smoke some of the American-made cigarettes, which he handed out like candy. He wormed his way through the group to Gerber and said, "You look like hell, sir."

"Thank you, Master Sergeant. I appreciate your concern and the compliment."

"Any time. What can I do for you?"

Gerber glanced at the billowing white clouds growing on the horizon and thought again that the day was going to be miserable. "Since we're getting short again, and since we spent all night in the field, I thought today would be a good day to stand down. Let Tyme or Bocker kind of run things here. We can just lie around or sleep or read. Just fuck off for a day. Start fresh tomorrow."

"Yes, sir," said Fetterman slowly, staring at the young captain. "Something happening that I don't know about?"

"No, Tony. Just seemed that we should take a day off to rest. There's nothing pressing and no reason for us to feel that we have to be on the job every minute of every day. Besides, we spent all night in the field. We deserve a holiday."

Fetterman noticed the bottle that Gerber was clutching by the neck. His knuckles were white, as if he had a death grip on it. "Where will you be, sir?"

"Out and about," said Gerber, waving an arm to indicate the camp. "Just out and about."

"Yes, sir," repeated Fetterman. "Well, I'll finish up here and then take the day off, too."

"Fine, Tony," said Gerber.

He angled toward the redoubt, passed the opening there, then turned back. He had found his hiding place. Slipping into his hootch, he grabbed one of the lawn chairs that he'd purchased in Saigon and left again, heading for the commo bunker. Once behind the bunker, he hoisted himself up on the waist-high double row of sandbags and flipped his bottle and lawn chair onto the top. Then levering himself higher with his arms, he found a toehold in the single row of sandbags and rolled himself over. He opened the chair, sat down and uncorked the Beam's.

He drank from it deeply, breathed out and stared into the distance at the mortar pits where Sergeant Tyme was working with a Vietnamese crew. Basically it was a hole in the ground ringed with sandbags, which had compass directions painted on them. A narrow trench led from each pit to a small bunker that housed the ammo.

Beyond that was an earthen wall topped with barbed wire, rows of concertina wire that guarded the approach to the camp and then open rice paddies sprinkled with clumps of trees and farmers' hootches. Some had rusted metal roofs that flashed orange and gold in the morning sun. To the west was the runway, just outside the wire, covered with the black, tarlike substance known as peta-prime.

Gerber unbuttoned his fatigue shirt and distractedly fingered the metal dog tags on his damp chest. They were taped together so that they wouldn't rattle. He smiled as he thought of the Hollywood soldiers whose dog tags jingled as they tried to sneak through the jungle, or the city, avoiding the enemy. Time for another snort. Placing the bourbon to his lips, he took two big gulps, then put a hand into his pocket so that he could feel the letter.

It was what he had hoped and prayed for—a letter from Karen Morrow. He didn't know what it could possibly say, but he knew the contents couldn't be bad because there was no way she could write to him with bad news. The break had been so final, so complete, that Gerber had eventually convinced himself he would never hear from her again. Now he had a letter from her, and although he hadn't read it yet, its very presence meant that she wanted to open the lines of communication with him again.

He set the bottle down on the sandbags and pulled the letter from his pocket. He didn't look at it right away. Instead, he kept his eyes on the men who were working in the mortar pits. The sounds of hammering came to him, and he wondered what Tyme could be building down there. Finally he let his eyes drop to the letter and looked at the cancellation. Two weeks had gone by. Gerber smiled, not knowing if he should be angry that it had taken so long, or happy that it had been delayed so that his DEROS was that much closer and he could possibly see her again.

Anxious now, he ripped the envelope open, took out the two lavender sheets, smelling faintly of Karen's perfume, and then read the salutation and glanced at the closing. He smiled to himself because it was better than he could have hoped for.

He read it quickly, too quickly, but could pick up the drift. Then he reread it slowly, looking for a message between the lines, the one sentence that would chop his feet out from under him. But it just wasn't there.

It started simply with a "Dear Mack" salutation that gave away nothing, but then it got serious. "I hope you'll read all this before you throw it away. I know I treated you shabbily when I left, but there was nothing I could do about it. A friend once told me that the thing you find hardest to do is the thing you should do. I violated that rule because I couldn't stand the thought of seeing you again and then having to leave you. It was easier to just pretend that I didn't care and slip away to the World.

"Now that I'm home I don't understand why I felt it necessary to leave. I guess my feelings about my husband—yes, I know that I failed to mention him—were a result of remembering only the best things about him. He has turned into a shallow man who is striving up the corporate ladder by devising ways of selling trivia to people who don't want it. His life seems to revolve around that, and it leaves little time for me. He sees my role as only to support him and produce children so that he can have a cluster of happy photos on his desk.

"I never realized how right you and I were. There was something about our relationship that started right, and if I hadn't been married, I'm sure that it would have developed. I doubt I've ever loved anyone else, including my husband. I felt a loyalty to my husband because he was my husband, but I'm not ready to smother my career and my desires so that he can climb another rung. I'm not ready to create babies for his career advancements. I've filed for a divorce.

"I know this is out of the blue and wouldn't blame you if you just tore it up without reading it. But I think I know you well enough to believe that you'll give me the opportunity to explain what happened. Maybe it does no good to tell you that I know I was wrong in just walking out the way I did. By doing that, I could pretend that you didn't care about me anyway.

"I'll end this by saying that I love you and hope that you can still love me. I hope you realize how hard it was to tell you my feelings after the way I acted, but perhaps you'll understand and write to me. Please forgive me."

It was signed, "All my love, Karen."

Gerber folded the letter and carefully put it into his pocket. He picked up his bottle and drank deeply. His face felt numb, but he wanted to shout. He wanted to dance. Somehow the sky looked bluer, the clouds whiter and the day was no longer uncomfortable, but actually quite pleasant.

Suddenly a thought occurred to him. What about Robin? Gerber had momentarily forgotten about Karen's sister. She had been around almost from the moment that Karen had fled to the World, and Gerber had tried, not too successfully, to keep her at arm's length. He knew there had been a good reason for not tangling with another Morrow. He should have run at the first opportunity, but he hadn't. He had let himself be forced into situations where he was alone with her. Situations that Robin worked hard to create.

No, that wasn't quite fair, Gerber thought. He hadn't been quite as cold as he could have been. He had encouraged her, had even engineered a few of those encounters, and now he had to find a way to let her down easily. He still remembered the pain of learning about Karen's return to the World and the news of her soon-to-be ex-husband. The despair had made it almost impossible to think or to function. It had robbed him of the desire to do anything but sit in his room and drink. He rubbed a hand over his face and knew that he would have to let Robin down easily, give her the scene that she would want, and send her off to finish her journalistic endeavors somewhere else. Send her off to find a Pulitzer story.

He thought about the physical pain and torture that Robin Morrow had endured because of him, how she had clung to him after the ordeal when the camp had been captured by the enemy. But she hadn't blamed him for any of it. Robin had been a friend when he'd needed one most. More than a friend. She had sat close by and listened as he had poured out his story of Karen and what she had done. And Robin had asked for nothing in return. She had given and never taken. Not exactly the attitude her sister had displayed.

He took the letter out again and read it slowly, as if trying to memorize the words. As his eyes raced across the paper, he thought that he had to be dreaming until he realized that the sun pounding on him was all too real. He was wide awake.

Now he wasn't being fair to Robin. He was doing to her what her sister had done to him. No, that wasn't quite right, either. Robin knew about his soft spot for her sister. She probably knew that if Karen came back to him, he would want to be with Karen.

He wouldn't worry about it. It was something that he would put out of his mind until Robin returned from Da Nang. He didn't have to deal with it now.

He finished his bottle, carefully corked it and wondered why he couldn't stand up without weaving. Sure, he had finished the bottle, but it had taken a long time, and he couldn't be that drunk. He lost his balance and fell to a sitting position. He began to giggle, thought that giggling was undignified for an army officer and laughed all the harder. He fell on his back so that he was staring into the almost cloudless blue sky directly overhead and thought that life was absolutely beautiful.

IT WAS LATE AFTERNOON when Fetterman began to worry about Captain Gerber. No one had seen him for hours, and although he hadn't gone through the gate, he was nowhere in the camp, either. Fetterman checked the rebuilt team house, erected after a mortar and rocket attack had destroyed it, searched Gerber's quarters and then talked to everyone who would listen.

Fetterman returned to the team house and sat down, sipping a beer from the brand-new refrigerator that Colonel Bates, the B-team commander, had sent from Saigon. It was a contrast to the others they had had. This fridge operated near absolute zero, and to try to snatch a beer from it was to risk frostbite and permanent injury.

In fact, almost everything in the team house had been received from Colonel Bates. The materials to build it, along the lines of every other structure on the camp, had been arranged for by Bates. There was a tin roof to reflect the sun and a couple of ceiling fans. There were four tables that each had four chairs around them. There was a bar that separated the rear third of the team house from the rest. Behind it was a stove, a large pantry filled with canned goods and a sink. A Vietnamese girl worked there, preparing the evening meal.

The beer was ice-cold and felt good after a long, hot day. Fetterman, still wondering where the captain had escaped to, drank it slowly. If Robin Morrow was around, he would assume that they were together. But Robin wasn't due back for a day or two. She was completing an assignment up in the Da Nang area. She had called on the makeshift telephone system to alert them she would soon return. So that was out.

Fetterman had nearly finished his beer and decided that it was time to organize a serious search party when Galvin Bocker entered the team house. Bocker, a big man with dark hair, dark eyes and the ability to build a radio from tin cans, sea shells and a couple of bits of wire, stopped, looked around and asked, "You seen the captain?"

"Not since this morning. Why?"

"Got a message that his presence is desired in Saigon tomorrow morning. Some hotshot at MACV Headquarters wants to talk to him."

Fetterman drained his beer and slammed the can on the table-top. As he got to his feet, he said, "Well, then I guess we'd better find him."

Together they left to search inside the redoubt. That was a dirt breastwork about five feet high and seventy feet across. The entrance was guarded by M-60 machine guns in bunkers. Inside was the dispensary, team house, the American quarters, including Gerber's hootch, and an ammo bunker. When they failed to find Gerber there, and failed to find anyone who remembered seeing him since early morning, they expanded the search.

As they left the redoubt, Fetterman said, "Why don't you crawl up in the fire control tower and take a look?"

Bocker was halfway up the ladder when he spotted Gerber lying on top of the commo bunker. He pointed at it and called, "Got him!"

Fetterman walked to the commo bunker, climbed up on the row of sandbags and stared at the top. Gerber was on his back, the empty bottle cradled in the crook of his elbow. His face was a brownish-red from the sun, and his uniform was soaked with sweat and stained with dried dirt.

"Captain," called Fetterman. "Captain Gerber."

Gerber stirred, pushed the bottle away and lifted his head, blinking his eyes rapidly. He groaned and let his head drop to the sandbag surface. "What'd want?"

"Don't you think you'd feel better if you got down off there, Captain?" asked Fetterman.

"I'm not sure," moaned Gerber. He held his hand over his eyes to shade them from the setting sun. "I'm not sure I'll ever feel good again."

"Anything you care to talk about, sir?" asked Fetterman.

Gerber didn't answer right away. He struggled to sit up cross-legged, his gaze on the sandbags. He didn't move for quite a while, as if he had gone to sleep in a sitting position. He gingerly touched his face and winced when he realized that after nearly a year and a half in Vietnam he had managed to get himself badly sunburned. Finally he said, "Nothing that we need to discuss. It's just that I needed to blow off some steam by myself."

"Yes, sir," said Fetterman. "You should've let us know where you were going to hide. Took us quite awhile to locate you."

Gerber turned his head and stared at Fetterman. "I wanted some time to think. Besides, I would have heard if anything happened."

"You get your thinking done?"

"Yes, I did." Gerber got unsteadily to his feet. He put a hand out and used the back of the lawn chair to support himself while he decided that he didn't want to throw up. His stomach settled down. It wasn't that he felt fine; he still knew that he had a stomach, could feel it churning away, but he didn't think he would be sick. He picked up the lawn chair, folded it and stepped gingerly to the edge of the bunker. As he handed it to Fetterman, he asked, "Why the big search?"

"Other than it seemed odd that no one had seen you all day," said Fetterman, "we got a message from Saigon that requests your presence at MACV tomorrow."

"They say who it was?"

Fetterman looked at Bocker, who had climbed off the ladder on the fire control tower and stood staring up at Fetterman. "They say who?"

"Maxwell," said Bocker.

Gerber sat next to Fetterman and said, "Maxwell. Can't believe the son of a bitch would request me to come to Saigon after the shit he's pulled."

"Sounded more like an order," said Bocker.

"An order," echoed Gerber. "Just fucking fine." He slipped from the top of the bunker and landed unsteadily on the double row. He grabbed at Fetterman to catch his balance and then dropped to the ground.

"Why do we do it to ourselves?" he asked. "I know sucking down all that bourbon is going to make me sick, make my head ache, but I do it anyway. Christ, Tony, I'm going over to the dispensary and see if T.J. has anything for me. For either the hangover or the sunburn."

"Yes, sir," said Fetterman. "What about the appointment in Saigon tomorrow?"

Gerber sighed. "If you're that worried about it, lay on a chopper ride for tomorrow. Probably coordinate it through the Hornets at Chu Chi since it's their turn for the ash and trash."

"Yes, sir. Should I plan to come along?"

"No, I think you'd better wait here, since we don't have an executive officer."

"Yes, sir."

"Tony, what the fuck has gotten into you? What's all this 'yes, sir' crap, anyway?"

Fetterman stared for a moment, then said, "Just a little concerned is all. I'll help Galvin make the arrangements for the chopper flight."

"Thank you. If you feel I've slighted you by my behavior today, I'm sorry, but I needed the time off."

"Of course, Captain. No problem."

3

THE HELIPAD SPECIAL
FORCES CAMP A-555

Gerber stood on the edge of the helipad, waiting for the morning chopper. His overnight kit sat on the ground near his feet, and he was holding his rifle. Fifteen minutes earlier Bocker had swung by his quarters to inform him that the aircraft was inbound. Bocker had then returned to the cool, dim confines of the commo bunker. Now he came out again, a smoke grenade clutched in his fist. With his other hand he shaded his eyes, searching the horizon for the helicopter.

When he found it, he tossed the grenade to the center of the helipad, then rushed back up the road into the camp and the commo bunker. Gerber watched the smoke billow, a dark cloud of green blowing gently to the west. The chopper circled north of the camp, as if to avoid overflying it, and made its approach from the west, the nose into the wind. At twenty-five or thirty feet above the ground, the helicopter flared, pushing the rotor wash forward so that it ripped at Gerber's uniform and stirred up the dust and debris around him. He put his hand on his head to hold down his beret and turned his face away from the sandpapering effect of the wind.

When the aircraft's skids touched the ground, Gerber moved forward and climbed into the cargo compartment. He pushed his overnight kit out of the way, sliding it under the troop seat. Then he sat down, buckled himself in and waited. Just inside the gate he could see a couple of his men and a dozen Tais, watching the takeoff. Gerber raised a hand to wave, and as the men responded, the helicopter lifted, rocking gently from side to side as the pilot made sure that he was clear of all obstructions.

They climbed out slowly until they were at fifteen hundred feet, outside effective small arms range. Sometimes the pilots circled the camp while climbing, but this time it was a straight shot east. Gerber glanced to the rear and saw the star-shaped configuration of his camp: five arms with rounded ends, each radiating from a large center with a C-shaped redoubt in it. He could see the sunlight glinting off the metal roofs of all the hootches, some of them already rusting and looking gold. Others were just dark splotches on the red of the dust because they were covered with the OD green, rubberized sandbags.

They turned slightly north toward Highway One and away from the wide expanse of swamp that sparkled and flashed in the south and east. There was a sea of grass and reeds that stretched as far as he could see, broken by clumps of trees that hid farmers' hootches, tiny villages and probably more than a few Vietcong. Directly under him were rice paddies filled with muddy water that was evaporating rapidly with the approach of the dry season.

With the roar of the wind, the pop of the rotors and the whine of the turbine, conversation with the crew was next to impossible. Gerber sat quietly, his overnight bag behind his feet and his rifle in one hand, the barrel pointing upward. The theory was that if a round was accidentally fired up, it would do less damage than one traveling downward. Beneath the deck of the cargo compartment there were control cables, communications wires, antennae and fuel cells.

Gerber closed his eyes and leaned his head against the gray soundproofing of the cargo compartment. He listened to the rhythm of the rotors and let it relax him. When the pitch of the engine changed, Gerber opened his eyes to find them only a few feet off the ground, weaving among the trees and buildings at the southern edge of Tan Son Nhut. They flew through a huge gap in the tree line, popped up again and then descended to the grassy area of Hotel Three.

As they touched down, Gerber leaped out, held up a hand to let the pilot know he appreciated the lift and trotted toward the terminal building. Before he reached it he was intercepted by a tall, skinny man in wrinkled and stained jungle fatigues. He was a young man with pimples and the hint of a mustache discoloring his upper lip. His face was lean, as if he hadn't eaten well in a long time, and since he wore Spec Four insignia, Gerber figured he didn't have access to the finer military clubs or the money for the downtown hotels.

"You Gerber?" he asked in a voice filled with ill humor.

"I'm Captain Gerber."

"I have a ride for you. Over to MACV Headquarters. Come on."

Gerber didn't move. Normally he didn't bother with reminding the enlisted men that there were military courtesies to be observed, even in a war zone. Most of the time he winked at the so-called breakdown of discipline because it was more a function of the nature of the job than a real decline in discipline. But this was an extreme case. One that couldn't be overlooked easily.

The man stopped and turned. He put his hands on his hips and asked, "You got a problem?"

Gerber returned the stare until the man dropped his eyes. Then quietly, almost under his breath, Gerber said, "Do you have a problem, sir? No, I don't, but you have a real attitude. I know it must be lousy duty, chauffeuring officers around, but it is a hell of a lot better living in Saigon than in the field. It is better driving people around Saigon than it is being shot at. So, even though we're in a combat environment, nobody shut off the rules."

The man slowly came to attention, started to salute, stopped and said, "Yes, sir. Sorry."

"No harm done. Now, if you would be so kind as to show me the jeep, we'll head over to MACV."

"Yes, sir."

They left the Hotel Three area, passed the World's Largest PX, with a movie theater on the east end, and walked through a small gate that separated that portion of the base from the rest. When they came to the jeep, Gerber dropped his over-

night bag in the back and climbed into the passenger's seat. He
kept his rifle in front with him. The Spec Four unlocked the
padlock that held a chain looped through the steering wheel so
that it couldn't be turned. It kept people from stealing the jeep.

At the gate to Tan Son Nhut, an air force security policeman stopped them and asked their destination. He eyed Gerber's weapon, and for a moment it appeared as if he was going
to say something. Then he waved them on. They wheeled along
the streets of Saigon, and Gerber noticed that some of them
were very wide and full of traffic. Military trucks and jeeps,
cars, Lambretta motor scooters and bicycles crowded the route.
Some of the streets were lined with palm trees, and the buildings sat well back from the curb. Others had narrow side-
walks, decaying buildings and miles of neon signs that remained
on even in the morning sunlight. Vietnamese women in incred-
ibly short skirts stood talking to men in a variety of uniforms
that represented all the American armed services in Vietnam as
well as those of the allies.

Gerber sat with a foot up on the dashboard of the jeep,
watching the traffic and the people. There were White Mice, the
Saigon equivalent of an MP, so called because of the white
helmets they wore. There were Saigon cowboys, young men and
women who rode Honda motorcycles up and down the streets,
weaving in and out of traffic and shouting insults at everyone,
waiting for an opportunity to steal something.

Gerber had seen it all before and found that his fascination
with the foreign capital was waning. Pearl of the Orient, my
ass, he thought. It had become a dirty city filled with refugees,
prostitutes, drug dealers, soldiers, journalists and criminals.
While there were still some beautiful sections, there were also
those with mud streets and hootches made from cardboard.
There were people sleeping in the streets, begging, hustling,
stealing or just waiting. Saigon had become the Cesspool of the
Orient. Those derelicts and petty criminals were waiting for
someone to save them, waiting for the war to end, or waiting to
die.

As usual the MPs at the gate to MACV Headquarters didn't
even blink as Gerber arrived. Since he was obviously an
American, he was allowed to pass without an ID check. They

didn't question his need for the M-14 he carried, although one of the guards wanted to look into his overnight bag. They found only a change of underwear and a shaving kit. Gerber climbed the concrete steps to the large glass doors, pushed his way through them, and then a second set, into the uncomfortable air-conditioning of the building. He walked along the tiled hallways, glancing at the posters that warned him that "Charlie was listening" and that "Comsec was everybody's responsibility." He ignored the men and women in uniform or civilian clothes until he came to a stairway leading down.

At the bottom, he was stopped by an armed guard who asked him for his ID card, checked it carefully, consulted an access list held on a clipboard and then opened his iron gate. He eyed the rifle but said nothing about it. Once again Gerber was forced to open his overnight case. Before he could get too far down the hallway, the guard asked him to sign in, being sure to include the time, and when that ritual was finished, let him go.

Once through there, he continued down a tiled floor that was stained by rust where cabinets, metal chairs and bookcases had once stood and then been moved. The cinder-block walls were painted light green and were dotted with black-and-white photos of the president and vice president as well as the secretaries of defense, army, air force and navy. Beyond them were photos of Vietnamese leaders. Gerber ignored everything until he came to a dark wooden door. He gave it three short raps.

A short stocky man with dark hair and dark eyes and a permanently sunburned complexion opened the door and stuck out a big hand. "Welcome," he said. "Glad you could make it." This was Jerry Maxwell, the man Gerber had come to see.

Maxwell stepped back so that Gerber could enter the office. Gerber hesitated and said, "I don't like this, Maxwell. I don't like it at all."

When Gerber was inside, Maxwell shut the door and moved to the scarred battleship-gray desk pushed into one corner. There was a row of Coke cans on one side and a pile of file folders in the middle. Red secret stamps glared up from them. He took off his white suit coat, which was badly wrinkled, and hung it on the back of his metal chair.

"Sit down, Mack, and let's talk."

Gerber looked around the office. He had been here before and little had changed in it. The far wall was still lined with four-drawer file cabinets, with a combination lock on the second drawer of the one in the corner. The top drawer stood open, and Gerber could see more folders marked Secret. The beat-up old leather chair still rested by the desk, but the picture that showed cavalrymen fighting the Sioux Indians had been changed. The new one showed cavalrymen fighting the Cheyenne Indians and was called *The Hayfield Fight*. Gerber noticed that there was a stack of pictures leaning against the side of a file cabinet, as if waiting to be hung.

Because they were below ground, there were no windows. Fluorescent lights burned from the ceiling, and a large one was sitting on the desk. It was cool in the room and smelled musty. Gerber figured the office was never aired out, and he wouldn't be surprised if mildew was setting in. Maxwell sat at the desk. He picked up the Coke cans one by one and shook them, hoping to find some remnants.

"Mack," he said, "I thought you understood that there was nothing I could do for you or your boys. If I had said that I knew your boys were in Cambodia, I wouldn't have saved them. I would have gone down with them. I explained that to you before you left here. Besides, they didn't go down. You got them off the hook."

"No thanks to you," said Gerber, still standing.

"You going to carry a grudge on that for the rest of your life?"

Gerber slipped into the chair, propped his weapon against the armrest and set the overnight bag next to it. He was studying Maxwell out of the corner of his eye, watching him squirm. Maxwell nearly always wore a white suit that needed pressing, white shirts that had been yellowed by the laundry and a thin black tie that always hung loose. It was as much a uniform as Gerber's jungle fatigues.

"I told you at the beginning of that mission that if you got into trouble I would have to deny I knew anything about it. I told you that up front. I was completely honest with you."

"All right, Jerry," said Gerber. "I'll let you get away with that one."

Maxwell smiled. "Okay, Mack. You want a Coke or anything?"

"No thanks. Just tell me what was so important that I had to rush in here immediately."

Maxwell hesitated, then searched his desktop until he found a map. "Naturally, everything I'm about to tell you is considered secret and we can't talk about it outside of this room."

"Naturally."

Maxwell leaned close to Gerber so that he could see the map. "Okay, we've got information that the Ho Chi Minh Trail has a major infiltration route that traverses the Parrot's Beak–Angel's Wing area of the border."

"That's nothing new," said Gerber. "Hell, I could have told you that within a week of building my camp."

"All right, here's what you don't know. We've had teams in Cambodia for the past six to eight weeks, monitoring the traffic along the Trail—provisional LRRP teams who are good at the sneak-and-peek operations. At first it was just what you'd expect—soldiers, bicycles loaded with supplies, a few trucks. But it began to change. Now there are antiaircraft weapons— S-60s, ZSU-23s, 37 mm, that sort of thing."

"Interesting," said Gerber, "but I don't see the importance."

"There are theories. One suggests that the VC and NVA are building a wall of triple A along the border to make overflight more difficult, more dangerous. Another is that they plan to ring Saigon with it to inhibit our fighter traffic—to inhibit all our air traffic. A third says that they're planning something big and are going to use the triple A to cover it."

"Again," said Gerber, "interesting, but I don't see what it has to do with me or quick trips to Saigon."

Maxwell set his map on his desk and rocked back in his chair, lacing his fingers behind his head. "Since we began our build-up, we've had a difficult time drawing the VC and NVA out into a large-scale battle. They hit us when they have the odds in their favor. It looks like they're planning something big, especially with the sudden influx of antiaircraft. What we need is to have someone monitor the traffic along the Trail for a few more weeks, someone who knows a little more about the capabilities of the enemy and can recognize the difference between a soldier and a supply clerk. And most importantly we need someone who can protect himself. The LRRPs are fine as far as they go, but they don't have the background to adequately assess what the VC and NVA can do. They don't understand the people here.''

"I am not a Trail watcher. Anybody can do that," said Gerber. "And I'm definitely not going to operate in Cambodia after what happened the last time."

"You're right. Anyone can do that," said Maxwell, "except now it's become dangerous. We had four teams in the field, and of those four we got one officer back. Barely. The rest are dead."

Gerber's interest finally peaked. "But we've had men observing the Trail for months."

"And in the past two weeks we've lost everyone of them with one exception. Now we want to put in a team that we're sure will survive, one that can get the information we need about the triple A, about the types of units moving along the Trail and that can get itself out if there is trouble. It's a complicated mess."

"Yeah," said Gerber slowly. He rubbed his chin. He would want to take fifteen, twenty men, find a good defensible position and stay put for a week. It was an interesting idea. The perfect mission to end his tour. Something that could be useful long after he had rotated home. But that was also the last thing he wanted to do.

"No," he said to Maxwell. "I won't do it."

"Sure you will," said Maxwell smiling. "Just tell me what it would take."

"First, a written order, signed by General Hull at worst, Westmoreland at best. And a full slate of replacements. I've got a number of holes in my TO&E." Both were things that would be impossible for Maxwell to arrange quickly. Replacements took weeks to get to the field.

Maxwell opened a folder and pulled a piece of paper from it. He read it quickly and then handed it to Gerber. "Your written order, signed by General Westmoreland himself, just as you requested."

Gerber took the paper and read it. It gave him permission, in fact ordered him, to operate in Cambodia. "How many copies have been made?"

"At least two," said Maxwell. "That one for you and one for the general to maintain in his files. Naturally he wouldn't like that to come back and haunt him."

"Uh-huh."

"You realize that isn't a request you hold. It is a lawful order drafted by the commander of U.S. forces in Vietnam. To refuse it is to invite court-martial."

"The legality of the order is debatable," said Gerber. "And that doesn't solve the problem with the TO&E."

"We'll get to that later," said Maxwell. "First, let me fill you in on everything that has happened along the Trail in the past few weeks."

Maxwell's briefing didn't take long. He described the mission that produced the single survivor, detailing everything about it. He talked about the traffic on the Trail, the abilities of the NVA and VC and the roving enemy patrols that had effectively blinded the American eyes on the ground. He answered Gerber's questions. Then he added a note about a defoliation program that had begun several months earlier. Maxwell mumbled something about "Ranch hand," claimed that it was an unofficial name for it and told Gerber that he was to assess its success. Did the chemicals strip the trees of their leaves? Did it kill the vegetation to a great degree? Was it exposing the ground to the air? Finally, when they began to cover the same information a second time, Maxwell said, "That should take care of it."

Gerber shook his head and studied his hand as if he suddenly found it fascinating. "You still haven't bothered with the holes in my TO&E," Gerber reminded him.

Maxwell stood. He opened the middle drawer of his desk, took out a shoulder holster that held a Swenson .45 Auto Custom and slipped it on. He grabbed his jacket as he headed to the door. He opened it and waited for Gerber.

"Come on, Mack," he said, "Let's take care of your TO&E problem now. Then we can stop fucking around and you can get back into the field."

Thirty minutes later Gerber found himself back at Tan Son Nhut in the building that General Billy Joe Crinshaw had built for his headquarters. Gerber tried to avoid the place as much as possible because it held so many unpleasant memories, such as the attempted court-martial of Fetterman and Tyme for murder in Cambodia. The last time he had been to it there had been dirt surrounding it instead of the neatly trimmed lawn there now. They walked up a sidewalk lined with brightly colored flowers that were being tended to by two enlisted men in sweat-stained jungle fatigues.

Gerber followed Maxwell inside, carrying his weapon in his left hand. They climbed to the second floor where they walked to the end of the hallway. There was a tile floor, two-tone paint, light blue under white, and pictures of the army in action. Without knocking on the door at the far end, Maxwell entered an office that looked more like a dayroom. There were two red leather couches, a card table surrounded by chairs, a television, radio and stacks of paperbacks and magazines. An ancient Coke machine with a handmade sign proclaiming that it was out of order stood in one corner.

There were three men in the room, two of them reading and the third watching the sign-on of AFVN-TV. The man watching the TV glanced up and saw Gerber. "Ah-ten-Hut!" he said.

"As you were," said Gerber. He studied the man who had called them to attention. He was a young man of Oriental descent, wearing bright green fatigues and the stripes of an army sergeant. He had on the new jungle boots being issued to the men as they came in-country.

"This is Tommy Yashimoto, a communications specialist we've assigned to your team," said Maxwell.

Gerber held out a hand and said, "Glad to meet you." Yashimoto was of medium height, five nine or ten and had dark eyes and jet-black hair. His face was round with a slightly pointed chin. Gerber noticed that he had exceptionally large hands and wondered if he would be too clumsy to work in the delicate interior of a radio. Bocker had slender fingers, like those of a brain surgeon.

"This is Philip Grummond," said Maxwell, "a medic now assigned to you."

Gerber turned and shook hands with Grummond. He looked to be older, maybe twenty-five or six, about six feet tall and a stocky build. Piercing blue eyes studied Gerber without wavering. He had a massive jaw, and when he smiled it looked as if he had ten or twelve extra teeth. His ears jutted out prominently, and he'd let his brown hair grow longer than regulations dictated, unsuccessfully trying to hide them. His uniform was faded, as if he had been in Vietnam for several weeks, but his boots were spit-shined, glowing like black mirrors.

"And finally," said Maxwell, "this is First Lieutenant Glen Mildebrandt, assigned as your new executive officer."

Mildebrándt was a big man. Huge would have been a better word, Gerber thought. He had black hair, light eyes, a pointed chin and Roman nose. He smiled at Gerber, seemed to be about to burst out laughing and said, "Glad to meet you, sir."

"Glad to meet all of you," said Gerber.

"Now that should put your team and your TO&E back to full strength," said Maxwell. "Captain Bromhead talked to each of these men yesterday and thought you'd approve the choices."

"All right," said Gerber, "if Johnny said they were good, I'll trust him on that. What about transport out to the camp?"

"Arranged. Chopper's standing by at Hotel Three to run you out there, as soon as you're ready."

"Then let's get going. Lieutenant, why don't you make sure that you're properly checked out of the transient billets and collect your gear. I'll meet you at the terminal at Hotel Three." Gerber glanced at Maxwell and wondered if he wasn't being sandbagged. Everything he wanted was being handed to him. He hadn't really said he would accept the assignment, and suddenly it was as if he was going to be leaving in a few hours.

Maxwell held up a hand. "There's one more for you to meet. We'll swing by another room here. Meanwhile, you men can do your thing. We'll be along in a few minutes."

As they left the room, Gerber said, "They seemed to be oddly uncurious about the camp."

"Captain Bromhead spent a couple of hours talking to them about it yesterday. Made you sound like a cross between George

Patton and U. S. Grant. I think they're a little bit afraid of you right now.''

They stopped in front of another door. Maxwell grinned at Gerber as if in on a private joke. ''Right in here.'' He opened the door without knocking.

Gerber followed him in and stopped dead in his tracks. A Vietnamese woman was sitting alone in the room, a thin, black cigar clamped between her teeth and her feet propped up on a table. She wore a black skirt that was hiked above her knees, displaying shapely legs, and Gerber got a glimpse of red panties. Her white silk blouse had four rows of vertical ruffles flanking the buttons, the top two of which were open. He could see the edge of her bra hiding the swell of her breasts. Perspiration stood on her forehead and upper lip. Her jet-black hair hung over the back of the chair and reached almost to the floor.

''This is Brouchard Bien Soo Ta Emilie,'' said Maxwell.

The woman didn't move or look up from her thick book. Gerber noticed that it was a French edition of *War and Peace*. She seemed not to care that anyone had entered the room.

''She's assigned as a scout for your mission.''

''Now wait a minute,'' said Gerber.

For the first time the young woman looked up. Gerber noticed that she had a thin narrow face, not oval like most Orientals. Her eyes held only a hint of a slant and were a light color, maybe blue, maybe gray. She turned her attention back to her book and then glanced at Gerber again.

She snapped the book shut, took the cigar out of her mouth and reached up to the buttons of her blouse, but could do nothing about it with the cigar in her hand. As she put the cigar back in her mouth, she dropped her feet to the floor and pulled her skirt down so it covered her knees. She pulled the cigar from her mouth and tried to crush it out but hit the edge of the ashtray, spilling it.

''I'm...I...'' she started, and then stopped. She put a hand over her eyes, as if she could hide behind it, and a blush crawled up her neck and spread across her face until it was lost in her hairline.

''Please,'' said Gerber, smiling. ''Relax. We should have knocked.''

Now she stood. She was tall for a Vietnamese, almost five two. She proffered a delicate hand and said, "It's my fault. It's so warm that I wasn't thinking. I shouldn't have allowed myself to relax quite so much."

"Hell," interjected Maxwell, "if you were that hot, you could have taken off all your clothes. We wouldn't have objected."

She looked at the floor as the blush broke out on her face again.

Gerber took her hand and looked into her eyes, realizing that they weren't light blue but a darker, nearly violet color. He had never seen eyes so blue.

She held his hand a moment longer then necessary and then stared up at him. "Pleased to meet you," she said, her French accent noticeable for the first time.

"Yes," said Maxwell, "I can see you are."

Gerber shot him a glance and then said, "Jerry, I want to see you in the hallway. Right now."

"If you'll excuse us," said Maxwell, bowing.

In the hallway Gerber shut the door and said, "This is too much. I'm not taking a woman on this. Especially her."

"What's wrong with her?"

"Christ, man, look at her. She's beautiful. I'm supposed to wander around the jungle with a bunch of horny men and one beautiful woman? You're out of your fucking mind."

"You wandered around out there with Morrow," countered Maxwell.

"That was different."

"How so?"

"She was an American journalist. We didn't wander around the jungle with her. Not on a mission like we're being sent on. It was a short-term recon, not an extended patrol into the heart of enemy territory."

"Well, she's going," said Maxwell. "I can haul out another piece of paper that makes it clear to you—another order—but I would rather report that you saw the light and didn't force the issue."

Gerber rubbed a hand through his hair. It was damp with sweat. He wiped it on the front of his fatigue jacket. "What makes it so important that this woman go with us?"

"For one thing, she knows the area. She lived in there for a couple of years. She understands the VC, understands the workings of their infrastructure."

"How did she learn so much?" asked Gerber, a sinking feeling in his gut.

"She's a Kit Carson. Came over to us after a VC captain decided she would be of more use as his bedmate than a soldier, ignoring her protests that she was married. He was a lot rougher than he had to be."

"Oh, that's just fucking great," said Gerber. "That's exactly what I need."

Maxwell clapped him on the shoulder and smiled. "That's good because that's exactly what you've got."

4

TERMINAL BUILDING
HOTEL THREE TAN SON
NHUT

Gerber rode in the back of the jeep while Maxwell drove and Brouchard Bien Soo Ta Emilie sat in the front, her hands folded in her lap. Her long, black hair flapped in the breeze as they sped along. Occasionally she stole glances over her shoulder, watching Gerber as he studied the surroundings of Tan Son Nhut.

They parked the jeep outside the gate that led into the World's Largest PX and Hotel Three. The guard was reluctant to let a Vietnamese civilian through, although most of his reluctance might have been a desire to talk to her. Gerber produced an ID card that failed to impress the MP, but Maxwell had the order signed by Westmoreland, and that did the trick. Once through, they walked by the PX and the fence that protected part of the helipad.

At the entrance to the terminal, Gerber said, "You wait here, and I'll see if the others have arrived."

Maxwell nodded and took the woman's arm. "Just hurry it up, please." Gerber stepped into the terminal. It was more crowded than he remembered ever seeing it. That had to be because of the continuing buildup of American forces. Men in jungle fatigues, most carrying weapons, stood in knots that filled the interior. Gerber knew there was a wooden counter in there somewhere, behind which the scheduling NCO and his assistants waited, but he couldn't see it. He had a hard time spotting the scheduling board on the wall.

He pushed his way in, stopped and tried to see over the heads and shoulders of the crowd, but he couldn't identify anyone. Then, from a corner, he heard someone calling his name and turned in time to see Mildebrandt waving at him.

Gerber made his way toward the man and shouted a greeting over the noise of soldiers lying to one another about their exploits the night before, telling each other bad jokes or arguing the relative merits of the expansion teams in baseball. As he got close, he saw that Yashimoto was in animated conversation with someone, and as a burly sergeant shifted his weight, Gerber felt himself grow cold.

Robin Morrow, dressed in a modified jumpsuit that left her legs and arms bare, was seated with the new men. Her light hair was pulled back off her face, and her green eyes blazed as she talked, gesturing with a slender hand. She looked like she needed sleep, the dark circles under her eyes standing out in stark contrast to her light skin. Her black combat boots looked as if they had never seen a brush, let alone polish, and now looked a dirty gray. Next to her was a camera bag and a suitcase.

When she saw Gerber, she leaped to her feet, but the press of soldiers prevented her from running to him. She called, "Mack! Mack, it's good to see you."

Gerber didn't want a confrontation with her in the terminal building at Hotel Three. He'd thought that Robin would just show up at the camp one day and he'd have a chance to put her straight immediately. In fact, he'd hoped that Karen would have written to her sister so that anything he said wouldn't come as a complete surprise. And then he realized that he didn't have to say much to her in the terminal. There were so many people crowded into it that she wouldn't have a chance to read his expression.

Robin forced her way through the throng and grabbed Gerber, hugging him tightly. He embraced her in response but tried to keep emotion out of it. He was acutely aware of Karen's letter in his pocket. He pulled away gently but firmly and said, "Robin. Didn't expect you."

"No," she said, laughing. "I guess you didn't."

"Captain," said Mildebrandt, "I assume we're ready to go?"

"Yes," said Gerber quickly, thankful for the diversion. He glanced at Robin and then back at the new lieutenant. "You've met Miss Morrow?"

"Yes, sir," he said. "She's been telling us some more about the camp."

"Grab your gear and let's get out of here."

Morrow whirled, nearly knocked down a skinny captain, and grabbed her suitcase and camera bag. Before Gerber could escape, she handed him her suitcase.

They managed to get out of the terminal and stopped in front of Maxwell. He held out his hand and said, "Thanks for coming down, Mack. Good luck with your mission."

"Yeah, Jerry," said Gerber. "Good luck." He set the suitcase down and said, "Robin, men, this is . . . say, what do we call you? Your full name is a little bit cumbersome."

"I will make it easy for you." She smiled. "You may call me Emilie, the name I received from my French father before he ran away to his homeland."

"Emilie, then," said Gerber. He was going to make the introductions more formal, but the whine of a Huey engine washed out the sound of his voice.

Morrow moved closer to him, and then the men began heading across the tarmac and grass toward the lone chopper that was sitting there. Maxwell lifted a hand and yelled, "Have fun, people," as he disappeared through the fence.

"Let's just board and get out of here," growled Gerber. "As quickly as possible."

THE FLIGHT TO THE CAMP was interesting. Robin sat on the floor of the cargo compartment, leaning against the backrest of one of the pilot's seats. She had her arms wrapped around her legs and her chin on her knees as she stared at Emilie, who had pulled some maneuvers so that she ended up sitting beside Gerber. Emilie kept her hands on the hem of her skirt to hold it down and leaned to the left so that her shoulder touched Gerber's.

Mildebrandt sat watching the whole thing, trying to figure out what was going on. He had been in the army long enough to know that most military units the size of a Special Forces A-team didn't have good-looking women hanging around them, didn't get their own journalists. It was going to be an assignment to enjoy.

When they were close to the camp, the crew chief leaned out of his well and shouted, "We're about five out."

Gerber nodded and yelled back, "Can you circle it a couple of times? Let the new guys have a look at their home for the next several months."

The crew chief disappeared for a moment and then his hand reappeared, his thumb up to indicate to Gerber that they would get the tour. Gerber leaned across Emilie and shouted at Yashimoto and Grummond to let them know they were about to get an aerial view of the camp.

As they circled, Gerber saw someone, probably Bocker, run from the commo bunker, through the gate and out onto the helipad. A moment later a thick cloud of green began billowing, obscuring the edge of the pad. The cloud drifted into the wire, hiding one of the arms of the star.

They made two more passes and then began a descent from the west. The moment they touched down on the helipad, Gerber grabbed his gear and weapon and leaped to the ground. He saw Fetterman and Tyme approaching from the direction of the camp, both strolling along casually. Gerber turned back to the aircraft and was handed Morrow's suitcase. He held on to it because the peta-prime that covered the helipad was soft from the sun.

Mildebrandt climbed out and turned to help Emilie down. Then Grummond gave him some of their gear, and he dropped it to the pad because he didn't know a thing about peta-prime. It was a substance that had been kept hidden from the World. Only Vietnam had the rare and distinct privilege of having it coat everything that anyone owned.

When Fetterman reached the helicopter, Gerber handed Morrow's suitcase to him.

"Ah, Miss Morrow," said Fetterman, grinning. He had already noticed one of the looks that the unidentified Vietnamese woman had given the captain. "This could be very interesting," he added.

"What could be interesting, Master Sergeant?" she asked.

"Oh, everything."

"This is, ah, Emilie," said Gerber, pointing at her, trying to divert the conversation.

"Emilie," said Fetterman. "Welcome to our camp."

"Who's she?" asked Tyme.

"I'll get everything sorted out just as soon as we get off this damned helipad," snapped Gerber. "Sergeant Fetterman, I want to meet with you, Sergeant Tyme and Sergeant Kepler in my hootch in twenty minutes. Find Sully or T.J. and have them arrange quarters for the new men. Lieutenant Mildebrandt will take Novak's quarters. Everyone understand?"

"Yes, sir."

Morrow reached out and jerked her suitcase from Fetterman. "I'll take that, thank you, and I can find my way to my own quarters," she said, stomping off.

"Miss Morrow," called Fetterman, hurrying after her. "Your old quarters no longer exist. They burned with the rest of the camp."

She stopped suddenly. "Burned?" Then she remembered the battle for the camp. "That's right, they burned."

Fetterman caught her and took the suitcase from her hand. "Let me have that. I think we'll be able to find something. Maybe have our guys vacate one of their hootches."

She waved a hand without looking at him. "Whatever you decide will be fine."

The rest of them left the pad, and the helicopter took off, low-leveling away, as if the pilot wanted to impress the ladies with his skill. He hopped over a tree line and disappeared on the other side of it, but when there was no orange ball of flame or pillar of black smoke, everyone assumed that he had managed not to crash.

GERBER WAS SITTING behind his desk when Fetterman knocked on the doorjamb and announced, "We're here, Captain."

"Come on in and have a seat." Gerber folded the letter he held in one hand, having read it for the sixth time, and jammed it into the top pocket of his fatigues. He automatically reached for the bottle of Beam's, hesitated, remembering that Fetterman had suggested he might be fostering alcoholism in the unit, and then decided he needed a drink. He pulled the cork, took a swig and handed it to Fetterman, who now sat in one of the lawn chairs opposite the desk. The bottle made the rounds as each man took a drink.

"Yeah. That's smooth," Gerber said, after Kepler returned the Beam's to him. He pounded the cork back into the bottle before he spoke again. "Okay, Tony, why don't you close the door. I don't want to be interrupted for the next hour or so, and I doubt it'll get much hotter in here anyway."

"Yes, sir."

"First . . . oh, did we get everyone settled?"

Fetterman explained that they had moved a couple of bunks into Sully's and Tyme's hootches. Washington had opted to move his gear into the dispensary, and although no one had asked, it was assumed that Bocker would sleep in the commo bunker until things settled down.

"And," Fetterman added, grinning, "I don't believe our female guests are too happy with the arrangements. I put them in the same hootch. Neither said a word, but the electricity was flying. They'll either become fast friends or kill each other sometime tonight."

"Whatever happens," said Gerber, "it'll solve a lot of problems. Okay, now the reason I've called this meeting." He lowered his voice. "We're going to Cambodia."

Tyme put a hand to his head and said, "Oh, Christ! Not again!"

Gerber ignored the mock distress and said, "This time it's with all the legitimate documents signed and orders issued. Normal patrol, maybe a week, to observe the action on the Ho Chi Minh Trail. Just observation. We're supposed to avoid contact."

"Airlift?"

"No, Tony. I think it'll be better if we walk it. You start flying aircraft all over the place and it becomes everyone's business. The farmers know where the airplanes go, the VC know and the NVA know. You might as well take out a billboard. If we walk, using the jungle for cover, we can avoid all that. Make it harder for the VC to find us and figure out what we're doing and where we're going."

"Yes, sir."

"Derek, your intel boys have anything new of interest for us?"

Kepler, who was wearing an OD T-shirt that was black with sweat, jungle pants stained around the waistband and brush-shined boots, rubbed his chin. He needed a shave, and his hair hung down as if he'd been caught in the shower. He ran a hand through it and said, "I've been getting reports of a lot of activity in the border areas. VC sweeping through the villes asking for rice, meat and water. No recruiting trips, just requests, hell, demands for additional supplies. Lot of movement, mostly at night with attempts to avoid contact."

"Anything else?"

"Got one weird one, sir." He smiled and shook his head. "Convoy of trucks crossed the border north of the Angel's Wing, drove east to Nui Ba Den and disappeared. I figure Charlie drove into the caves that riddle the place."

"You reported it to Nha Trang?"

"Yes, sir. Told them that it was from a single source but that they might be interested. We've got a couple of camps in that area."

"So all you've really seen is an increase in the activity, meaning more people running around here?"

"In a nutshell, sir. Too early to pick up any real trends. Just more people wandering around."

"We the target?"

"I doubt that. Most of the problem is way north of us. If they were interested in us again, they'd be staging the buildup west of here, in Cambodia, not north. Keeps them away from the air force that way."

"Then if we're going to see anything of importance, we need to operate north of our normal AO."

"Yes, sir."

"Okay, thanks, Derek. Tony, you see the general drift of this?"

Fetterman got to his feet and looked at the map spread out on Gerber's desk. "Yes, sir," he said. "Airlift into Tay Ninh. Maybe one of the fire support bases west of there would save us a lot of time and shoe leather. So much going on out there that an extra flight landing shouldn't raise any eyebrows."

Gerber nodded. "Right. Without Derek's info, we'd have walked due west and maybe not seen anything. Justin, when we break up here, I'll want you to talk with Galvin. Have him start trying to arrange airlift."

"I can't see any real difficulties, sir," said Tyme. "How big a force are we taking?"

"Given the nature of the mission and what I was told in Saigon, I'd say half the team and an equal number of Tais. Fourteen in all, fifteen with our scout."

"Scout?" said Kepler.

"Yes, Derek. Scout. We've been provided with a Kit Carson for this mission."

Kepler shook his head. "I don't want to be negative about this, but I don't like it. We're going into enemy-held territory with a fairly small force, no real possibility of air or artillery cover, and we're being led by someone who was a traitor once. Just because he was VC and now wants to help us is no reason—"

"She," said Gerber.

"What?" asked Tyme.

"She. The Vietnamese woman who came back with me is supposed to be our scout."

"Oh, for Christ's sake, sir," said Kepler.

"She's going. Orders," said Gerber.

Fetterman said, "So fifteen people to monitor the Trail. Wouldn't four or five be enough?"

"They've had some trouble with their teams in there. That's why we've been given the task, with orders to take a large enough force that we'll be relatively safe. I figure on leaving most of the new men here with our new XO in charge. Tony, I'll want you with me. Derek, you're in because we'll need someone who can determine the importance of anything we see on the Trail. Justin, you're in, of course. I'll talk to Washington because we'll want a medic, Anderson for demo and Bocker for commo."

"Which Tais?" asked Fetterman.

"Contact Sergeant Krung and have him pick a team of six. That means Krung goes, too."

"When do we leave?" asked Tyme.

"If Galvin can arrange for the airlift tomorrow, I'd say about 0700 hours. Derek, you and I'll go over the map to pick a route. Justin, make a detailed weapons check. Only the best. Select the squad weapons that you think will be the most helpful."

"Yes, sir."

Gerber consulted his watch. "All right. Full briefing tonight after evening chow. Everyone who is going except the Tai strikers. Krung, yes."

"Our Kit Carson?" asked Kepler.

"Whoa," said Gerber. And then, "Yeah, I think we'll need her, but then we've got to keep her isolated from the other Vietnamese. Don't want her to have a chance to pass any information to them if she's so inclined. Someone will have to stay with her the whole time, and we'll have to watch her hootch tonight to make sure that she doesn't sneak out for any reason." He looked around the room. "Anything else?"

"No, sir," said Fetterman, speaking for the group.

"Then let's meet in the commo bunker after chow. It'll be cooler, and it'll provide us with a little better security."

AN HOUR AFTER he dropped Gerber and the Kit Carson off at the terminal at Hotel Three, Jerry Maxwell was back in Brigadier General Billy Joe Crinshaw's building. He entered the outer office where an old master sergeant, a graying, thin man who did nothing but watch the clock, sat behind a large desk. He was obviously waiting for the end of the day, the end of the week, the end of his tour. When Maxwell entered, the sergeant flipped closed a copy of *Stars and Stripes* and asked, "Can I help you?"

"I'm supposed to brief General Crinshaw."

The sergeant turned to a large appointment book sitting on the corner of his desk, opened it to the right page and ran a finger down it. "You're Maxwell?"

"Yes."

"Please have a seat, and I'll see if the general is free."

Maxwell chose not to sit. Instead, he seemed to find the outer office interesting. The walls were paneled in dark wood, with light blue carpeting on the floor. He took in the potted and hanging plants that seemed to camouflage one corner, and the four plush high-backed chairs. There was a short square table in front of the chairs that held copies of *Time, Newsweek, Life,* and strangely, *Analog Science Fiction* magazine.

The sergeant picked up the receiver on a field phone, spun the crank and talked quietly into it. As he hung up, he said, "You may go in."

Maxwell opened the door leading into the inner sanctum of Brigadier General Billy Joe Crinshaw. It was like stepping into another world, a world where it was always cold and dark. The general had rearranged and replaced almost everything since Maxwell had last been there.

Crinshaw, a big, stocky man who had played tackle on the Georgia Tech football team, sat behind his opulent desk of polished mahogany, writing on a yellow legal pad. He wore a starched and pressed field jacket with embroidered stars on the epaulets. The walls around him were paneled in rich, dark woods. Venetian blinds, which were closed, covered the windows, almost completely hidden behind OD green curtains. In one corner were twin air conditioners, blowing cold air with the force of a Midwest blizzard.

Maxwell stood between the two leather wing chairs that faced the desk. To his left were floor-to-ceiling bookcases filled with volumes, some of which were actually army manuals, he noted. Opposite the books was a wall full of captured weapons, each with a plaque detailing the date, weapon type and circumstances. Crinshaw had had nothing to do with the capture of any of the weapons. He had collected them from combat soldiers by threatening their careers. The carpeting was thick and dark.

Crinshaw continued and then, without looking up, waved at one of the chairs. "Siddown, for Christ's sake. I'll be with you in a moment."

Maxwell collapsed into one of the chairs, fastened the top button on his shirt and slipped his tie up in an attempt to keep from freezing. Crinshaw took a file folder from the middle drawer, placed his pad in it and then locked everything away. He jammed his pen into the holder on the front of the desk, folded his hands and waited.

"I've just left Captain Gerber after his briefing," said Maxwell.

"And?"

"And he's preparing for the mission, just as he was ordered to do."

"No complaints from him?" asked Crinshaw. "I thought the boy would be up in arms about it."

"I had to give him the written orders . . ."

"I'll fucking bet you did." Crinshaw rocked back and clasped his hands together behind his head. "I'll just bet you did. That dumb ass. Goes charging into Cambodia on a whim and then makes us give him written orders to do the same thing. I'll just never understand that boy."

"No, sir," said Maxwell. "Anyway, he's been briefed on the mission."

"Good. Now I'll want you boys to keep in touch with him so we know what's going on out there."

"That's no problem. And since he has a fairly large force going in with him, it'll give us a clue about how important the VC think their secrecy is. I believe," said Maxwell, tenting his fingers under chin, "that this will tell us if the buildup is leading to something big or if it's just an attempt to place more people in the area, for whatever reason."

"Now we have to be very careful," said Crinshaw. "We don't want to tip our hand. We can't have the NVA and the Vietcong realizing that we know they're planning something. We don't want them to back off."

"I understand that, General."

"What I'm saying is we have to rethink this airlift if Gerber should get into trouble. Right now Charlie doesn't have a clue about what we know or how much. He's just out there, sneaking through the fucking jungle, thinking the Americans are a bunch of candy asses who don't know shit from shinola."

"I understand all that," said Maxwell, not sure that he did at all.

"Boy, you got to see the big picture. That's something Gerber and his kind fail to do. See the big picture. We go pullin' a big rescue, if Gerber and his boys get into trouble, and Charlie's gonna know that we know."

Maxwell leaned forward, his hands on the arm of his chair. "Excuse me, General, but you're not suggesting that we—"

"Mr. Maxwell, I'm saying that Captain Gerber is going to have to get out of anything that he gets himself into. We have to play this very close to the vest."

"You can't be serious," Maxwell said. "You're not suggesting that if Gerber gets out there, gets the information we want, and then gets into trouble, we leave him there with his ass blowing in the breeze?''

Crinshaw reached out and pulled the pen from its holder. He twirled it in both hands. ''The military sometimes finds it necessary to sacrifice men. Travis and the boys at the Alamo so that Sam Houston could build an army. The rearguard that dies to ensure the majority of the army escapes. It's a fact of life and a fact of war.''

''But not when you can get them out.''

Crinshaw waved a hand. ''Maxwell, we're arguing something that might not even happen. If Gerber does his job properly, Charlie won't even know he's there.''

''General, those LRRPs were very good at their jobs, and we only managed to get one of them out. And that was with airlift and close air support.''

''Doesn't matter, boy. Mission requirements dictate that we provide no army airlift to extract them. There'd be too much publicity if any aviation assets were lost on the wrong side of the border. I'm already catching hell over the LRRP mess. The moment Gerber crosses into Cambodia, he's on his own. We won't send him help because of the international ramifications and the possibility of accidentally telling the enemy what we know.''

Maxwell sat there for a moment, staring at Crinshaw, trying to force the general to lower his eyes first as if that would somehow make him rescind his order, but Crinshaw won the skirmish. Maxwell looked away and then said, ''None of this is right.''

''Doesn't matter if it's right or wrong, it's an order.''

5

THE HO CHI MINH TRAIL
PARROT'S BEAK REGION
CAMBODIA

The airplanes came in the afternoon. They crisscrossed the sky above Corporal Tran Minh Ngo's platoon, as if searching for them. Ngo and his comrades crouched among the bushes and trees and refused to move. Ngo clutched his rifle with all his might, his knuckles turning white. He kept his eyes on the sky, as if by looking at the American airplanes he would somehow protect himself from them. He felt fear knot his stomach and a cold, clammy sweat slide down his back.

The terrors of the Cambodian jungle hadn't really fazed him. He had pulled leeches from his body and chopped the head from a cobra before it could strike. He had heard the screams of the tigers as they prowled in the night and had listened to the trumpeting of elephants in the distance. He had suffered the heat of midday, the cold rains that came at four in the morning and the chilling predawn breezes. He had eaten the soggy rice and the stolen meat. And he had believed, almost, when the political officer had told them of the great glory that awaited them in the South.

But now he hid, paralyzed with fear, as the American jets circled overhead like vultures waiting for something to die. He realized that he was mumbling under his breath, a prayer of deliverance, and then knew that it wasn't. He was quietly calling for his mother.

One of the jets dived toward the ground, and as it pulled up suddenly, something tumbled from its wings. A second later, the top of a nearby hill burst into orange flame and black smoke. Ngo could imagine the flames engulfing him, roasting him, killing him. There was nothing more horrible in the world, he was certain, no more horrible way to die.

For thirty minutes the jets pounded the ground with their napalm and machine guns. They were far enough from Ngo's platoon that the men were never in danger from the jets, but they were close enough for them to see everything the airplanes did. The jungle erupted in flames under the bombardment of napalm, vegetation shredding under the relentless stream of machine gun bullets.

Then, as suddenly as they had appeared, the jets vanished. Except for the quiet whimpering of one of the men, everything was silent. Ngo looked to his left and saw the man, his arms wrapped around the tree, crying. He had dropped his rifle in the mud of the jungle floor, thrown his pack into the bush and had tried to rip off his uniform. His eyes were tightly closed, and he had wet himself.

Ngo looked away. He didn't feel like laughing at the man. Ngo understood completely the terror the man felt, understood the despair. Even after the inspiring story told by the Chinese officer, Ngo couldn't believe that he and his comrades could do anything against the might of the Americans. They were too strong and had too much. How could a man with a rifle fight an airplane that swooped from the sky to kill and destroy.

The lieutenant walked to the man hugging the tree. Ngo expected him to receive a tongue-lashing about cowardice in front of his comrades, but that didn't happen. The officer knelt and talked to the soldier quietly, explaining that everyone had been frightened, but now it was over. The airplanes were gone, and none of the platoon had been harmed. It was time to forget about that, forget about the Americans, and get busy with the job they had come to do.

Within minutes they were moving again, but their attitude was solemn. The laughing and joking were gone, replaced by the fear of the Americans and their war machines. Ngo kept his eyes on the ground in front of him. It was as if he believed the American planes would return if he looked at the sky. He now ignored the heat and humidity, thinking only of orange balls of flame that would melt the flesh from his face and cook his lungs as he tried to breathe.

GERBER SAT ON THE MAP TABLE, which was pushed against one of the sandbagged walls of the commo bunker, and watched as his men filed in. When Emilie came down the stairs, he was tempted to pull the chart from the wall that had the suspected locations of enemy units and the coordinates of American bases marked on it, but he realized that the VC already knew where their men were, and the American bases were out there for all to see.

Most of the men sat on the floor, ignoring the light coating of red dust on it. One or two jumped up to sit on the plywood counter that separated the rear of the bunker from the rest of it. Behind the counter, Bocker stood, the radios on, but the microphones unplugged. He leaned between Tyme and Washington.

When Anderson saw Emilie, he leaped to his feet, brushed the seat of his fatigue pants and opened one of the metal folding chairs leaning against the sandbagged wall. He held out a hand and said, "Please."

Emilie smiled at the big, blond man. Standing next to him, she looked like a tiny doll. She was still wearing her black skirt and white blouse that now had perspiration stains on it. She brushed at her hair, pushing it off her forehead, which was beaded with sweat. She looked up at Anderson and said, "Thank you."

A moment later Krung came down and stood at parade rest next to the entrance. Gerber looked at him, the Americans, saw that both Kepler and Fetterman were there, too, and hopped off the table. "Sergeant Fetterman," he said, "is Sully standing by outside?"

"Yes, sir. He won't let anyone get close to the door. We're as secure here as we could be anywhere on the base."

Gerber dusted his hands together and then pinned a map to the acetate-covered board behind him. He pulled a string on the lamp that hung over the board and then faced the men. "This will be the predeployment briefing for this mission. Any questions should be answered tonight. We'll begin with Sergeant Kepler's intel update.''

Kepler moved to the front and said, ''I guess I don't have to tell you that this is secret or that it's not to be discussed outside the confines of this bunker.''

''That include the woman?'' asked Bocker.

Gerber looked at Emilie and then at the communications sergeant. ''Yes, Galvin. It includes her. She's our Kit Carson on this one.''

''Well, then, by all means, let Kit stay,'' said Bocker. ''I just wondered.

Kepler hesitated, watching the woman for a moment, and then launched into his briefing. He covered the suspected locations of the enemy forces they might encounter, probable weapons those forces would have, terrain features that could affect the mission and the best escape and evasion routes, if those were needed.

Gerber thanked him and said, ''Master Sergeant, you have a route of march?''

Fetterman moved to the front of the room and leaned across the table. He marked a couple of places in grease pencil on the acetate map. He had to move the one that Gerber had tacked up. ''Sergeant Bocker's arranged airlift for tomorrow at 0700 hours. I've found an LZ west of Tay Ninh City between the Suoi May and the Song Vam Co Dong, which is called the Prek Tate in Cambodia. That means we've only got one river to cross. And since it marks the border, we'll know when we're in Cambodia.''

He turned and drew a long line on the map. ''Now this is the approximate location of the Ho Chi Minh Trail. Using the secret topographical charts and the aerial photos provided by Derek, I've located a number of good spots from which to observe the Trail. Of course, working from a map means we might have to remain flexible once into the AO, since some of our maps are unreliable.''

''You check this out with Kit?'' asked Gerber. As he said that, he realized that she had acquired a nickname, and it was easier to think of her as the Kit Carson rather than Emilie.

''No, sir. Didn't have time. I thought I might check some of it out with her later.''

"Proceed."

Fetterman outlined the route and approximate locations for overnight camps. He also suggested the supplies that would be needed for a week-long patrol.

When Fetterman finished, Tyme briefed everyone on the weapons, who would carry what and the breakdown of the spare ammo for squad weapons, who would carry the grenade launchers and which personal weapons should be taken. Although he wasn't sure about the reliability of the M-16, he suggested that they all be equipped with it because of its lighter weight and the smaller size of the rounds. The men could carry more ammo for it. And if they all had the same type of weapons, they could share the spare ammo, if the need for that arose.

Bocker talked about the radios, and Washington made a couple of suggestions about ways to remain healthy. He told them to take the malaria pills, knowing that they wouldn't because the pills gave everyone diarrhea, and the last thing anyone needed was diarrhea in the jungle. Anderson had nothing to say about demolitions, and Kit just sat there, almost as if the briefing had put her to sleep.

"Now, are there any questions?" asked Gerber.

"Just one," said Fetterman. "What about Miss Morrow? She's going to be very interested in our activities."

"A good point," said Gerber. "Obviously we can't tell her a thing about it because it's a clandestine operation."

"And you're going to be hard-pressed to keep her out of it, since we're taking a woman with us," added Fetterman.

"She has to know that something is up," said Gerber. "Hell, we've had meetings, and she found us in Saigon coming from briefings." Gerber shrugged. "I guess we'll, or rather I will just order her to stay here if it comes up."

"Good luck," said Fetterman.

"Yeah, good luck," repeated Gerber. "Anything else? No? All right, gentlemen, we have work to do. Let's get at it. Kit, I'd like to talk with you and Sergeant Fetterman as soon as we're done here. The rest of you can leave."

When the men were gone, Gerber sat down with Kit and Fetterman to check the map and make sure the routes were going to do what they wanted them to do. Kit nodded and studied them but had little to say.

It took them an hour to work through everything, but when they were done Gerber suggested they head over to the team house and he would treat them to a quick beer before they turned in for the night. He told them to go on ahead of him because he had to find Captain Minh and brief him, alone with Lieutenant Mildebrandt and Sully Smith.

When Gerber broke off to head to Minh's hootch, Fetterman gently steered Kit to the team house. They entered, and he held out a chair for her.

"You don't really have to drink a beer if you don't want one," said Fetterman.

She sat down and slowly crossed her legs. "No. A beer will be fine."

Fetterman got two from the refrigerator, opened them and set one in front of Kit. "Be careful, because it's very cold. Do you mind if I call you Kit?"

"No." She laughed. "You Americans are so fond of nicknames. Everyone seems to have one."

"You have to admit," said Fetterman, "that Kit is handier than your real name."

"If you insist," she said.

Fetterman sipped his beer and stared. Finally he asked, "How do you like your accommodations?"

"They are just fine. Very comfortable. It is nice to have a bed and not a handful of straw. Not as nice as Saigon, of course, but still nice."

"Well," said Fetterman, "I think it's a cot, not a bed, but it's definitely better than a handful of straw." He hesitated and then said, "I hope you don't think I'm prying, but you're not pure Vietnamese."

She looked at him over the top of the beer can and set it down deliberately. "Are you suggesting . . ."

"Oh, no," said Fetterman. "I phrased that badly. I was just wondering about your background."

"A personal question or professional?"

"Kit, you're here on the orders of a higher authority. They have faith in you, and I have no reason to doubt you. So, the question is personal." What he didn't say was that he had no faith in the higher authority and had every reason to doubt them. They would take too much at face value, rarely looking below the surface, because that would cut into their time in the club. They were easily fooled because they wanted their record to look good, and the more of the enemy who defected, the better they looked. Never mind that the defecting enemy might really be a VC spy.

"Then I'll be happy to answer," said Kit. "My father was a French paratrooper who was here during the Second World War. After the war, he went home, but then he came back for my mother. He was killed in our war."

"I'm sorry," said Fetterman.

"It was a long time ago."

"Yes, I suppose."

"But it did some good for me. Not his death, but the fact that he was French. I received some schooling that I would otherwise never have received. I learned things that I would never have known, and I was allowed to do things that a good Vietnamese girl would never do. By that, I mean I was allowed to leave the village for my schooling. I do not have to live in a village that belongs in the Stone Age at best, hoping to one day have an electric lamp. I have seen some of the world and know what's out there. I'm not like the other girls of my village who have no idea what is beyond the next tree line."

Her voice took on a bitter quality. The knuckles of her hand grew white around the bottle, and her eyes were locked on the edge of the table.

"Then you have been quite fortunate?" suggested Fetterman.

"Fortunate? Yes, I suppose I have been. But then I've paid the price for my luck. I have lost my husband and my father in a war that neither wanted to fight."

"That is the way of the world," said Fetterman, knowing that the words were inadequate. Her emotions sounded genuine. She seemed to be just what she said, but Fetterman was concerned about it. He wished he knew more about her.

"Yes, the way of the world." She shook herself and said, "Your Captain Gerber seems to be a man of great compassion, however."

Fetterman didn't speak for a moment. Something had suddenly changed, and he didn't know if she had shifted the subject because she was unsure of her ability to carry off her act, or if she was interested in Gerber.

Then, before he could say anything, Gerber appeared in the doorway. He glanced at the beers they both held, got one for himself and dropped into the chair next to Kit. "I see that you two couldn't wait."

"Didn't think you'd mind, Captain," said Fetterman. "I was learning a little about Kit."

"Then don't let me stop you," said Gerber.

"Actually," said Kit, "we were talking about you."

"Oh. I'm not sure I like that."

Fetterman decided it was time to change the subject again. He said, "Kit? You look very nice, but do you have some other clothes for the mission?"

"We could get you some fatigues if you need them," said Gerber.

"No, I have some clothes that are suitable for the field. I also have my own pack and canteen. Everything I need. I shall be fine."

Gerber caught Kit staring at him, and for some inexplicable reason he suddenly remembered the letter from Karen in his pocket. He let his eyes slide away and then said to Fetterman, "We'd better wrap it up here. Get some sleep." He stood, "If you'll excuse me, I have a few last-minute details to take care of. See you in the morning."

FETTERMAN ESCORTED KIT back to the hootch that she was to share with Robin Morrow. She thanked him and then turned, stepping up into the hootch. As she entered, she saw that Morrow was sitting cross-legged on one of the bunks, a camera in one hand and a tiny brush with a red bulb in the other. She wore only a pair of flimsy panties, but she didn't look particularly cool.

Kit cast a glance around the room. Her gaze came to rest on the metal locker sitting against the wall, on the pile of gear in front of it, the dresser on the other side of the room and the other locker there. The floor was dirty, and a soiled canopy from a parachute flare was draped over the rafters. An ancient ceiling fan hung through the center of the canopy, but it wasn't turning. From one corner a naked light bulb glowed, and a Coleman lantern sat on a metal chair near Morrow.

"Hello," said Kit.

"Hello," responded Morrow without looking up.

Kit opened the locker and took out a hanger. She unbuttoned her blouse and shrugged it off. Then she took off her skirt and hung both garments in the locker. With just her underwear on, she moved to her bed, watching Morrow. "You have something going with Captain Gerber?" she asked point-blank.

For an instant, Morrow froze, jolted by the directness of the question. Then she started working on her camera again as if she hadn't heard a thing.

Kit watched her and then said, "The captain is a very nice man."

Morrow set her camera down and turned so that she faced Kit. "He is indeed a very nice man. He is kind to everyone, yet ruthless in battle. He can be very nice. And to answer your question, we have a kind of an understanding."

"Yes, an understanding." Kit lay back on her bunk, her hands under her head as she stared up at the ceiling.

Morrow slid her camera away, stood and walked to the dresser. She stopped and turned. "What do they call you? Emilie? Soo Ta?"

"The men here have started calling me Kit. That seems to fit nicely."

"Why Kit?"

"I am Kit Carson scout for them."

Morrow moved back to her bunk and sat down looking at Kit. "I thought the Kit Carson scouts were all VC who had changed sides."

"Yes."

"Oh."

Kit sat up and looked at Morrow through the mosquito netting, supported by two long poles on the right side of her cot. "Is there something wrong with that?"

"Not at all. I just find it interesting. Very interesting." She looked at her camera bag and the reporter's notebook that was sticking out of it. "Say, this might make an interesting story—

what it was like to be a VC, why you changed your mind. Pictures and everything.''

Kit rolled to her side so that she didn't have to face Morrow. ''I don't think it would be such a great story,'' she said.

''Why not?'' asked Morrow. ''Your picture in the paper all over the world. You'd be famous. The heroic female fighter for democracy.''

''No,'' said Kit quietly. ''I don't think so.''

NEXT MORNING Gerber found Fetterman sitting in the team house, eating a breakfast of cold cereal in warm milk and orange juice that was darker at the bottom of the glass where the powder had settled. The toast was dark brown in the center and nearly black at the edges.

Gerber slipped into the chair opposite Fetterman, took a slice of toast from the plate and made a face at it. ''I don't suppose we have any jelly?''

''A little,'' said Fetterman. He slid a flat can from a C-ration meal at Gerber. ''This is the best I can do.''

''Well, thanks, anyway.'' Gerber ate the toast dry. When he finished, he said, ''We've got another problem. I want you to take the lead aircraft off ahead of us and show the pilot the LZ. That'll give them a chance to arrange an arty prep.''

''What do we need an arty prep for?'' asked Fetterman. He dropped his spoon into the now-empty cereal bowl.

''I doubt that we do, but the way the army has been running their combat assaults dictates an arty prep. It's more of an exercise for the cannon cockers and to detonate any booby traps that might be scattered in the LZ. If we want this to look like a normal mission to anyone who's watching, we'll need the prep.''

''Okay, Captain. I'll take Boom-Boom to coordinate the artillery.''

''That's not necessary. Oh, you can take Tyme if you want, but once you've shown the pilot the LZ, he'll coordinate the arty with his C and C.''

''When's the aircraft due in?''

''It'll be coming with the others. We'll just sit on the strip for ten, fifteen minutes, giving you a head start. We won't need much in the way of artillery.''

At that moment, Tyme stumbled in, looking as if he hadn't slept in a week. His fatigue shirt wasn't buttoned, his belt wasn't buckled and his boots hadn't been laced. He had a soft hat jammed onto his head and carried a towel over his shoulder as if he was coming from the shower, although it didn't seem as if he'd taken one. As he entered, he yawned and scratched his belly. "We got any breakfast?" he asked.

"Jesus!" said Gerber. "We're going to war with this?"

"Don't worry, Captain, I'll be ready by the time we get out into the war," said Tyme.

"I'm not worried," said Gerber. "You see the others?"

"Yes, sir. Galvin's in the commo bunker, playing with his radios and eating a monstrous jelly roll, but he won't tell me where he got it. Kepler and Washington are in the dispensary doing something. Maybe drinking all the medicinal brandy or something. I didn't see Anderson."

"He had the last watch on the girls' hootch. Probably still out there watching it," said Gerber.

Fetterman checked the time. "I make it about twenty minutes before the aircraft arrive."

"Okay. Why don't you swing by the Tai area and make sure that Krung has his people up and around. I'll gather the rest of the men and meet you on the helipad in about fifteen minutes." Gerber smiled. "That means you'll have to gulp your food, Justin."

"Yes, sir."

GERBER, WEARING HIS RUCKSACK and pistol belt and carrying his M-16, stood at the gate to the camp. The road there led to the runway. He watched the five army Hueys touch down in formation near the men who would make up the loads. The lead ship shot the approach to the cloud of yellow smoke from the grenade that Bocker had thrown, and as his chopper flared, so did the four aircraft behind him. His skids touched the soft peta-prime with the nose of the lead helicopter over the smoke grenade. The last two ships, caught in the turbulence created by the swirling rotor wash of the first three, bounced high as if the skids contained springs. Then they dropped suddenly. It wasn't a pretty landing, but both choppers settled in a cloud of dust stirred up by the rotors.

"I'm not sure I would care to fly with those guys," said Mildebrandt from a position just behind Gerber.

"It's a lot harder landing in a formation than you'd think. They did a fairly good job."

"If you insist."

"Okay, Glen," said Gerber, "there won't be that much for you to do. Familiarize yourself with the camp, the defenses and the immediate area. Sully Smith will be a big help to you. Listen to him. I know I'm not doing you any favors, leaving all the new guys with you, but Captain Minh, my counterpart, is top-notch. He may be the best that the South has."

"Yes, sir. I understand."

"You get into a situation you're uncomfortable with, don't be afraid to ask either Minh or Smith for advice. If you're in a real bind, call on Colonel Bates at the B-Detachment in Saigon. He's one of us and understands. They'll all take care of you and help you."

"Yes, sir."

Gerber smiled and held out a hand. "Good luck, and I'll see you in about a week." Gerber left then, heading for the second aircraft. He watched Fetterman, Tyme and two strikers climb on board the lead ship. A moment later the chopper leaped up, its nose tilted toward the ground as if the pilot was going to dive into the dirt. Instead, it raced forward, gaining speed but no altitude. Then it disappeared from sight quickly.

Gerber walked to the second load. Kit stood there wearing black silk shorts, a khaki shirt, webgear with two canteens and a rucksack. She was holding an M-16. Her long black hair was piled on top of her head and hidden under a boonie hat.

As he approached her, a dozen things ran through his mind. Things to say, orders to give, a feeling that he was arming an enemy soldier with the best of the new rifles. Instead of any of that, he simply said, "Good morning, Kit."

She turned and looked at him, smiling warmly. "Good morning, Captain. I trust you slept well."

"Yes," he said. "And you?"

"As well as could be expected in a new place, with people who do not trust you. Your guards made very little noise as they rotated last night."

"That was for your protection," Gerber said, a little too quickly.

"If you say so."

Gerber was mildly embarrassed that she had picked up on the guards so quickly, but to him it was just a sensible precaution. Before he could say anything about it, there was a shout from the camp, and he turned. Morrow, wearing jungle fatigues, her pistol belt with canteens, knife and first-aid kit, and carrying a large camera bag, ran through the gate.

"Hey, Mack! Wait!"

Gerber looked at the four remaining helicopters, their blades spinning slowly at flight idle, and wished that he could just leap on one to escape. He faced her, and over the noise of the helicopters said, "Good morning, Robin."

"Thought you were going to get away without me, didn't you?" She stopped two feet from him and set her bag on the soft, red dirt at the side of the runway.

"Didn't think a thing about it since you're not going," said Gerber.

"What do you mean, not going? Of course I'm going. I always go."

"Not on this one," said Gerber.

"Then I'll just have to get on the horn to Saigon and talk to General Crinshaw about it. He'll clear me," she said.

"That I seriously doubt. First, you're not one of his favorite people anymore, and second, the nature of this mission dictates that we operate only with combat-experienced troops."

Morrow pointed at Kit. "You're taking her." Morrow's voice was filled with derision.

"I'm taking her because she's combat-experienced, she knows the area, and I was ordered to take her. All three things work for her, but not for you."

Morrow stared at Kit with hate-filled eyes. "I could force my way on this little mission."

"No, you can't. I'll have you forcibly removed and restrained if I have to. Robin, be reasonable. You know there are missions where we can't have amateurs, even well-trained amateurs, with us. This is one of those times. When we return, I'll give you the full details and you'll have your story. But you can't go."

"I don't like this, Gerber. I thought we had a deal, an arrangement."

"We did. Do. I try to respect your job. You've got to respect mine. There are times when our jobs work against each other. This is one of those times that you'll just have to trust me."

"Thanks," she said sarcastically, "for pulling that trust routine out like that. Shit. Okay, Gerber, you win this one. You just watch your butt and not hers." She grabbed her camera bag, spun and stomped up the road.

"What did all that mean?" asked Kit.

"Never mind," snapped Gerber. "It's none of your business." Then he softened and said, "Sorry." Before he could say more, he noticed that the pilot of his aircraft was waving at him. The rest of the men had boarded the ships. "Come on, let's go."

They climbed aboard but didn't strap in because Gerber wanted to be ready to get out the instant they touched down in the LZ. Over the increasing noise of the Huey turbine, he felt like shouting, "This is it," but realized it sounded like a bad line from a hundred war movies. Instead, he leaned back against the soundproofing and thought of the letter from Karen Morrow. He didn't feel right about leaving it at the camp, especially with Karen's sister running around. Reporters had a tendency to go snooping. But there wasn't anything he could do about it now.

He felt the chopper break ground and couldn't help himself.

"This is it," he said.

6

ABOARD A HUEY HELICOPTER WEST OF TAY NINH CITY EAST OF THE CAMBODIAN BORDER

Fetterman studied his map closely, checking it against the landmarks that were readily visible in the early morning sunlight. He was surprised at the size of Tay Ninh, a city with more than a million inhabitants. The streets were wide, with high buildings and countless cars. He identified the Cao Dai Temple, an impressive structure, which it was claimed had more than a million dollars worth of gold statues, artifacts and treasures. On the west side of the city, they passed the American base, a sprawling complex of red dirt that looked like a badly infected sore in the bright green of the jungle and rice paddies surrounding it.

To the northeast, dominating the landscape for miles around, was Nui Ba Den, the Black Virgin Mountain. It was a name that fit because the mountain rose from the verdant landscape around it like a giant black blemish. From the top, observers could see almost to the South China Sea and into the interior of Cambodia.

They continued to the northwest, flying over rice paddies that gave way to swamp in the south or forests and jungle in the north. Fetterman saw the point where the Suoi May and the Song Vam Co Dong met. There was a road that crossed one of the rivers and turned almost due north, avoiding Cambodia. Jungle grew around it, some of the trees nearly two hundred feet high. The canopy was becoming thicker so that Fetterman rarely saw the ground, just a sea of green broken by rice paddies to the east and some swamp to the west. Finally he spotted the LZ, a large open area bordered by tall teak, mahogany and palm trees and carpeted with scrub brush and grass.

They circled it once at fifteen hundred feet so that Fetterman could get a good look at it. Then they broke out of the orbit, moving farther to the north. Fetterman instructed the pilot to circle a couple of other areas, just in case there was an audience.

Once they had moved off far enough, Fetterman requested a radio linkup to the other pilots at the camp to tell them it was time to take off if they hadn't done so already. He then sat back on the troop seat and watched as the sun rose higher, burning off the mist.

He was staring at the LZ when there was a single flash of fire and a gigantic white plume, smoke rolling upward from the center. He lost sight of it when the helicopter banked, and then it reappeared on the left side. Now the LZ was hidden under a cloud of brown dirt and dust thrown up by the artillery rounds detonating in it. A silver column flashed in the sunlight, water exploding upward under fire from the 105 mm artillery pieces.

There was a moment's hesitation, and then another six rounds detonated. They added to the smoke and dust that was drifting off to the east, obscuring the ground but marking the LZ. Then, far to the south, avoiding the gun target lines of the artillery at the fire support base, Fetterman could see the tiny black shapes of the other Huey helicopters.

Fetterman's chopper broke back to the west, skirting the Cambodian border, trying to avoid the gun target lines. They joined up with the other four helicopters and orbited south of the LZ. From the right, two Huey gunships, each with two seven-rocket pods and two XM134 miniguns, appeared.

When the flight was formed, they turned north, heading toward the LZ. Through the windshield, Fetterman saw flashes of light twenty-five to fifty feet high. He knew they were the last six rounds, exploding in the air. They would rake the ground with shrapnel and detonate any small booby traps that might have escaped the heavier bombardment.

In his mind, Fetterman could hear the radio communications between the pilots and the arty officers. The pilots would be told that the last rounds were on the way, and they would then report that the rounds had hit the ground. Someone at the far end would say that the tubes were clear. The ritual was designed to prevent the pilots from flying into the last six rounds of the arty prep. A check against a check, and since Fetterman had seen the results of an artillery round exploding too close to an aircraft, he approved of it.

Normally there would have been a gunship to lead the flight in. It would hover through the LZ, and someone would toss a smoke grenade out of the cargo compartment. This time, without a C and C directing the mission, the lead ship would shoot the approach with the other ships following. Both gunships were on the west side of the flight now where they could use their weapons for suppression. There had been no indications that Charlie was in the area, but that didn't matter. They would hose down the trees in an attempt to keep anyone who happened to be around from shooting at the flight.

As they neared the LZ, the lead gunship's nose dropped, and it dived at the trees, clouds of smoke erupting from the rocket pods as it fired. From his vantage point, Fetterman saw the tiny yellow flames of the rocket motors until they disappeared into the dense vegetation. He lost sight of them for only a second. Then, through gaps in the jungle, he saw an orange flash as the warheads exploded, and an instant later a column of smoke boiled upward. There were more flashes in the jungle as other rockets hit. Then that ship broke away from the flight, the door guns hammering and the ruby tracers slamming into the trees as the second ship began its firing run.

Fetterman turned his attention to his own ship. The crew chief and door gunner both opened fire with their M-60 machine guns. Even over the whine of the engine, the roar of the wind and the popping of the rotor blades, Fetterman could hear the hammering of the M-60s. To the left, a line of tracers smashed into the base of the trees as the choppers got close to the LZ. Dirt splashed upward like water slapped by a giant hand. Leaves and bark stripped from the branches rained on the ground. Ruby-colored lights flashed into the dark green of the jungle and disappeared.

But there was no return fire. No higher, flatter staccato bursts from AK-47s or yammering from .30 caliber machine guns.

They were flying close to the ground now. Fetterman could see it rushing under his aircraft, a blur of greens and grays. He reached up and buckled the chin strap of his helmet so that he wouldn't lose it as he leaped from the back of the chopper. He slipped off the safety of his weapon with his thumb as he moved from the troop seat to the edge of the cargo compartment, crouching in the doorway so that he could leap out first.

When the aircraft flared, a maneuver that killed the forward motion, Fetterman put a hand out against the edge of the troop seat to steady himself. A second later the skids leveled, and they dropped the last few feet to the ground. The instant the skids touched the earth, Fetterman was out, moving rapidly through the thick brush, thorns grabbing at his uniform. Once he put some distance between himself and the aircraft, he dropped to his stomach, watching the trees, waiting for the enemy to open fire.

Each of the helicopters lifted off then, their door guns momentarily silent. Once they were clear of their human cargo, they opened fire. Five M-60s opened up at the trees as the gunships roared overhead. The miniguns made a sound like that of a buzz saw, firing so fast that the tracers formed an unbroken line.

In seconds the gunships had peeled away, taking up a station to the south, waiting for their release. It was suddenly silent again in the LZ. The quiet seemed overwhelming after all the noise of the combat assault. Fetterman hesitated where he was, watching the jungle, waiting for the trap to spring, but there was no trap, no enemy. It was a typical, cold LZ.

Without waiting for a command, Fetterman was up and moving. He didn't speak to the men. They followed him, spreading out as they swept toward the trees. He glanced to the south and saw that Gerber was moving, too, his weapon held at the ready. Kit was near him, almost as if she was guarding him. Anderson was close by. Spread farther to the south were Bocker, Washington and Kepler. Krung and his four Tais were on the far end. Fetterman turned and watched as Tyme and the other two Tai diverted around a bush and entered the trees.

Once they had gained the trees, the line collapsed toward the center. Fetterman made sure that security was out and then stepped close to Gerber. Kit was right beside him.

Gerber crouched and pulled his map from the pocket of his fatigue pants. He opened it and then refolded it so that the patch of jungle where they stood was in the center of the map. There was nothing marked on it, no routes drawn in, no proposed campsites indicated. Absolutely nothing on the map that would prove useful to the Vietcong if he was captured, or if he lost it.

"We're here," said Gerber, tapping the map with a forefinger.

"Route due west would put us into Cambodia the fastest, but we've got some swamp to cross and one river. If we swing north and then west, we can slip in between a couple of the swamps," said Fetterman.

"Kit?"

"The sergeant is right. There is a good place to cross the border, but we used that before I quit the VC. It is a dry area of no swamps, and the river there is shallow and wide."

"So, if we try to make the crossing there, you're saying that we'll run into the VC?"

"It is possible."

"Tony?"

"We're supposed to be looking for Charlie. It might be a good place to look for him."

"What's the cover like?" asked Gerber.

"Light jungle," said Kit.

Gerber held the map closer to his face and studied it. The grids were about ten klicks on a side. That meant the area was maybe two klicks across. In light jungle that was plenty of space to get lost in. If they moved carefully, quietly, assuming that the enemy was all around, they could probably get through it, if Kit wasn't lying. And there was no real reason to suspect that she was.

"Tony," said Gerber, "take the point. Kit, I'll want you up there with him."

"Yes, sir."

"I'll be in the center of the patrol with Bocker, but not real close to him. I'll have Krung and Tyme bring up the rear." Gerber consulted his watch, surprised that only an hour had passed from the time he had stepped onto the helicopter to this point. "Let's move out."

They began marching through the jungle, an area that reminded Fetterman of a landscaped park. The trees here were over a hundred feet tall, their branches woven together lightly. There were shorter ones with broad leaves. Some scrub grew around their bases, and thick vines spiraled upward around the trunks, but the ground was relatively clear. A thick carpet of dead leaves lay piled high, moist with the humidity of the jungle. There were some obvious paths, chopped by farmers moving to their rice paddies, and some game trails. But the jungle was light enough, so Fetterman avoided them in case they were booby-trapped.

He checked his compass, moving to the northwest at a fairly rapid pace. In minutes Fetterman was covered with sweat. He could feel the beads dripping from his face and running down his sides. Drawing one sleeve of his fatigues across his face to dry the perspiration, he tossed a glance over his shoulder. Kit was right with him, moving like a feline in search of prey. The heat didn't seem to be bothering her. Fetterman could see no evidence that she was even warm.

They skirted one deserted village, but the mud-and-thatch structures were too dilapidated to suggest any habitation. Fetterman stopped long enough to see a few pockmarks in the mud walls, some scorch marks on the ground and a couple of craters that suggested a firefight, but not in the recent past.

Fetterman held up his hand and let the men take up firing positions around him. Using the break, he drank some water, but he didn't empty the canteen as he normally would have. There was no telling how long it would be before they came to a stream where they could refill, and he didn't want to waste the water. In daylight it wasn't quite as important to maintain absolute noise discipline.

Before they moved out again, Fetterman circulated among the men. The captain was sitting with his back to a tree, sipping at his water, letting some of it trickle onto a go-to-hell rag around his neck. His face was sweaty, but he didn't look very tired. He smiled at Fetterman and pointed at Bocker.

The commo sergeant was on the ground, propped up in an uncomfortable-looking position on his rucksack. His uniform was drenched with sweat, giving it an almost all-black appearance. He had put his helmet on the ground next to him and held a canteen in the right hand, but he wasn't drinking.

Fetterman moved toward him, crouched and asked, "You going to be okay?"

Bocker opened his eyes and said, "I knew there was a reason that I didn't go out on these things—too much work." With a Herculean effort, he looked at his watch and groaned. "Good God! It's not even noon. Tony, promise you'll bury me at the side of the trail. I don't want to be eaten."

"Sure," said Fetterman, grinning. "We'll just plant a bush over you so that we can find the spot."

"That'll be fine. Maybe add a nice stone after the war, so I don't have to worry about the VC smashing it."

Like Kit, Krung and his men didn't seem bothered by the heat. They were facing in opposite directions, scanning the jungle all around them. When Fetterman approached, Krung said, "Sergeant Tony. I think someone behind us. I think VC near."

"You see anything?"

"No. I just believe they there."

"Then keep your eyes peeled, but I don't want you shooting any of them. If you finally see them, you alert me or the captain. We'll want to deal with anyone behind us quietly if we can."

"I understand. Let's go."

The group descended into a thicker patch of jungle where the canopy blocked out the sun and the surroundings were lost in a perpetual twilight. The humidity hung in the air, choking them, making it hard to breathe, and everything appeared hazy. Fetterman pushed his way through the tangle of undergrowth, his pace slowed until he was only moving a couple of hundred meters an hour. He didn't want to hack his way through, clearing the vines and bushes with a machete, because that left a definable trail for the enemy to follow.

They started up again, climbing the gentle slope as the jungle thinned and the traveling became easier. They reached the top where they had a good view of the surrounding countryside. Fetterman halted, and the men spread out around him in a make-shift perimeter.

The meal was cold C-rations. Fetterman had the boned chicken, salted heavily. He ate some peaches and the crackers with jelly. When he was finished, he buried the remains, the tin cans, the cardboard, in a shallow hole. He finished the water in one of his canteens and then moved to the west, at the edge of the perimeter. Here he took up position to watch the territory around them, searching for signs that the enemy was near.

After an hour, they were on the move again. Fetterman continued on the point, Kit walking near him. Gerber and Bocker remained near the center of the short column, and Krung was still in the rear. The pace changed with the terrain, sometimes rapid and sometimes slow. By midafternoon they were at the edge of the jungle, looking out over a narrow plain bisected by a wide river, whose slow-moving water sparkeled in the afternoon sun.

Fetterman was still looking for signs of the enemy when Gerber came up behind him. He crouched there and said, "Probably be best to cross at night."

"Yes, sir." He wiped a hand across his forehead, then looked at the sweat smeared on it. "Besides, it won't hurt for us to take a break."

"No, it won't. Every other man on alert and switch every hour," said Gerber.

Fetterman moved among the men, issuing orders. He talked to Bocker briefly and found out that the commo sergeant had recovered during the afternoon march. Maybe it had been the opportunity to rest and eat, but he looked improved. He was sweating heavily, but that was better than having his skin appear dry and florid.

He positioned Krung and two of his Tais across the trail separated from the group by a hundred meters. Krung told him that he still believed someone was following, although he hadn't seen anyone back there.

"Just keep us posted," said Fetterman. "You see anyone, you let the captain or me know."

He returned to the front of the column, where Kit sat away from everyone, although Anderson was in a position to keep an eye on her. Fetterman dropped to the soft jungle floor next to her. She had taken off her boonie hat, and her hair hung down her back. It swept the ground when she moved her head.

"All that hair has to be hot and uncomfortable," said Fetterman.

"I am fine," she said.

"Yes, I suppose you are." Around him, he could hear the buzzing of flies, while up in the trees, the occasional bird and monkey rustled the branches. A patch of blue sky showed through a gap in the foliage overhead.

He wanted to talk to Kit, to find out more about her. She was such a beautiful woman, and he had a hard time accepting her at face value. Surely someone on one side or the other would have realized her potential as a spy. Too many men lost their heads over a beautiful woman. Fetterman felt that he was immune to the tactic only because he had realized long ago that he wasn't the kind of man who had to fight the women off with a club.

He took out his map and studied it. He looked at the Cambodian border where the river touched it between the two swamps. There was an unnamed hamlet close to the Cambodian side, but they should be far enough from it that it wouldn't cause a problem for them.

To Kit he said, "How far is the Trail from here?"

She looked at the map and pointed to an area near Kampong Trach. "Maybe ten, twelve klicks. There are many side trails diverting from the main one."

"What's the terrain like?" he asked. Fetterman already had a good idea, based on the aerial photos he had studied, the features marked on the map and his observations of the ground around them, but he wanted to give Kit a chance to answer. Maybe catch her in a lie.

"South of Prek Tate there is some open country. Rice paddies and meadows. North is jungle, some like this, some heavier, thicker. And hills. Up and down country. There are some swamp lands near the river. A few people. Most have been run off by the NVA and the Americans with their airplanes."

"Okay," he said as he folded his map. He looked at her closely, but she seemed to be holding up better than the men. She had sweat stains on her shirt and beads of perspiration on her upper lip, but she showed no signs of the exertion of marching through some fairly rough country. "How are you doing?"

She turned her head so that she could stare at him. "Why, I am just fine, Sergeant. You expected something less?"

"Not at all," he answered, smiling. "You look like you're ready to run through the jungle."

"What does that mean?"

"Nothing. Nothing at all."

Gerber appeared then and crouched next to Fetterman. He glanced at Kit and then said, "Krung has them spotted. Three guys. Shadowing us."

"We going to take them out?" asked Fetterman.

"You, Krung and Kepler."

"When?"

Gerber was watching Kit. "As soon as we can get into position to do it."

"Yes, sir," said Fetterman getting to his feet. "I'm on my way."

7

SPECIAL FORCES CAMP
A-555

Robin Morrow spent the morning searching through the wall locker where Kit had stored the equipment and clothing she'd brought to the camp. The newswoman had examined the front of the wall locker carefully, looking for a sign that it had been booby-trapped. Not an explosive trap, but one that would tell Kit if it had been opened in her absence—a hair across the door that would fall when it was opened, or a sliver of paper slid into the crack that would drop. But there were none of those things. In fact, the door hadn't even been closed properly, and Morrow tried to remember exactly how it had been shut so that she could duplicate it.

Inside, she found very little: a pair of Ho Chi Minh sandals made from the worn tread of a truck tire and the black pajamas that everyone in Vietnam seemed to favor. Morrow examined them closely, but only discovered that they could use a washing. There were no labels, and there was nothing concealed in the seams.

She went through the other equipment, some of it Russian-made, including a combat knife with a small rust stain near the hilt. Morrow was surprised at that, until she realized that it wasn't rust, but dried blood. She shoved it back into the sheath and set it in the locker.

There was nothing that seemed to be incriminating. Hell, she knew there were nearly two dozen weapons of Russian manufacture in the arms locker and twice that many that had been made in China. A Russian knife meant nothing on its own. She needed more.

Morrow got down on her hands and knees and pulled out the drawers in the bottom of the locker, but she came up empty. Kit apparently had brought nothing with her except the black pajamas, the clothes she had worn on patrol and the black skirt and white blouse she had arrived in. Morrow found no underwear, no personal items such as face powder or lipstick or anything else that might suggest Kit had a life outside her new existence at Camp A-555. Morrow didn't like it, but then she couldn't find anything to suggest that Kit was an enemy agent. Of course, an enemy agent wouldn't leave incriminating evidence lying around.

She moved back to her cot and sat down, staring at Kit's wall locker. Her training told her there was something more to the woman. There had to be, but she wasn't sure how to get a handle on it. Gerber and his men were out in the field with a woman whom no one knew, a woman who had dropped on them yesterday and whom they were now to trust. She didn't like it at all.

Suddenly an idea struck her. She leaped up and stepped to her wall locker. Stripping she took out a towel and wiped the sweat from her body. She realized she could use a shower, but it was too much of a hassle now. Dabbing on some perfume, she dressed in a light blouse and a short skirt. She didn't bother with a bra, leaving her shirt partially unbuttoned. Then she slipped on a pair of sandals that she'd bought in the PX, and which were not made from truck tires. Satisfied, she left the hootch and made her way to the team house.

The new executive officer was sitting at one of the tables looking miserable. He was wearing a brand-new fatigue uniform of bright green. His rank and branch insignia were pinned to the collar because he hadn't gotten the cloth ones sewn to it. There was no name tag above the breast pocket. The heat must have been bothering him greatly because he was fanning himself with the latest copy of *Playboy* rather than looking at the pictures. A cup of coffee sat in front of him, and next to it was a glass of orange juice and a sandwich on a cracked plate. He was staring at the food as if he was about to be sick.

"Mind if I join you?" asked Morrow.

"No ma'am. Have a seat." Mildebrandt stood up and waved at the chair opposite him. "It'll be nice to have someone to talk to for a while. I was beginning to feel like the fifth wheel around here."

Morrow sat down and said, "Why's that?"

"Well, I didn't go out on the mission, nor did I have anything to do with the planning of it. Sergeant Smith seems to have everything under control here, and Captain Minh is a superb officer, just as Captain Gerber said."

"I know how you feel. I usually have more to do myself, but everyone is gone," said Morrow. She glanced at the orange juice. "Is that cold?"

"Cold? Yes. But it tastes funny. Like I'm drinking the container it came in rather than the juice. Would you like a glass?"

Morrow shook her head. "No, I don't think so. Not after that glowing description you gave it. What I would like is to get a flight into Saigon."

"I'm afraid there's nothing I can do for you. I wouldn't know how to go about that. Oh, I guess I could get on the radio and request something, but I'm not sure about the authorizations."

"That's no problem, Lieutenant," said Morrow. "We just go into the commo bunker and have the commo sergeant let it be known that we need airlift to Saigon. He coordinates it with someone in there."

"You can call me Glen," he said. "Do you see what I mean? I know how to fieldstrip any of the weapons we have, field an ambush, establish a camp, but I don't know how to whistle up a helicopter."

Morrow smiled. "You'll learn. It's all just learning the procedures being used here. I once asked Mack something about the coordination of an air assault, and he told me he really had no idea how it was done. He put in his request through B-team Headquarters. All he had to know was who he wanted to take and where he wanted to go. The flyboys took care of coordinating the rest of it."

Mildebrandt sighed. "Yes, I know that. It's just hard to drop into a new unit like this. I mean, normally the CO would stay around for a couple of weeks to teach the new guy the ropes." He held up his hand. "No, I'm not complaining. I understand the circumstances. I just wish I could find something useful to do."

"Then find me a way to get into Saigon," said Morrow smiling.

Mildebrandt picked up his coffee and drained his cup. He stood up and said, "Let's head over to the commo bunker, and I'll see if I can get you a chopper. How long are you going to be gone?"

"Just as long as it takes to find out the background of someone, someone who is probably telling lies to the whole bunch of us."

GERBER WATCHED AS FETTERMAN crawled to the rear of the formation and then disappeared into the jungle. Gerber turned his attention to Kit and said, "We'll press on, cross the river now and take a chance on the enemy being in a position to see us. You wait here."

Gerber found Anderson lying under a bush and said, "I want you with me. We're crossing now."

Anderson nodded and began silently working his way out from under the bush.

Near Anderson, Gerber found Bocker. "Report to the camp that we're being followed and plan to take care of the problem. Make the coded transmission once, then wait for an acknowledgment. If you don't get it quickly, turn off the equipment and prepare to move."

"Yes, sir."

Quickly Gerber spread the word. The men moved from their defensive positions near trees and under bushes, their weapons readied. As they formed into a column, flank security slipping deeper into the light jungle, Gerber headed back to the front.

They slid down the slope, through the thinning jungle and away from its protection from the sun. It had been hot in there, but at least the sun had been blocked. Now it was like moving from a steam bath into a broiler. The sun baked them as they walked from the jungle onto the plain that led to the river. The terrain was broken, riddled with ravines, holes and depressions, created when the river overflowed. Scraggy bushes with dry leaves rattled in the breeze, concealing the holes and ravines. They had to slow down, watching their step, and Gerber realized that they would have never been able to cross the plain in the dark. There would have been a dozen broken bones.

They used the cover that was available, moving slowly from the ravines to the scattered trees until they reached the riverbank. Gerber crawled out on the bank so that he could see the river clearly. The water was muddy brown and slow-moving, almost like molasses. There was a mud bar in the gentle curve of the river. It had obviously been submerged recently. There was nothing on it except some animal tracks.

Even though he couldn't see the bottom because of the silt in the water, he had the impression that the river wasn't deep. He slipped away from the bank and found Kit. He leaned close to her and asked, "How deep is the river?"

She shrugged. "Here, I'm not sure. Other places it's not more than three or four feet deep."

Gerber retreated farther and found Tyme. "Justin, take two men and cross the river while we cover. Set up security there and wait for us. Once you're on the other side of the river, you'll be in Cambodia."

Tyme nodded, reached over and tapped Bocker on the shoulder. He got one of the Tais, and the three of them moved to the riverbank. Tyme dropped his pack but kept his bandolier of M-16 ammo and his combat knife. Bocker left the radio behind, and the Tai took only his weapon.

When they were set, Tyme glanced at Gerber, who nodded. Tyme stepped from the bushes onto the mud flat. His foot sank into the soft earth. He froze there, ready to spring back to the cover of the riverbank, but no one seemed interested in him. He stepped forward, crouched and waited.

Behind him, there was a sucking noise as Bocker moved onto the mud flat. His boot sank into the foul-smelling mass, and when he pulled it out there was a loud pop.

Tyme stood up and rocked his foot to the toe so that the mud couldn't grip him. He moved forward to the edge of the water, hesitated, then stepped in. There was almost no current to speak of. The bed of the river was also mud. It pulled at his boots, tried to trip him, or to pull him down, under the surface of the water.

With his weapon held high he waded out, as if he expected to fall into deep water and didn't want to get it wet. But the water came only to his knees. When he was halfway across, the Tai jumped in, following. Bocker hesitated at the edge of the mud, and as Tyme scrambled up the steeper bank on the other side, Bocker entered the river.

In moments the three of them were on the far bank, disappearing into the dense bush there. Gerber waited for some sign from them but kept shifting his gaze to the rear, wondering how Fetterman and his tiny ambush team were faring.

Then Tyme was on the bank, waving them over. Kit crouched on the mud flat, then rushed across it, barely leaving footprints. She entered the water that came up to her bare thighs, and when she was on the other side, a hand snaked out of the bush to help her up the bank.

The rest of the men with the equipment, including Bocker's radio, spread out along the mud flat to work their way to the river. They crossed it on line quickly, the dark water splashing as they moved. In the swirls of current created by their movement, he could see chocolate patterns of stirred-up silt that slowly dissipated.

Gerber reached the bank, climbed into the bush and spun, looking at the river. He was concerned by the footprints that his men's combat boots had made on the mud flat. It showed that Americans had been there recently, but Fetterman would take care of it when he crossed the river.

Tyme appeared next to him. "What now, sir?"

"We get the fuck away from here." He pulled out his map and studied it quickly. There was a trail or track not far from where they were. "Due west until we reach the Ho Chi Minh Trail," he said.

"Yes, sir."

"Kit," said Gerber, "what can you tell us about the terrain from now on?"

"Same as before. Hills and valleys, but the jungle gets thicker. Swamps that we can avoid. Travel will be tougher the farther we go."

"Okay, Justin, you heard. Let's get the men ready to move out, but keep the pace slow. We don't want to get too far ahead of Sergeant Fetterman."

"Got it, sir."

As they began to move through the bush and scrub, Gerber turned once and looked at the jungle on the other side of the river. There was nothing there except the empty landscape. Again he wondered how Fetterman was doing.

FETTERMAN, KRUNG AND KEPLER stole along the trail, heading back east, the way they had come. They were paralleling their old path, moving slowly, cautiously, concentrating on stealth, on not stirring up the small animals hiding from the heat of the afternoon. Fetterman led the group, reaching out once to push a branch out of the way and then carefully replacing it so that it didn't spring back. He moved like a man riddled with arthritis, as if each movement was painful, taking his time, watching the jungle and listening to the sounds.

To one side he heard the quiet scrape of a snake as it wound its way up the trunk of a tree so that it could sun itself on an exposed branch. Around his head was the buzz of flies and a flickering of gnats, but he ignored them, his mind focused on the men that Krung had spotted.

It didn't take long for Fetterman to find the first one. He was alone, standing next to a teak tree, his hand out against the smooth trunk as if supporting himself. He wore black shorts and a torn, sweat-stained khaki shirt. Fetterman realized that it was the same uniform that Kit wore but forced that thought from his mind. Instead, he noticed the pistol belt holding a single canteen and a small pouch that looked like an American-made civilian first-aid kit. There was a knife on the belt next to the first-aid kit. Fetterman shook his head in disgust. Damned student protestors hating war but prolonging it by providing the enemy with "humanitarian" aid, he cursed silently.

The man had slung his weapon, an SKS. He wore a green pith helmet with a cloth down the back to protect his neck from the sun. He seemed to be oblivious to everything around him, his attention focused on the trail in front of him. In his hand he held an unlit cigarette. It was as if he was waiting for permission.

Fetterman turned, pointed at Kepler and then at the enemy. He held up one hand and flashed the fingers twice, which told Kepler to wait at least ten minutes. Kepler nodded, stepped for-

ward and crouched at the base of a giant palm where he could
watch the enemy soldier without being seen.

Fetterman and Krung moved then, inching to the north across
their trail. Krung spotted the second man. He was leaning in a
depression formed by two trees that had grown together. Krung
saw his hand move as the man slapped at something near his face.
Krung smiled and stopped to tell Fetterman that he would kill that
man.

Fetterman nodded and wondered how Krung would dig him
out. The VC had found a nearly perfect hiding place. No way to
sneak up behind him and cut his throat.

A moment later Fetterman found the last of the VC. He was
kneeling between two trees, his AK-47 clutched in his left hand.
He wore black pajama bottoms, a khaki shirt and had a pistol
strapped to his side. That probably meant the man was an officer, since the VC and NVA rarely gave pistols to the enlisted men
or the NCOs. He also wore a dark green pith helmet, and Fetterman had no doubt there would be a red star painted on the front
of it.

The man was waiting patiently, his head cocked to one side, as
if listening. Slowly Fetterman slung his own weapon, the magazine digging into his side as his pack pressed into him. He drew
his Case combat knife, the blade dulled so that it wouldn't reflect
the sunlight. He moved until he was only a few feet from the man
and then crouched in the protection of a tree, his eyes on the enemy's boots.

Fetterman wasn't sure if he believed in ESP or not, but too
many ambushes had been ruined by the enemy suddenly sensing
something strange. Fetterman remembered a dozen times when
he had felt enemy eyes on his back. He glanced at the VC but
didn't stare. Instead, he checked the time and realized that Kepler and Krung would be making their moves soon.

Cautiously Fetterman advanced, his eyes scanning the ground
around his feet, looking for trip wires and booby traps that could
ruin his plan. He didn't expect to find any, but he looked anyway. He shifted his weight slowly, rocking his foot from heel to
toe so that he didn't snap a twig or crush a leaf that would give
him away.

When Fetterman was within striking distance, he snaked his hand out and grabbed the VC by the face, jerking him backward. Using his knee as a fulcrum, he bent the enemy until he could see the man's round white eyes. With a single stroke, Fetterman's knife flashed, cutting the VC's throat. There was a gurgling sound and a splash of warm liquid. The man spasmed, going rigid, his hand trying to grab his attacker's wrist. He missed the mark but left four ragged lines where his nails dug into the American's flesh. The VC's foot kicked out, drumming on the ground.

Fetterman plunged his knife into the man's chest under the breastbone, and the man died. There was a sudden foul odor as the VC's bowels loosened. The sergeant rolled the body onto its stomach, took the AK from the ground where the man had dropped it and moved to the right, searching the jungle around him. No one appeared, and there was no shooting. Fetterman glanced at the body, then began to search it, looking for documents and unit insignia. He took the man's wallet, which included a small notebook and pictures of a family, and the scarf the man wore. The latter was a red-and-white piece of cloth that was now soaked with blood.

He moved back the way he had come. In the distance he saw Krung leaning against the side of the large trees where the enemy soldier hid. He wondered what Krung planned until he saw the snake held in his left hand.

Krung looked as if he was about to kiss the tree, but instead he tossed the snake into the air so that it fell on the man. There was a grunt of surprise, and the man danced from hiding, slapping at his back. As he moved, Krung sprang at him, grabbed him and shoved his knife into him. The blade penetrated upward into the lungs, and the man fell forward, dragging Krung with him. There was a halfhearted attempt to push himself up, but he collapsed into the dirt of the jungle.

When he saw that Krung had dispatched his man, Fetterman continued on. He found Kepler standing over the body of his VC. The skin of the dead man's face had been stripped from the chin, as if Kepler had slashed him too high the first time. Fetterman noticed blood on Kepler's right sleeve and on his pants. He was leaning against a tree trunk, half hidden in the jungle.

Fetterman approached and pointed. "Any of that blood belong to you?"

"No, his. Bled real good."

"Doesn't look like a textbook case," said Fetterman. "What'd he do, duck his head?"

"Yeah, but I got him anyway."

Fetterman held out the cloth that his man had been wearing. "Anything significant here?"

Kepler took the cloth and looked at it. "Not really. I think the colors identify it as part of the Ninth NVA Division, but this guy is VC, not NVA. Got a contradiction here. Unless the VC and NVA are mixing their units now, which wouldn't be all that surprising."

"Okay," said Fetterman. There were other questions he wanted to ask, but he decided to wait until they were out of that portion of the jungle. "Hide the body as best you can. Take the weapon and ammo, and we'll get the fuck out of here."

Kepler bent to drag the man deeper into the bush. Fetterman saw the pool of crimson liquid on the ground already drawing flies. He kicked dirt and leaves into it to conceal it. Kepler saw what was happening and nodded. He understood that the blood had to be covered over just as the body had to be hidden.

With that, Fetterman returned to the man he had killed. He picked up the body, carried it ten or twelve feet to the right and dropped it into a deep depression. He went back, picked up the pith helmet and tossed it into the hole. He checked the ground. If someone looked closely, he might see signs of the struggle, see that someone had been there, but the person would have to know what he was looking for. In a day, the jungle would claim even those traces.

They finished disposing of the bodies and then headed for Gerber and the main column. They reached the river, saw the place where Gerber had forded it and followed. Fetterman hesitated long enough to wipe out the traces made by the first group and then finished the crossing. Once again a close examination might reveal that someone had been there, but it would take someone who knew what to look for and who knew where to look. Fetterman didn't worry about it.

He found Gerber's trail easily. He knew the captain was making it easy for him to follow and not trying to conceal anything yet. After they had camped for the night, they would begin moving with more care, worry then about someone stumbling over their trail. But at this point it wasn't something to be concerned about.

Within thirty minutes Fetterman had caught up to Gerber. He approached the captain's group cautiously, waiting for visual contact before trying to enter the camp. Once it was established, along with their identity, Fetterman came in.

Gerber met him and asked, "How'd it go?"

"No problem. Got all three of them and hid the bodies. No evidence of anyone else around with them." He glanced at Kit who was sitting just out of earshot. "Got a couple of things we might let her look at and see if they mean anything to her. Might identify the enemy units or something."

"We'll have her take a look at it later. Right now grab something to eat. I think we'll want to move another klick or so before we hole up for the night."

"Yes, sir."

8

MACV HEADQUARTERS
SAIGON RVN

Jerry Maxwell, wearing another of the wrinkled white suits, sat at his desk and stared at the phone. It was a real telephone, not the field phone that almost everyone else used in Vietnam. He had spent an hour talking to various colonels and majors, trying to find an aviation unit that would remain on standby in case Gerber and his boys got into trouble. Most of them agreed that they would help if they could, based on their other mission requirements, but none wanted to violate the Cambodian border. They hinted that Maxwell was on a fishing expedition, looking for someone who would disobey orders and regulations. A couple said they would cross into Cambodia if the proper authorizations could be found.

Since it was all speculation, no mission details, no units identified and no code words thrown about, Maxwell wasn't violating security. He was making an unofficial survey, with results that he found sickening.

Finally he gave up. He picked up one of the Coke cans that lined the edge of his desk and was mildly surprised to find some liquid in it. He tipped the can to his lips and swallowed the remains of the warm Coke. He pulled a map closer to him and looked at the locations of army aviation units. They were scattered at the major American bases, but could be called on quickly to get Gerber out of the field if the recon degenerated into the disaster that the

LRRPs had run into. These units could get to the border quickly if Gerber managed to get his people back across it to be rescued.

He got up and walked around the office, looking at the stack of framed pictures that leaned against the side of a safe. Maxwell had a bad habit of throwing his Coke cans when he got mad, usually aiming at the pictures hanging in his office. Then he was forced to change the picture. Because of that, some army sergeant, with nothing better to do, had given him fifteen framed prints, most of them of the Wagon Box Fight.

The phone buzzed insistently, and Maxwell grabbed it. "Maxwell."

"You stay there, boy," said the voice at the other end. "I'll be down in a couple of minutes to talk to you. So you stay put."

The line went dead as Maxwell recognized the voice, and he stared at the receiver for a moment. Then he hung up and dropped into the leather chair that was there for visitors. The last thing he wanted to do was talk to Crinshaw. He was an asshole.

He had expected Crinshaw to knock on his door, but Crinshaw believed that since he was a general, normal courtesy didn't mean him. He could do what he wanted. He didn't have to worry about others.

As the door opened suddenly, Maxwell almost got to his feet and then decided not to. He watched Crinshaw enter and look around in distaste, sweat beading his forehead and staining the underarms of his starched jungle fatigues. He stood in the doorway as if rooted to the spot.

Maxwell waved a hand and dropped it to the arm of the chair. "Seeing how the other half lives?"

"You just watch your mouth, boy. You're in a peck of trouble as it is and your smart mouth won't win you any prizes," Crinshaw warned him.

Maxwell sat up and rubbed his hands on his knees. He breathed deeply, as if controlling his temper, and said, "What's the problem?"

"First problem is your manners. I have to stand here in the doorway like some buck ass private?"

Maxwell pointed at the chair by the desk. "Knock yourself out." He glanced at Crinshaw's feet, saw spit-shined boots and knew that Crinshaw hadn't touched a can of shoe polish in ten years. Probably shined by one of those buck ass privates that Crinshaw had just mentioned.

Crinshaw dropped into the chair, crossed his legs and ran his fingers along the crease in his jungle pants. He glanced around the office again, the distaste obvious on his face. He shook his head, as if he couldn't believe what he was seeing. He said, "You're pushing it about as far as you can, boy."

"Excuse me, General," snapped Maxwell, "but I am not in the army and not in your chain of command and therefore not one of the men who has to listen to shit from you. There a problem? Let me know. If not, just get the fuck out of here and I'll get back to work."

"I could call the ambassador and let him know that I find your attitude offensive," said Crinshaw. "Maybe the ambassador has a different attitude. Maybe he could straighten you out so that you fly right."

Maxwell sighed and said, "Call whoever you want. What are they going to do? Draft me?"

"Smartass, boy. Real smartass," said Crinshaw. He pulled a camouflaged handkerchief from his hip pocket and mopped his face with it.

"That's right."

"Well," said Crinshaw, "I'll let you in on a little secret. You can stop wasting your time trying to line up an aviation company to pull Gerber out of the field. All such requests come through my office, and even if you find a company commander who will commit to your plan, I can tell you that all such requests will be denied." Crinshaw stood up so that he could look down on Maxwell. "I think that concludes our business, except for me to say that I will forward a report of your activities through channels. I don't like all this infighting. If you have something to say, you come to me. Don't try to sneak around behind me."

"I don't understand this at all, General," said Maxwell.

"Nothing for you to understand. You keep your superspook nose out of my business. There are some things that you are not privy to. They dictate the policy that's in force right now. Captain Gerber will just have to live with it and cover his own ass."

Before Maxwell could respond, Crinshaw reached the door. He grabbed the knob and then turned around, jerking the door open.

"I don't like learning that some smartass civilian spook is trying to make an end run around my office. You keep your nose out of my business, or I'll chop it off for you. This is your one and only warning." Crinshaw was gone in a flash, the door slamming behind him.

Maxwell didn't move. He couldn't understand Crinshaw's decision, but knew that the general meant it. Crinshaw just didn't venture out of the icebox he used for an office unless something was important to him. Maxwell realized that it meant he would get no help from an army unit. Crinshaw had taken less than an hour to learn that Maxwell was trying to line something up and had wasted no time in coming to his office to stop it.

"Well," he said out loud, "there's always Air America."

THE RECON TEAM didn't move for the hour that Gerber had waited to see if anyone else was following them. Then they passed through a low swampy area, the water never much higher than the knee. But there were overhanging branches, clinging vines, bushes with thorny leaves that scratched at the bare skin of hands and faces and ripped at the uniforms, and there were hidden holes under the water. They moved through it rapidly, making noise as they splashed around in it. As they reached the drier ground, moving into a twilight area of thick jungle, Gerber noticed a small black shape wiggling up Kit's thigh. He reached over to brush it off and realized that it was a leech.

"Shit," he mumbled. He said nothing to her, moved around her and caught Tyme, who had taken over the point duties. "Find us a place to hole up quick."

"What's the problem, Captain."

"Leeches. We've got to get them off."

Tyme looked sick. "Oh, fuck. I can take everything but the fucking leeches. Oh, Jesus, not leeches."

"Take it easy, Justin," said Gerber. "Find us a place to hole up and we'll get them off."

Tyme unconsciously brushed at his sleeve, as if he could knock the leeches from him. His face was suddenly pale. He wiped his hand over his face and rubbed it on the front of his fatigue shirt.

"You going to be all right?"

Tyme nodded. He rolled his shoulders as if he could feel something crawling on his back. He shifted his weight from one foot to the other. He swiped at his lips with the back of his hand. "I'll be fine."

"Listen, why don't I have Anderson take the point for a while? Give you a break."

"I don't need the Cat to do my job for me," snapped Tyme, forgetting where he was.

"I know that," said Gerber quietly. "I want the Cat to take the point."

"Yes, sir," said Tyme. He had stopped vibrating for a moment, as if he had forgotten about the leeches.

Gerber slipped to the rear, found Anderson with his canteen tipped to his lips and said, "Cat, take the point. Find us a good hiding spot and do it quickly."

Anderson capped his canteen and slipped it into the pouch on his hip. He moved forward, his rifle held in both hands and disappeared into the bush. The patrol strung out behind him, moving rapidly through the trees and around the light scrub on the ground. The canopy was thick enough to keep sunlight from filtering down, which made the undergrowth thin and easy to penetrate.

Within ten minutes they were spread out in the jungle at the top of a small hill that overlooked all approaches. Half the men were on the perimeter, watching, while three others tried to light the stale cigarettes from C-ration cartons. Tyme had dropped his pack and stripped his shirt, throwing it away from him like it was about to explode. Fetterman reached the younger man quickly, put a hand on his shoulder and forced him to sit down.

Gerber moved closer to Kit and said, "We've run into leeches."

She looked up at him, dropped her rucksack and began to unbutton her shirt. "Get them off me, please," she said.

She handed him one of the tiny cigars that he had seen her smoking in Saigon. He lit it quickly, drew through it until the tip glowed orange and waited.

Kit held her shirt so that it covered her breasts, but bared her back. He spotted a fat black leech hanging on just under her shoulder blade. He touched it with the tip of the cigar, heard a quiet hiss and watched it drop away. He stomped it, splattering Kit's blood on his boot.

He knelt behind her, lifted the shirttail and examined the rest of her back. He noticed some old scars near her waist, which seemed to indicate she had been whipped sometime in the past. He said nothing about them, found a leech on her hip and burned it off. As it dropped, it left a smear of blood that Gerber wiped away with his thumb.

He then moved in front of her, looking at her shoulders and the tops of her breasts. She smiled at him as he touched the tail of her shirt, moving it so that he could examine her belly. There was a third leech there, and as he burned it away she jumped.

"That hurt?"

"A little," she said. "It reacted badly to the fire. I felt it."

Gerber nodded and continued to examine her, realizing that he wasn't quite as detached as he had hoped. He could feel the beginnings of desire, but shoved the thoughts from his mind.

She bared one breast, grinning, but there was nothing hiding near it. When he was sure that he had gotten them all from her back, chest and stomach, he made her stand so that he could look at her legs. She turned slowly, letting him look at her closely, one knee flexed so that the muscles under the skin stood out.

She tugged at the hem of the shorts, pulling them up. He found a final leech hidden near her crotch. She yanked at her shorts, and Gerber saw a flash of dark pubic hair. He burned the leech off her.

As it fell, she reached for the cigar and said, "Now I'll do you."

Gerber nodded, thinking that she had already done him. He wondered if the old men in Congress who year after year refused to discuss the possibility of women in combat units didn't have the right idea. The forced intimacy of searching each other for leeches had certainly affected him in ways that looking for them on a man never did. He could see where it might be a problem in a combat environment. Then, grinning, he realized that he was in a combat environment, and it *was* a problem.

He unbuttoned his shirt and pulled it off, trying to ignore his emotions. He felt her hands on his body, touching his arm, his shoulder and his back. He heard the sizzling of a leech as she burned it off him. She got a couple more and then was standing in front of him, a hand on his hip as if they were about to kiss.

She put the cigar in her mouth and inhaled deeply. She fiddled with the buckle of his pants. He reached down and grabbed her hands, stopping her. She glanced up, her eyes sparkling with mischief.

"Is there a problem, Captain Gerber?"

"Oh, yeah, there's a problem." He sat down and pulled off his boots. There were no leeches on his feet because his boots were too tight, but he found one on his knee, and Kit burned it off quickly.

"There could be some higher up," she said, tracing her tongue slowly across her lips.

Gerber got to his feet and dropped his pants. Kit looked at him, but found no more leeches. In seconds he had his pants up again. Then he put on his shirt, but left his pack on the ground. Glancing over, he saw that Tyme was now working on Fetterman. Apparently Fetterman had managed to get all the leeches off the younger man, and with that he had calmed down.

They rotated positions. Those on perimeter defense replaced those who had already removed the leeches. It didn't take long. When they finished, Gerber studied his map, but there was nothing of interest around them. He found Fetterman and said, "This seems to be a good spot to camp for the night. Let's get the men fed, give everyone half an hour of free time and then get them on line. Half alert for that."

"Yes, sir. And then?"

"We'll get an LP out about fifty meters away and go to two-thirds alert after midnight. We'll move tomorrow at first light and then find a good spot to rest through the middle of the day."

"Any special way you want to run this? I mean, who does what?"

"No." He thought for a moment and then said, "How's Tyme?"

"Doesn't like leeches at all," said Fetterman, "but I think that phobia is taken care of. Once I got them off him, his attitude improved, and I don't think it'll affect him like that again."

ROBIN MORROW WAS ABLE to promote a jeep once she landed at Hotel Three. She pushed her way through the crowd in the terminal, sweet-talked a young sergeant and got him to call someone else who promised to send transportation. Then she spent the next half hour trying to convince the sergeant that she didn't want a date, that she had seen everything at Tan Son Nhut and Saigon that she cared to see and that she wasn't interested in learning about the *real war* in Southeast Asia. And there was no meal available in Saigon that would change her mind.

A corporal, angry because he had been tagged to drive a journalist around, came in, yelled for Morrow and then nearly fainted dead away. He glanced at her, smiled so wide that his face had to hurt and was glad that he had drawn the assignment. He picked up her camera bag and ushered her outside.

He held out a hand to help her climb into the jeep and then didn't even try to conceal the fact he was looking at her legs. He walked around the front of the jeep, smiling at her, but Morrow didn't respond.

"Where to?" he asked as he climbed behind the wheel.

"General Crinshaw's headquarters."

"Shit," he mumbled. "Yes, ma'am."

As he started the engine and fumbled with the gear lever, she asked, "You don't care for General Crinshaw?"

"Don't know him, ma'am, and I'd just as soon keep it that way. I don't think he much likes us enlisted swine."

"Then you can wait in the jeep while I go talk to him," she said.

They passed through the gate where a single military policeman holding an M-16 stood. They turned east, and a moment later pulled up in front of the two-story building that was Crinshaw's headquarters. He put the jeep into neutral and turned off the engine.

"I don't think I'll be here all that long," said Morrow. "I may need one more ride, and if I do I'll buy you a dinner."

"Yes, ma'am. That'll be nice."

Morrow took her camera bag, slipped it over her shoulder and walked up to the glass double doors. She noticed a bullet hole in one of them, near the top, with a network of cracks that reached almost to the middle of the door. She was surprised that Crinshaw hadn't had it replaced and then realized it was just the sort of thing Crinshaw would order his men not to repair. Looked impressive. Crinshaw the great warrior; in danger even in his office.

She pushed her way through and walked down a short hallway to the stairs that led to the second floor. Once there she turned, walked halfway down the hall and opened the door that led into Crinshaw's outer office.

The old master sergeant was still there. He glanced up, said nothing and picked up the field phone. Morrow watched him spin the crank and then turn so that his back was to her. Finally he turned and said, "You may go in."

She smiled and started for the other door. Before she reached it, it opened and Crinshaw was in front of her, grinning at her.

"Miss Morrow. So nice to see you. Come in," he said, stepping out of the way.

Once inside Crinshaw's office, Robin wished she had brought a jacket. After the heat outside, it felt as if the snow would start at any moment.

Crinshaw gestured at the couch along one wall. She noticed the weapons hung above it, each with its plaque telling the story of its capture. Just more proof that Crinshaw was the typical chairborne commando and not a line officer like Gerber. He had all kinds of war-related mementos to decorate his domain, and none of them had been captured by him.

She sat at the far end of the couch, set her camera bag at her feet and waited. Crinshaw leaned close and asked, "May I get you something to drink?"

"No, General, I'm fine. I'll only take a few minutes of your time."

Crinshaw joined her on the couch, his eyes falling first to her breasts and then to her legs. He smiled and asked, "What can I do for you?"

She looked at him, trying to find some clue that he had a trick up his sleeve. This was the general officer whom she had helped crush when he had tried to court-martial two of Gerber's men on trumped-up charges. He had literally thrown her out of his office then. Now he was trying his best to be charming. The only reason had to be the power of the press. She remembered what Gerber had said about her not being one of Crinshaw's favorite people, but here he was, being as cordial as possible to her. It had to be because she could advance his career with a couple of strategically placed stories in the newspaper for the folks at home.

She leaned forward, pulled her reporter's notebook from the bag and flipped through a couple of pages. She found a blank one and stopped.

"Is this on the record?" asked Crinshaw, smiling.

"If you don't mind, although I'm not certain where this story is going to take me."

"Anything I can do."

"Okay. Are you familiar with a Kit Carson scout named Brouchard Bien Soo Ta Emilie?"

"Yes, I am. What about her?"

"What can you tell me about her? What kind of background check has she had?"

Crinshaw leaned back and locked his fingers behind his head. He stared across his office at his massive desk with its large green blotter and at the venetian blinds, closed against the late afternoon sun.

"She came to us through the Chieu Hoi program. Walked into our base at Bien Hoa, carrying an AK-47. She was interrogated by MI and then turned over to us. Told them that she was half Vietnamese and half French. Her father and her brother had been killed by the Vietminh. She was tired of living in the jungle, supporting a cause she wasn't convinced was the best for the oppressed peoples of South Vietnam. MI believed her story. There was enough solid information, so they were able to confirm a lot of what she said. Gave us some very good intelligence in the bargain, I understand."

"Then you're convinced that she's loyal to the South?"

Crinshaw smiled. "Well, how loyal can you expect her to be? She changed sides once. What's to prevent her from doing it again? I mean, she was a traitor once. Why shouldn't she switch her allegiance again?"

"Yet you sent her out into the field with our men?"

"Sure, as a Kit Carson scout. They all know what that means. She was VC. Now she's not. At least she claims she's not. Anyone working with a Kit Carson knows what it means."

"Any reason to suspect that she might be any good or that she might switch back?"

Crinshaw got up and walked to his desk. He pulled the top right-hand drawer open and got a cigar. He snapped the end off it with a silver tool, picked up a lighter and said, "You mind?"

"No, please. Now, is there any reason to suspect she might switch back?"

"I'm not sure how to answer that, Miss Morrow. She seems to be just what she claims to be—a loyal believer in the South Vietnamese government. But I do know that her brother is VC. Not the one who was killed, but the other one. She told us that much, which she didn't have to. With the record-keeping in this country in the state it's in, there's actually no way we would have discovered it if she hadn't told us. If there is something more you want, I would suggest you talk to the people over at Military Intelligence."

Morrow nodded. As she had listened to Crinshaw talk, she'd realized that most of his Georgia accent had disappeared. It was as if it was something he used to reinforce his anger, to prove to the victim that he was angry. She grinned and bowed her head, hoping to shield her grin from Crinshaw.

Again she asked, "Can she be trusted?"

"That, Miss Morrow, is the question."

9

THE CAMBODIAN
JUNGLE SOUTHWEST OF
KAMPONG TRACH

Captain MacKenzie K. Gerber didn't sleep well that night, a fact that was hardly surprising, considering his situation.

He was with a fifteen-man patrol, well, fourteen-man anyway. You could hardly call Kit a man. Not unless you'd failed miserably in high school biology class. He and his patrol were several klicks inside publicly neutral Cambodia in clear violation of Cambodia's sovereignty, looking for Vietcong soldiers, who were also there in clear violation of Cambodia's sovereignty and alleged neutrality. But Gerber was aware that the Phnom Penh government turned a blind eye to this as long as it was convenient, and in any case was able to do little or nothing when it stopped being convenient.

Having slept on a rare spot of hard ground in the middle of a swamp full of leeches, rats, poisonous spiders and assorted insects, did little to improve his mood. Damn it, he thought, with enough venomous snakes to keep a herpetological toxicologist happy for a lifetime plus a few that could only swallow you whole, not to mention a mean distribution of mosquitoes measurable in kilograms per cubic centimeter of skin surface area, even Rip Van Winkle might have trouble getting a little shuteye.

Except that Mack Gerber was a professional soldier, a Green Beret, with nearly a year and a half of experience in Indochina, and he'd learned not to sweat the small stuff. The day-to-day problems that were always with you, but which you couldn't do anything about, you learned to accept and finally came to notice only on a subconscious level. That left the mind and the senses free to deal with the more important problems of staying alive and killing the enemy. Indeed, the chill rain that had fallen shortly after midnight, soaking his uniform thoroughly, had gone unnoticed until several hours later when the wind had picked up slightly and he'd begun shivering.

Yet Gerber's sleep was far from tranquil. His dreams were haunted by images, not of things that killed or ate you or sucked your blood, but of things that could nevertheless destroy a man. The two creatures that vied for dominance in his dreams were women, remarkably similar in physical appearance except for the strikingly dissimilar eyes. But once you got beyond gross anatomy, the similarity ended.

One was a self-confident, sunburned young woman with an ever-present camera hung about her neck, a deep throaty laugh and the ability to drink beer like a Russian on the outskirts of Milwaukee. She had been a friend and a lover and because of her close association with Gerber had twice been subjected to the most brutal and degrading of treatment, yet had never complained about the cruel hands that fate had dealt her. Nor had she considered blaming Gerber for the situations, as others might have done. The other woman often complained, had once blamed Gerber unjustly for the death of a young soldier he had nothing to do with, preferred a glass of good wine over any other form of alcohol and seldom laughed in deference to biting her lip while grinning. She had been the kind of lover Hugh Hefner only dreamed about. Gerber couldn't honestly say she'd been a friend. In his dreams, that night at least, she wore a stethoscope around her neck, and nothing else. Both women claimed to be in love with him.

Gerber's dilemma was that he wasn't in love with the first woman, although exactly what his feelings toward her were did seem a bit confused at times, most of the time in fact. And while he was desperately in love with the second, past experience had given him good reason not to entirely trust her when she now professed a renewed love for him. Whatever the reason for the mistrust, it evaporated when she took off her stethoscope and turned around to show him a pair of buns so perfect you could ski off them. Gerber was just snuggling up to their marvelous curves when that part of the unconscious that never really sleeps nudged him awake and his eyes snapped open.

He knew that in the jungle at oh-dark-thirty in the morning there was nothing for the eyes to see, but his nostrils were aware of the faint musky smell of a woman's hair and the warm, gentle pressure of her buttocks against his side. Belatedly his mind became aware that the woman with the stethoscope had existed only in his dreams, and that here, in the middle of the Cambodian jungle, there should be no delightful curves pressed up against his body. Gerber felt the hairs stand up on the back of his neck and tensed involuntarily.

"I'm sorry. I did not mean to wake you," the faintly accented voice whispered softly. "I was cold from the rain, and two bodies are warmer than one."

The fact that Brouchard Bien Soo Ta Emilie had once been a Vietcong soldier and might just as easily have been seeking to cut his throat as seeking warmth was not lost on Gerber. Nor was the observation that had she wanted to kill him he'd be dead by now an entirely comforting thought.

"It's okay," said Gerber softly. "Just don't sneak up on me like that again. We don't want any accidents."

"I am sorry, Captain. As I said, I was cold from the rain."

"Forget it. Go back to sleep."

The young woman snuggled up tight against him, but made no effort to touch him with her hands. After a time, her slowed, regular breathing suggested to Gerber that she had, in fact, gone to sleep, but lying in the cold and wet of a jungle cuddled up to a former VC soldier wasn't exactly conducive to a good rest. Gerber realized the woman pressed against him might well have been responsible for the deaths of an unknown number of American and South Vietnamese soldiers.

Jerry Maxwell had somehow managed to avoid mentioning anything about that part of Kit's background. Gerber wondered idly if she'd ever killed anyone he knew, then somewhat embarrassed, wondered if the reverse might not also be true. It had to be an interesting situation for both of them, sleeping with the en-

emy. Kit seemed to be doing a better job of coping with it than he
was. While she'd managed to get back to sleep fairly promptly,
Gerber could not.

For a long time he lay listening to the false, empty silence of the
jungle, trying without success to bring on sleep. At last he tried
to submerge his concerns about the mission in thoughts of Karen
Morrow, the air force flight nurse with the incredible posterior
and the sexual proclivity toward being a bit kinky. He was only
partially successful. Occasional images of Robin, hurt and looking very vulnerable, kept intruding, and when he entertained the
warmest of thoughts about Karen, the closeness and smell of Kit
produced an annoying arousal that he had to fight down.

Finally fatigue overcame him, and he drifted off. As he did so,
his last thoughts were of Karen's perfect backside. But as she
turned toward him, her face took on fine, dark Eurasian details,
her hair became long and black, and the stethoscope about her
neck was slowly transformed into something else, becoming an
M-16 held in her hands and pointed straight at his heart.

WHEN FETTERMAN WOKE him just before dawn, Gerber was a
little disappointed, but frankly relieved not to find Kit still sleeping beside him. The Kit Carson scout was squatting on her
haunches about ten meters away across the tiny clearing, brewing her morning tea in a canteen cup set atop a couple of hexamine tabs in a tiny trench she'd scraped out of the ground.

Gerber's first reaction was to bite her head off for building a fire
in enemy territory, but he realized that her tiny fire would make
no smoke and leave less evidence behind than the mere passage
of their patrol. Leaving some sign behind you in the jungle was
unavoidable if you were being followed by a really good tracker.
The trick was to leave as little as possible, so it wouldn't get noticed by some dummy who could then call in a really good tracker
for assistance. And the smell of the tea brewing, while it might
carry a short distance in the jungle was, unlike the uniquely
American aroma of coffee, a typical Vietnamese mealtime odor,
and thus, a sort of protective coloration of its own. Besides, the
troops would need something warm to get them started this
morning.

Gerber's sodden uniform was like a clammy second skin from last night's shower. And anyway, he told himself, while the smell of tea might attract unwanted guests, they were likely to be a lot less alert upon arrival than either coffee or just the distinct odor of fourteen cold, wet Americans and Tais would make them.

Gerber noted with mild amusement the somewhat comical efforts of Sergeant Anderson to assist Kit in a task for which she obviously had no need of his help. Anderson seemed to be taking an intense personal interest in the attractive young Vietnamese woman. Gerber had to admit that a comparative analysis of the gross physique of Sam Anderson, a blond Nordic giant, and Emilie Brouchard, the diminutive, dark-haired, dark-complexioned, half-French Vietnamese, made for some interesting speculation. Seeing Anderson towering above the woman as she crouched, checking her tea and paying him only the slightest attention, it was difficult to imagine how the two of them would fit together, if they ever did get together physically.

From a personality standpoint, a match between the two was even more improbable. Anderson was a quiet, self-reliant man of few words, whose only previously exhibited vice had been an affinity for absorbing the same sort of zest at making things blow up that Sully Smith, the team's senior demolitions specialist, exhibited.

Anderson was something of a health nut. He had an electric blender back at Camp A-555 that he used to produce godawful vegetable juice concoctions, which he drank in preference to a rarely sampled beer. He also owned a ceramic electric yogurt maker, which usually failed him because of the inefficiency of the camp's refrigerators, at least until recently. He usually allowed himself one bowl of a wonderfully smelling, disgustingly tasting Danish pipe tobacco each evening while in camp, but never on patrol. While he would participate in the ritualistic *smooths* involving Beam's Choice that had become part of the routine in Gerber's A-Detachment, it was generally believed that no other bottle had passed his lips since infancy. He was the only man on the team who still bothered with a complete set of morning calisthenics.

Kit, on the other hand, smoked small black cigars with a passion, had disdained the offer of one of Anderson's health cocktails back at camp and had, as Gerber had observed, an affection for Kentucky sour mash bourbon that rivaled his own. Indeed, twice during their trip, he'd seen her produce a small flask from her pocket and have a nip when she thought no one was watching. Gerber had been a bit concerned by it at first, but since she didn't seem to be doing it to the extent that her judgment was influenced by it, Gerber had let it pass. As long as it wasn't affecting her performance on the mission, Gerber didn't care if she drank fifty gallons of the stuff. It was an affliction he could understand.

"I suppose we all have our own personal crutches to help get us through this war," he mused softly.

"How's that again, sir?" asked Fetterman, who was still kneeling beside him.

"Nothing, Master Sergeant. I was just thinking out loud about how everybody has certain needs, no matter what situation they're in. Forget it."

"Yes, sir," said Fetterman. "I quite understand." Which, being Fetterman, he did. Far more perfectly than Gerber could have imagined.

"Let the men heat up their rations for breakfast. Routine security, half on guard while the other half eats, then switch. Right after that we'll move out. Tell the men to use their hexamine tabs only. No open fires."

"Yes, sir. Do you think that's a good idea, sir? I mean, the smell will carry farther when we heat the stuff up."

Gerber nodded in the direction of Kit. "I'd say as far as that's concerned, the damage has already been done. Wouldn't you, Tony?"

"Yes, sir. Just making sure you'd thought of all the ramifications and felt the same way. I'll pass the word to the men."

Gerber opted to set up the little folding metal stove he dug out of his recon pack rather than scoop out a shallow trench as Kit had done. It was about as easy to do one as the other, and while the stove would take a couple of minutes to cool down after use, the ground was too hard to scrape out a trench with your hand. Besides, Gerber had an inbred aversion to dragging the blade of his knife through the dirt when he didn't have to. It dulled the edge and necessitated cleaning the knife afterward. If you didn't wash the blade, there was no telling what kind of intestinal parasite you might pick up from the germs left behind by the fecund Vietnamese soil. Just wiping it would never get them all. And if you washed the blade but didn't oil it, it would start to rust in a matter of hours out here in the bush. Never mind that the blade was stainless. As long as it was steel, it could still rust, and the climate of Indochina was ideal for promoting oxidization.

Gerber unfolded the tiny stove, in reality a small hinged framework of flat pieces of aluminum alloy, designed to hold a canteen cup. He shook a couple of hexamine tabs out of their small tube and placed them on edge beneath the stove. The instructions written on the tube said that two of them would boil a canteen cup of water in three to four minutes. Gerber knew from personal experience that it usually took three tablets and a little over five minutes. He tried half a dozen of the army-issued damp-proof matches without getting one to light and finally started the hexamine with his Zippo. Then he filled his canteen cup about two-thirds full of water and set it on to boil.

Sergeant First Class Derek Kepler, the team's intel sergeant, had managed to acquire a quantity of LRRP rations for the A-Detachment during his last trip to Nha Trang. In fact, he had acquired quite a large quantity of LRRP rations, so large that he had also been forced to acquire a two-and-a-half-ton truck to haul them in. Kepler had developed quite a reputation among the men for acquiring things needed around Camp A-555. So much so that the men had taken to referring to him as Eleven Fingers Kepler.

Kepler's latest acquisition had made fascinating listening when Gerber, in a brief moment of forgetfulness, had made the mistake of asking him where the truckload of food had come from. Gerber had wisely stopped listening shortly after the part where Kepler explained how he got the two MPs to help him load the cases of rations onto the truck as he was stealing them. It had seemed wiser not to ask how Kepler had managed to get the rations and the truck across a few hundred miles of Vietnamese countryside to the camp.

The LRRP rations were light in weight, simple to fix, could be eaten cold if necessary, although they left a lot to be desired that way, and left little residue to be buried or packed out when you were finished with them. In short, they were perfect for the sort of reconnaissance or ambush patrols frequently conducted by Gerber's men. So naturally every request Gerber filed for them was denied by General Crinshaw in Saigon. After many failed attempts to procure the rations, which weighed less than half of a comparable C-ration and tasted a lot better, Gerber happened to mention the problem to Kepler one day.

Less than a week later, a couple of tons of the rations and the deuce-and-a-half had mysteriously materialized at the camp along with a smiling Sergeant Kepler, immaculately dressed in the crisply pressed uniform of a full bird colonel assigned to the inspector general's staff. The truck, carefully repainted and with a new set of skillfully altered serial numbers, was now being used for general utility duties at Camp A-555, complete with some very official-looking paperwork indicating that it had been issued to the South Vietnamese contingent there during the tenure of Dai Uy Trang, A-555's first Vietnamese commander, now deceased. A small part of the enormous quantity of LRRP rations was now filling the packs of the men in Gerber's patrol.

Gerber pulled out one of the ration packs and checked the label. Spaghetti in meat sauce. It wasn't exactly Gerber's idea of an ideal breakfast, but he'd eaten worse on many occasions. He tore open the waterproof outer wrapper and shook out the contents, pocketing the coffee packet for later. He nibbled on the granola-like cornflake bar while he waited for his water to heat, and when it was hot enough, tore open a corner of the main-course pouch and added enough water to reconstitute it. The rest he mixed with a cocoa packet. The stuff was even better than he'd anticipated, and he was contemplating not saving the coffee for later, after all, when he looked up from his meal to see Kit standing next to him. Gerber was so startled he nearly dropped his spoon. The damned woman could move more quietly than anyone he'd ever known, with the possible exceptions of Fetterman and Krung.

Even Cat Anderson, who'd gotten his nickname because he could move his enormous bulk with such uncharacteristic stealth, sounded like a wandering water buffalo by comparison. She wasn't in the same class with Fetterman and Krung, of course. Nobody was. At least he didn't think so, but Kit did it so easily, so naturally, that it was more than a little unnerving.

Free digital watch—on time and on target

Rugged digital calendar watch displays exact time, date and running seconds with flawless quartz precision. Water-resistant, too. Comes complete with long-life battery and one-year warranty (excluding battery). Best of all, it's yours FREE!

Peel off grenade from front cover and slam it down here

PULL THE PIN ON ADVENTURE

Rush my 4 free books and my free watch.

Then send me 6 brand-new Gold Eagle novels (2 *Mack Bolans* and one each of *Able Team*, *Phoenix Force*, *Vietnam: Ground Zero* and *SOBs*) every second month as they come off the presses. Bill me at the low price of $2.49 each (a savings of 12% off the retail price). There are no shipping, handling or other hidden costs. I can always return a shipment and cancel at any time. Even if I never buy a book from Gold Eagle, the 4 free books and the watch are mine to keep.

166 CIM PAJ8

Name	(PLEASE PRINT)	
Address		Apt. No.
City	State	Zip

This offer is limited to one order per household and not valid to present subscribers. Price is subject to change.

The most pulse-pounding, pressure-packed action reading ever published

Razor-edge storytelling. Page-crackling tension. On-target firepower. Hard-punching excitement. Gold Eagle books slam home raw action the way you like it—hard, fast and real!

"Good morning, Captain Gerber," she said politely. "May I offer you a cup of tea? There is plenty left."

Gerber was about to tell her that he preferred coffee, but couldn't see any point in seeming unfriendly, especially toward a former Vietcong who was sneaky enough to slip up on you and cut your throat before you could hear her. He nodded and held out his cup.

"I want to thank you for last night," said Kit, lowering her voice.

"Last night? Thank me for what?" Gerber asked, momentarily confused by the statement. He noticed that he, too, had unconsciously lowered his voice.

"For helping me to keep warm," Kit replied innocently. "It was very kind of you. However, I thought it best to move before the others woke so that none would think anything happened between us."

"I didn't think anything had happened," said Gerber flatly. He wasn't sure he liked the direction this conversation seemed to be taking.

"Of course not. You were merely showing me a kindness, for which I thank you. I thought it best to move so that no one else would think anything unusual happened, and, of course, nothing did. Besides, although sleeping with you was much warmer, it was not very comfortable," she said, turning away. "All night long something very hard kept pressing into the back of my legs. I think I must have been lying on your pistol."

Gerber was thankful she had turned away. It helped hide the flush on his cheeks.

THEY MOVED OUT after breakfast, Fetterman taking the point while Krung and Corporal Bhat shadowed their back trail. For over four hours they sloshed through more of the swamp, picking up another batch of leeches in the process. When they finally reached firmer footing at about eleven, Gerber called a halt so they could burn the leeches off.

Remembering the experience of the day before and not wishing to repeat it, Gerber quickly sought out Fetterman, and the two men checked each other for the blood-engorged worms. Kit, Gerber noticed, seemed a bit miffed at his avoidance of her, but

was getting plenty of voluntary help from Anderson while an un-
abashed Kepler watched the proceedings with ill-concealed de-
light. Despite the large amounts of near nudity and Kepler's
good-natured leering, which Anderson appeared to find mildly
annoying, Gerber noticed that today's ritual of removing the small
black vampires was devoid of the sexual innuendos that had accompanied yesterday's bloodletting.

Gerber also noticed that Sergeant Tyme, although clearly not
amused by the situation, showed no indication of repeating his
previous nearly hysterical reaction to the leeches. Instead, looking a bit pale, he sat off by himself, burning the leeches away with
grim determination and slowly grinding each one beneath his boot
heel.

They laid up for a couple of hours during the hottest part of the
day, those not on guard sleeping in the sun in the middle of a small
clearing because the hordes of mosquitoes made sleeping in the
shade impossible to bear. Gerber, having wrongly assumed he
would be safe from Kit's advances during the daylight, and having already stood his turn at guard, had just flopped down when
a familiar shadow fell across his chest.

"Captain Gerber, please, may I speak with you?"

"Certainly, uh, Kit," answered Gerber, catching himself just
in time. He'd almost said Miss Brouchard, but some little voice
had warned him that doing that might be an even bigger mistake
than being nice to her. "What do you want to talk to me about?"

"I have the feeling that you are angry with me for some reason.
All day you have avoided me. Did I say something at breakfast that
offended you?"

"Not at all," said Gerber. He tried to look her in the eye for the
next part, but couldn't quite carry it off. "It's just that I, that is,
we've all been rather busy, what with crossing the swamp this
morning and all, and I really haven't had time to waste, uh, I mean
to engage in conversation with you. Or anyone else for that matter."

"I have said or done nothing to offend you, then?"

"No. Of course not. Nothing at all."

"And you do enjoy talking with me?"

"Certainly."

"That is good. I like very much talking to you. You seem to really listen, and to care about what I have to say, and it has been such a long time since I have had someone I could really talk to. There has been no one I could really talk to since my husband was imprisoned by the Hanoi government."

"Your husband was put in prison by the North Vietnamese?" Gerber couldn't keep from sounding a bit surprised.

"Yes. He was an educated man. A teacher. But he would not teach what the Party political commissars wished him to teach. He believed that a representative form of government was the best kind of government and that the government the Communists had established in the North was not a true representative democracy, despite the fact that the Party insisted it was a people's democracy. He taught this to his students, and when one of them reported my husband to a political commissar, they put him in prison. That was the last I ever saw of him, nearly four years ago."

"I'm sorry," said Gerber. "I didn't know. Jerry Maxwell had told me you were married, but he didn't say what happened to your husband. I suppose I should have figured out something had happened to him because you weren't using your married name."

"Yes. I took back my maiden name when I became convinced that my husband was dead."

"Dead? I thought you said he was in prison."

"They told me at first that he was being reeducated so that he would understand the Party and the workings of their people's democracy. But how long does it take to reeducate someone? When our baby died and I tried to write to him, my letters were returned unopened. I made inquiries of the authorities, but for weeks I heard nothing. Then one day I was informed that my husband had been released from the reeducation center six months earlier and, having seen the error of his previous ways, he had voluntarily joined an army unit that was going south to fight in the war of liberation there. My husband was a man who placed family above all else, Captain. He would never have done such a thing, and certainly not without first contacting me somehow. That is when I knew my husband was dead."

"I'm very sorry," said Gerber.

"Sorry? Why should you be sorry, Captain? You did not kill my husband, nor withhold the medicines that might have saved the life of my child. The Communists did that."

"I meant that I share your sorrow. That I grieve for your loss, both of your husband and your child," said Gerber. "I meant that you have my sympathy."

"I do not want your sympathy, Captain. I want only your respect, and your trust and perhaps…something…more. You are a strong and intelligent man, like my husband was, and like my father. I do not think that I can call you a nice man because of your profession, but I think maybe you are a good man, yes?"

"Kit, Emilie, I, that is… Let me try this again. You've behaved in a most professional manner throughout the mission thus far. You've already earned my respect."

"But not your trust. You do not need to say it. I can see it in your face. There is no need to apologize. Yet perhaps there will come a time when you will need to trust me. I have told you that the Communists caused the death of my husband and my child, so you are wondering then, how is it that I became a soldier for the Communists."

"The thought had crossed my mind," Gerber admitted.

"I was not given any choice, Captain. I have no family. I never saw my father after he returned to France. After my husband was imprisoned, my mother did her best to look after me and my child until she, too, became ill and died of tuberculosis. Then I had no one. Although I had some education, I had no skills. There were only three choices open to me. I could work as a common laborer and turn old and sickly before my time. Or I could volunteer to fight in the South with the army. Or I could become a prostitute. The latter I could not bring myself to do.

"Things were not so bad in the army, I told myself. At least I would have food and clothing. And I had heard rumors that things were better in the South. I do not think I really believed those rumors at the time, but I thought that if they were true, perhaps once I got to the South, I would be able to slip away and blend in with the civilian population, maybe even someday make my way to France and find my father. Perhaps, too, I still held out some hope that the lies the Party had told me were true and my husband was still alive, and if I went South with the army I might find him. I do not think I really believed that either, but at the time I desperately needed something to believe in. I was not—what is the expression you Americans have?—I did not have my head on very straight then. I did not have my shit together.''

Gerber smiled at the metaphor.

''But instead of going to the South, my unit was sent into Cambodia to help build a training and indoctrination camp for new recruits conscripted from the South. That is how I came to know something of this area. Building the camp was very hard work, and there was little food. Many of the soldiers in my unit took sick, and some died. Conditions were even worse than they had been in the North, and they were made more unpleasant for me by one of our officers who seemed to think that I could serve the Front best by serving him personally. I repeatedly refused his advances, but he persisted until it became unbearable. Then one night he sent a runner to tell me that I was ordered to report to him in his quarters. I went, thinking that he wished to see me on some matter regarding the unit. When I got there, he raped me.

''He was very cruel, and he hit me several times and called me names, and then he held a knife to my throat and raped me. It was very strange. All the time, while he was lying on top of me, he held the knife to the side of my throat. I thought surely he would kill me. But when he had finished, he got up and put his uniform back in order, sat down at his desk and lighted a cigarette. Then he started working on some papers, as though I was no longer there.

''After a time, when I no longer thought he was going to come back and kill me, I got up off the floor. And when I did, he said to me, 'That will be all. You may go.' My clothes were in tatters, I had bruises all over my body, and I had been raped, and he acted as though nothing at all had happened.

''I started to walk out, but he called me back and made me stand in front of his desk. I was so afraid that I obeyed. 'You must salute me before you may leave,' he said. He made me stand there in front of him with my breasts falling out of my torn shirt and my trousers in rags about my ankles, the blood oozing from my nose and mouth, and salute him. Then he said, 'That's more like it. Now you may go.' I ran out the door and straight into the jungle and kept on running until I collapsed.

"They caught me and brought me back, of course. Where can you run to in the jungle without food or clothing or a compass. I told my story, and he denied everything. That was when I learned the full measure of the Front's justice and mercy. For trying to desert, I was publicly flogged. I know that you have seen the scars yourself, yesterday, while we were burning the leeches from each other.

"It took me nearly three months of planning and biding my time before I could attempt another escape. Interestingly, the man who had raped me no longer seemed to have any interest in me, once he had had me. Perhaps he was developing an interest in one of the other women. Or perhaps he would have come back to me for more eventually. I do not know. At any rate, he never got the chance. One night after they had stopped watching me to make sure I didn't try to desert again, I gathered all my gear, and some food I had been hiding, and I left. But not before I paid him one last visit.

"Part of the equipment I had been issued was a knife. It was a Russian-made knife, and the steel was very hard and difficult to sharpen, but I had been working on it for three months, and it was very sharp. It would have given me more satisfaction to have emasculated him first, but I could not risk the noise he would certainly have made. I killed him as he slept, and then I cut off his genitals and nailed them to the top of his desk before I left. That is how I came to be a Vietcong soldier, Captain, and that is why I will now help you kill VC."

There was a long silence that seemed to stretch interminably in the hot sun of the little clearing. At last Gerber cleared his throat uncomfortably.

"Maybe I ought to introduce you to Staff Sergeant Krung. The two of you seem to have a lot in common."

"Krung? I'm afraid I don't understand," said Kit.

"Never mind. I'll explain it some other time."

"Thank you for listening to my story, Captain," said Kit abruptly. "I apologize for burdening you with the story of my problems, and I do not seek your sympathy. As I said, it has been a long time since there was anyone I felt I could really talk to, and I needed someone to listen. I picked you because I felt that you were different from the rest of the men and might care enough to take the time to really listen, and not just humor me as a prelude to getting into my pants. When I gave you every opportunity to take advantage of me but you didn't, I was sure that I could trust you. You will have to decide for yourself whether or not to trust me. It is strange. In a way, a part of me regrets that you did not take advantage of me, but I am glad you did not. I will not bother you any longer. We still have a long way to go, and I am very tired and need to rest before we move again."

Gerber couldn't have said why he did it, except perhaps for the natural protective instinct some men exhibit toward a bird with a broken wing, even if the bird happens to be a sharp-beaked, sharp-clawed falcon. Many months later he marked it down to the fact that he was just a natural sucker for any good-looking woman with a sob story. As Kit rose and turned to go, he reached out and touched her arm lightly.

"There's a nice, warm spot right here," he said.

She looked at him, and their eyes locked for a long moment. Then she sank slowly back to her knees.

"You are not afraid of what the others might think?"

"Here in the daylight the others will be able to see that nothing unusual happens," Gerber told her.

She smiled, remembering their conversation at breakfast.

"Nothing unusual is going to happen," she told him. "At least not yet."

She stretched out next to him on the ground and laid her head against his chest. After a minute or two, Gerber spoke again.

"Kit, may I ask you a question? You don't have to answer if you don't want to."

"What is it?"

"When you killed the man who raped you, how did it feel?"

There was no hesitation in her voice. "It felt good."

"Mmm," said Gerber. He did not speak again.

After a time, they both fell asleep in the hot afternoon sun.

10

CARAVELLE HOTEL
SAIGON

Robin Morrow detested the rooftop bar of the Caravelle Hotel. Not because it wasn't a nice enough bar. The bar was just fine. It was the clientele she couldn't stand.

Especially this time of the day. The Five O'Clock Follies had just ended down at MACV headquarters, and the Caravelle bar would soon be crawling with pseudojournalistic creeps and media personality newsreaders. Already there were too many of them hanging around to suit her taste.

Morrow had no use for those members of the Saigon press corps who seldom, indeed never in most cases, ventured into the war with one of the combat units to find out what was really happening in the countryside. The pretty boy TV screen faces with their camera crew and sound engineer hangers-on made her feel sick to her stomach when she overheard them refer to themselves as journalists.

The worst offenders, though, were the reporters for the big papers and magazines. The TV entertainment specialists at least had the excuse of all the staff they had to drag along with them. What military commander in his right mind would allow a bunch of noisy, undisciplined civilians, burdened down with cameras and klieg lights and sound equipment, who stomped around in the brush like a herd of water buffalo, to accompany his unit on a mission to the field? With that kind of albatross hanging around his neck, the only contact he'd be likely to make with the enemy was when they ambushed his men.

The print reporters had no such excuse. They could go to the field. Ernie Pyle had done it in the Second World War, and Morrow did it practically every day. But most of the real reporting on the war was being done by stringers for small-town newspapers and little-known magazines, frequently free-lancers who had wrangled themselves a set of credentials from half a dozen small-town weeklies, and served as both reporter and photographer. They weren't overly afraid of being shot at and didn't have well-padded expense accounts to keep them living like kings in Saigon. When Morrow occasionally ran across one of them, it was like bumping into an old friend from home, but the others were disgusting. They acted as though they actually believed that sitting around Saigon drinking booze at company expense and attending the daily press briefings at MACV HQ, where some disinformation officer from Pentagon East told them all about how we were winning the war, was all there was to reporting on the situation in Indochina. The TV camera crew brave enough to actually go out and visit a relatively secure fire support base was a rare bird indeed. And if they weren't busy telling one another what great journalists they were, or soaking up Scotch on the home office tab, they were hitting on the few round-eyed women about, like Morrow.

But today Morrow had no choice. She had to visit the Caravelle. That was where Jerry Maxwell, resident superspook for the CIA could be found, savoring the single rum and Coke he allowed himself daily at this time. The Caravelle would be relatively free of snoopy reporters who might ask him questions they knew he had no intention of answering, and then make up the answers he hadn't given them, crediting the answers to "a highly placed source in the intelligence community."

Morrow couldn't put her finger on it, but something had been bothering her ever since her visit to General Billy Joe Crinshaw's office earlier in the day. Part of it, she admitted with reluctance, was just a gut-level feeling that something was amiss with the mission Mack Gerber and his bunch had gone out on. But another part—and she didn't like to admit this—stemmed from a suspicion of the Kit Carson scout assigned to Gerber that was probably founded more in jealousy than in journalistic curiosity.

What really had her bugged though, was Crinshaw's attitude. He had been cooperative, almost friendly. And Billy Joe Crinshaw wasn't one to behave in a friendly fashion toward anyone. Not unless he wanted something in return. But Crinshaw had asked for nothing, and that had Morrow worried.

Morrow knew that getting anything out of Jerry Maxwell that might alleviate some of the worry was about a billion-to-one shot. Maxwell had a reputation of being so tight-lipped with journalists that the Saigon press corps called him the dirty white clam, a reference to the permanently rumpled white suits he always wore, and to his uncommunicativeness. Morrow didn't know if a good-looking woman might have any more luck getting information from Maxwell or not, but she was prepared to give it one heck of a go. Having flown to Saigon only with a change of shirt and cutoff shorts because she'd expected to return to Camp A-555 on the next available flight, she'd had to go out and spend money she really couldn't afford on a new skirt, blouse and shoes. Maxwell, she knew, also had a reputation for having an appreciative eye for the female form, and Morrow hoped that if he saw her as a woman first and a reporter second, she might have a bit better luck getting what she needed out of him.

She stood next to the elevator, scanning the bar for a bit, and finally spotted the familiar form, looking like a giant crumpled piece of paper as he hunched over a small table near the railing with his back to her. She braced herself for the encounter, daringly unfastened the top button of her blouse so Maxwell would have just the hint of the upper curve of her breasts to hold his attention and walked over and introduced herself.

"Excuse me. Aren't you Jerry Maxwell? I don't know if you'll remember me. I'm Robin Morrow, Mack Gerber's friend."

Maxwell sighed deeply, as though greatly distressed by the intrusion.

"I'm sorry, but I'm really not feeling very well. Would you mind terribly—"

He broke off abruptly as he turned slightly in the chair and looked up at her. For a long moment he gave her a look of frank appraisal, then smiled and indicated the empty chair opposite his, gesturing for her to sit down.

"Well, well. Of course. Take a pew. It would be pretty hard not to remember you, Miss Morrow, after that court-martial charge you helped Gerber get his two boys off of. I didn't recognize you without your camera and your combat boots. I must say this is quite an improvement."

"Thank you," said Morrow, taking a seat, not at all sure she should be thankful for such a left-handed compliment.

"You were at the airport as I recall. If you don't mind my mentioning it, I thought you flew off with Gerber and his bunch for a look at the Triple Nickel. What happened? Did that cute little fortune cookie with the black hair and the violet eyes upset your plans?"

Morrow felt like throwing the ashtray at him. It took every ounce of self-control she could muster to smile.

"Yes, in a way she did. But not the way you mean it, and you know it. What's Mack Gerber doing in Cambodia this time, Mr. Maxwell? And why does he have a female Kit Carson scout along with him?"

"Cambodia? What's Cambodia?"

"Come on, Jerry. Don't try to play dumb with me. I saw you bring them to the airport."

"Bring who to what airport?"

"Gerber and his new replacements and that Kit Carson you dredged up from one of the houses on Tu Do Street."

Maxwell smiled. "Carson, Carson. Kit Carson, you say? He was some kind of western hero or other, wasn't he?"

"Christ, Maxwell, you're hopeless. You'll never get to buy me dinner if you won't answer any of my questions."

"Seems to me that you're the one should be buying me dinner. After all, you're the one looking for answers."

"I can see the headline now. 'CIA Agent Tells All for Price of Dinner.' I didn't realize you could be had so cheap, Maxwell."

"I can be had, lady, but not cheap," said Maxwell sourly. "Some days I can be had cheaper than others, but the price is never really cheap."

Maxwell's tone, as well as his statement, seemed a bit out of place to Morrow, a sort of combination of depression and disgust.

"Well, anyway, you have to buy if we're going to have dinner. I spent all my money on clothes so you wouldn't have to take me out in combat boots."

"What's the matter? Don't you have an expense account like the rest of these vultures?" Maxwell quickly held up a hand to stave off the impending storm from Morrow. "Okay, okay, you win. Dinner's on me. But not here. This place will be full of TV news boys in another twenty minutes. Let's have a drink and then get out of here."

He signaled for a waiter and ordered a Scotch and water for Morrow and a rum and Coke for himself. Morrow noticed that there were already two empty glasses before him. For Jerry Maxwell to be drinking three rum and Cokes in the same day, something must be very wrong indeed.

The waiter brought the drinks and left, taking the empty glasses with him this time. Maxwell didn't fail to notice the meaningful look Morrow gave the departing empties. Indeed, there was little of anything that Jerry Maxwell failed to notice. Beneath the strategically rumpled white suit and the carefully cultivated crude mannerisms was a mind like an IBM mainframe computer. Maxwell was one of the finest intelligence officers in the business, and one of the Company's very few experts on Southeast Asian politics and culture. One of the main reasons he was so effective was because he didn't look or act like he would be effective at anything. The man didn't even seem to know how to tie his necktie properly. And for the past seven years while the Communists scattered about Asia had been largely ignoring Jerry Maxwell as a figure too comical to be any kind of real threat, Maxwell had been carefully building one of the finest networks of agents since the Cheka of Czarist Russia.

That amazing ability to appear incompetent, without carrying it to the extreme where it would become suspect as a clever cover ploy, coupled with the ability to think fast on his feet and look you square in the eye and convince you the sun rose in the West, had gotten Maxwell out of a couple of pretty tight spots in East Berlin before he'd come to the Company's Asian bureau. This time, though, it wasn't quite enough.

"You're right, of course," said Maxwell. "I have been drinking too damned much lately. Starting earlier and earlier in the day, too. Pressures of the damned job, I guess. Maybe I'm just getting too damned old for this kind of work."

"Cut the bullshit, Maxwell," Morrow told him. "About the only thing anybody really does know about you is your drinking habits. One rum and Coke a day, always at the same time, always here at the Caravelle. You ought to change your drinking habits. One of these days some VC spook is liable to recognize the pattern and decide to take you out while you're going out the door downstairs. Any day you have three drinks it's got to be a bad one. What happened? China decide to send ten million advisors to the Vietcong, or did all of South America declare war on Guam?"

Maxwell made a mental note to do exactly that, reevaluate his drinking habits. The one drink each day at the Caravelle was part of his carefully prepared cover. It gave him an excuse to be in a public, crowded place every twenty-four hours in case he needed to arrange a message drop or pickup, or a direct meeting with one of his many field agents. They could pass each other in the crowded bar and exchange information without seeming to make contact. But the damned woman reporter was right. Setting a pattern of any kind left you vulnerable to attack. He'd have to reexamine the situation and decide whether the advantages outweighed the risk.

"Miss Morrow, you are absolutely right. About setting patterns, I mean. Why, I was thinking that myself just the other day. Self, I said, you need to drink in other bars more often. But you know, I'm so used to coming here I just plain forgot to go somewhere else, so I decided the only way to break the pattern was to have several drinks. If that works, maybe in a month or two I'll try giving up drinking altogether for four or five months, and then go on a real good binge. What do you think? Will that be enough variety to keep me from becoming a marked man, or should I try a new drink as well, maybe give up my rum and Coke for a vodka Collins or something?"

"I think you should try less bullshit and more politeness, or I may just decide to eat alone and throw this Scotch right in your nasty face."

Maxwell actually chuckled, then looked serious.

"Miss Morrow, Robin, look. We both know I'm not going to tell you anything about Gerber's mission. I can't. I can't even confirm that I've seen or talked to him, although we both know that I have. That's just the way it is."

"I already know they're going to Cambodia and they took that so-called scout with them."

"So you say. As I said, I can't confirm any of this."

"You don't have to. It isn't important. What is important is that something's gone wrong. Very wrong."

Maxwell's left eyebrow twitched ever so slightly, and he leaned forward a few millimeters in his chair. "What do you mean, something's gone wrong? What's gone wrong?"

"Damn it, that's just it. I don't know. But I know something is wrong. I can smell it. I can feel it in my bones, Maxwell. Without even knowing what this mess is all about, I can tell you that it's as rotten as a barrel full of year-old apples. I don't care what Gerber and his bunch are up to. If the Agency is involved, the world's probably better off never knowing. But what happens to those men is important to me. Especially what happens to Gerber. And there are a lot of things happening here that just don't add up."

"Such as?" asked Maxwell, doing his best to look as if he really wasn't interested.

"Number one, that scout of yours. How much do you really know about her? How thoroughly was her background checked?"

"She was given a clean bill of health by Military Intelligence," said Maxwell. "We have no reason to believe that she is anything other than what she appears to be."

"Yeah, that's pretty much what Crinshaw told me. But what exactly is it that she appears to be?"

Maxwell rolled his eyes and prayed for strength. "You spoke with General Crinshaw about the mission?"

"Of course not. But I did ask him a couple of questions about this Brouchard woman's background."

"And what did he tell you?"

"The same thing you just did. She was cleared by Military Intelligence. Only nobody says who at Military Intelligence cleared her, and nobody gives any indication of how her background and story were verified. Frankly, I don't see how they could be. Did you know she has a Russian-made knife?"

Maxwell shrugged. "Why shouldn't she? She was carrying a Russian-made AK-47 when she *chieu hoi*ed and came over to us. The woman was a Vietcong soldier for over two years, for Christ's sake. What do you expect? She should have the Statue of Liberty tattooed on her ass?"

"It wouldn't surprise me to find out she had something tattooed there, but you're missing the point. The Russian knife. Wouldn't MI have taken such a thing away from her when she surrendered?"

"That would be the normal procedure," replied Maxwell.

"Right. So even if it were reasonable for her to have a Russian-made knife, she shouldn't have one now, right? And something else. She has no personal effects. No photographs of her family. No little mementos, nothing except that French translation of Tolstoy she was carrying when she came to the camp, and I never saw her open it once we got out to the Triple Nickel. It's as though the woman has no past. She had a good pair of boots and all the webgear and equipment necessary for going out in the field, but she didn't even have a change of underwear in the stuff she left behind in camp."

"How do you know all this?"

Morrow hesitated just a moment. "I went through her locker after they went out into the field."

Maxwell offered no comment on that.

"I'm telling you, Maxwell, there's something not right about the woman. There's just nothing there. It's as though she'd sanitized her belongings. Sanitized, that's the word your people use, isn't it? Remove anything that could be identifiable, right down to the labels in an agent's clothes? The only problem is that the very absence of such things is noticeable in itself. The woman just doesn't read right. It's like looking at a silhouette instead of a person.

"There's something else odd, too. I went to Crinshaw to find out what I could about the woman. I expected he'd have to make some inquiries if he gave me any help at all. I didn't really expect him to do anything. He's always very careful not to alienate me, but since that court-martial business you mentioned earlier, he hasn't exactly gone out of his way to assist me. Yet when I asked him about Brouchard, he not only bent over backward being polite and trying to assist me, he knew exactly who the woman was and that she'd been cleared by MI. In fact, he made a big deal about having no reason to question her loyalty, and then in practically the same breath he did exactly that, raised doubts about whether or not she could be trusted. Now doesn't that strike you as being just a little bit odd?''

It did indeed, but Maxwell was tempted to just write it off as Crinshaw straddling the fence on the question of Brouchard's reliability, hoping to be able to cover his own ass if it turned out the woman was less than totally dependable. It was a typical enough Crinshaw move. And, of course, Crinshaw knew about the woman because he knew about the mission, a connection Morrow had apparently missed. Added all together, it still produced nothing but a sort of general uneasiness that something was amiss. Nothing, that is, until you added in two little bits of information Morrow couldn't possibly know about.

First, there was that bizarre insistence by Crinshaw that Gerber's team was not to be extracted if they encountered trouble. It was a stupid decision, and Crinshaw had made such a big deal out of it that Maxwell suddenly found himself wondering if there was something more to it than just a childish whim followed by a general throwing a temper tantrum.

Second, Maxwell's boss had been in Saigon for two days, coming in aboard a scheduled airline flight returning GIs from R and R in Hong Kong. He'd been in-country for more than forty-eight hours and had thus far made no effort whatsoever to contact Maxwell, a situation that could politely be described as highly irregular. What was more, one of Maxwell's Vietnamese informants had told him that during that time, Maxwell's superior had been seen going to General Crinshaw's office on three separate occasions, twice for approximately half an hour each, and once for nearly two hours. That was a lot of time for anyone to be taking out of a general's schedule.

Maxwell's boss was a man know within the CIA's Asian bureau as Smiling Jack Jirasek because of a wound he'd once received that had severed some of the nerves in his face, leaving him with a perpetually gaunt grin. But Jirasek hadn't always been known as Smiling Jack. In the late fifties and early sixties, at the height of the cold war in Europe, they'd called him Jack the Ripper.

In those days Jirasek had been fast building a reputation within the Company, a reputation for tackling supposedly insolvable problems and rapidly resolving them. Those kind of results had insured Jirasek a spot on the management ladder, but it hadn't won him any friends among the agents in the field. A characterizing trademark of those solutions had always been sudden, brutal resolution by means of overwhelming force, and Jirasek had never hesitated to be willing to spend a few friendly agents, or even a couple of his own people, setting the situations up. Jirasek had been a man for whom the end always justified the means. Moving inside to a desk after he'd received the facial wound on an assignment where he'd used himself as bait hadn't apparently changed his attitude about getting the job done.

In the first six weeks of Jirasek's tenure as chief of the Asian bureau, there had been more resignations, reassignments, and terminations in staffing than in any other bureau in the history of the Company. Maxwell had survived the purge only because he got results in his station, and Jirasek valued results above all else. Maxwell had no doubt about what would happen to his career if he ever failed to continue producing those results.

And Smiling Jack the Ripper Jirasek had once more left his desk and returned to the field. In Maxwell's station. And after two whole days he still hadn't bothered to let Maxwell know he was there, but he had made three visits with General Crinshaw, one of them nearly two hours long.

Maxwell was beginning to think that maybe Morrow was onto something after all. He had to admit that things did seem to be just a little bit odd.

11

THE CAMBODIAN
JUNGLE

From a small rocky outcropping near the military crest of the hill, Fetterman and Gerber looked down across six hundred meters of broad-leaved jungle interspersed at irregular intervals with huge pine trees.

It still seemed strange to Gerber, even after spending more than a year in Southeast Asia, to see pine trees cropping up among the palms, teak and bamboo. He knew that conifers were among the oldest of trees and that they were found in virtually all climates in all parts of the world. But they were most prevalent in northern temperate zones, and he always associated them with such, perhaps because of their traditional use as Christmas trees, which reminded him of snowy winters back at his parents' home in Iowa. Still, the greatest variety of species was to be found in eastern and southeastern Asia, and in the Mexican and Central American highlands, places one didn't normally associate with Christmas trees. Dredging up old and seldom-used knowledge from his college major in botany, Gerber eyed the nearest pines and wondered whether they were of the subgenera *Haploxylon* or *Diploxylon*, but without knowing the precise species there was no way to tell without a microscope.

A stream cut through the shallow valley floor below. Back in Iowa, Gerber mused, it might have been called a river. There were places in Appanoose and Wayne counties where the Chariton was less impressive than the stream below, and the Chariton was a pretty average-sized tributary of the Missouri, with a lot of interesting switchbacks and rapids.

This stream wasn't listed on his maps as a river, however. In fact, it wasn't listed at all. Gerber knew that meant little. The maps had been drawn by the French cartographic service over twenty years ago and were notoriously inaccurate. Still, it obviously wasn't just some seasonal runoff, and you would think they would have noticed something its size.

So it could have been a river, but Gerber didn't think so. Kit had accurately predicted they would find it when they reached the valley and had stuck to her prediction even after it was pointed out that there was no such feature indicated on the maps, but she had not been able to name it. To her it was just a ''very big stream here,'' that she had crossed while escaping from the Vietcong. Since she had lived not all that far from it for over two years, building and then working at the training camp west of Phum Thant Peam, it seemed unlikely that she wouldn't know the name if it was important enough to the locals for them to consider it a river. Gerber assumed it to be some minor tributary of the Prek Cham.

''Jesus, sir, what do you make of that?'' whispered Fetterman, indicating an area on the other side of the valley floor. ''It looks like the end of the world.''

Beyond the stream was a scene of utter, stark desolation. Shattered tree trunks stood dark and naked amid a crumbling black-and-gray valley that should have been a tangled mass of lush green. Even the pines had been stripped of their needlelike leaves. Running down the valley in a broad band roughly parallel to the stream was a dead zone nearly three hundred meters wide. The whole area was pockmarked with craters like the face of the moon, many of them superimposed on one another from repeated impacts. Yet no amount of mere bombing could have created such a no-man's-land on its own, especially not one with such clearly defined edges.

''I've got a feeling that it's just the beginning of something else,'' Gerber replied. ''When Maxwell briefed me, if you could call it that, he mentioned a field test of some kind of new chemical defoliant being studied as a means of depriving the VC of cover along infiltration routes. Part of the mission profile calls for us to assess the efficacy of the project if we encounter any defoliated areas. Maxwell presented it as such a minor adjunct to the main mission that I didn't think it worth mentioning.''

''Well, I'd say from the look of that shit we've encountered a defoliated area and the stuff is damned efficacious. They must have sprayed the area first and then bombed it, unless they disperse it in bombs. Did Maxwell tell you what they're calling this stuff?''

Gerber searched his mind a moment. ''No. I don't think so. Like I said, he mentioned it almost in passing, as if it weren't terribly important, just something that it would be nice for us to check on if we ran across it.''

Fetterman eyed the powdery gray-black landscape, with its blackened, broken trees. The trees weren't twisted or splintered by the obviously intense, repeated bombing of the area the way ordinary, living, green trees would have been; they were broken like old, brittle bones, and crumbling as though they were ancient plaster sculptures. Trees that had been dead long before they had been shattered, and then burnt into charcoal stalks with fragile, slowly disintegrating branches. He studied the area first through his binoculars, then through the eyepiece of the compact eighty-power spotting scope they'd brought along for detail work in their observations of the Trail network. Finally he eyeballed the whole area again. In all that vast expanse of denuded, blasted landscape nothing moved. Not so much as a single bird was visible to the eye.

''Captain,'' said Fetterman uneasily, ''when Maxwell mentioned that minor little adjunct to our mission out there, he didn't happen to mention anything about how safe it was to pass through one of these defoliated areas, did he?''

''No. Something bothering you?''

''Not really, I guess. Just a little spooky seeing that out there. Sort of like walking through a midsummer patch of forest and finding yourself staring through a doorway into winter. There doesn't seem to be anything left alive out there, at least nothing's moving. If that stuff is persistent, I'd sure hate to go stomping around down there without a protective mask. Wouldn't want it to defoliate us, if you know what I mean, sir.''

"I would think if Maxwell thought it might be dangerous, he would have said something," Gerber mused. "Besides, I don't see where we have much choice. Kit says the OP where we can observe the Trail network is still two ridge lines away. I don't see any way for us to get around this area, so I guess we'll have to cross it."

"Yes, sir. Are we going to wait for nightfall? I don't like the idea of us crossing all that open terrain in daylight. Those burned-out and rotten tree trunks won't offer much in the way of cover if someone spots us out there," Fetterman observed.

"Agreed. But I don't much like the idea of stumbling through that area in the dark, bumping against those tree trunks and shaking God only knows what down all over us, just in case your uneasy feelings aren't groundless, Master Sergeant. We'll move down to the edge of the area and hold there, then cross right at dusk. We'll make a little less of a target that way and still have enough light that we ought to be able to see to get across without bruising our shins and bumping our knees too many times. Needless to say, once we do get down in that area, I don't want anybody stopping for any reason until we're clear across. I'll expect everybody to keep moving until we're well clear of the area. We don't want to be hanging around down there."

"Of course, sir. Shall I start moving the men into position now?"

Before either of them could move, Kepler slid in alongside them, breathing hard.

"Captain," he said, speaking between gasps. "We got trouble."

"Let's hear it."

"VC working our back trail," Kepler wheezed.

"What, again? How far?"

"Fifteen, maybe twenty minutes tops, if they keep at their present rate," Kepler said, panting "Say ten if they decide to di most ricky-tick."

"Numbers?"

"Looks like a squad. At least seven, maybe more. I couldn't get an accurate count."

"That many must be point element for a company," offered Fetterman.

"You sure they're looking for us?" asked Gerber.

"Well, sir," said Kepler, gulping air, "they're sure as hell looking for somebody. They got a tracker out front, walking point with a two-man security team."

"Jesus! Where in the hell did those guys come from?"

"Sir," said Fetterman, "I don't like to say this, but they must have found the bodies of that other patrol we neutralized. I thought we'd done an adequate job of concealing the evidence, but perhaps we weren't quite as thorough as I thought we were. Maybe we should have buried them instead of just hiding the bodies."

"This is no time to be thinking about what we should have done, Master Sergeant. What we need to do now is think about what we're going to do."

"Yes, sir. We'll have to kill the tracker, sir. It's the only way we'll lose them if he's any good at all."

"He's done all right following us so far," offered Kepler.

"I suppose it can't be helped. It sure is going to blow our being here."

"Not necessarily, sir. The VC may not know what they're onto yet. Those three we killed earlier we took out without firing a shot."

"So?"

"So we didn't leave behind any brass or other clues that would point to the job being done by us. Those turkeys could have been taken out by any three mean guys with knives. South Vietnamese smugglers, Cambodian border bandits, even other VC who had a grudge against them or were trying to defect to the South and *chieu hoi* like our Kit Carson did. So long as those guys tracking us didn't find any of Anderson's size thirteen triple E boot prints, all they know is somebody killed their buddies. They don't know it was us."

"You're forgetting one thing, Tony. Any of those other groups would have stripped the bodies."

"I know. But think about it. We took their weapons and ammunition, and Derek collected all their personal papers for analysis."

"Which is what any *military* unit would have done. But nobody took their clothes or their boots, which is what bandits would have done."

"I did."

Gerber stared, aghast at his master sergeant. "You did what?"

"I took the guy's boots off. Left them under a bush about fifty feet from where I hid his body. Did the same with his sun helmet. Figured if anyone did find the body, it would confuse them for a little bit. And I'd be willing to bet that Krung's man is now sporting a modification in his anatomy, which is exactly what any military unit would not have done."

"Yes," admitted Gerber. "I hadn't thought about that."

"Sir, Master Sergeant Fetterman may be onto something," said Kepler, warming to the idea. "I'm afraid I was too slow and my man tried to duck the blade. Got the job done, but made a bit of a mess of it. It wasn't exactly a textbook kill. Add it all up, and it might be enough that those guys back there are wondering just who in the hell they're following."

"Gentlemen, the key word is *following*. As long as they're still doing that, it doesn't matter who they think we are," Gerber pointed out.

"Granted, sir," said Fetterman. "You agree then that we'll have to kill the tracker?"

"Absolutely. And as soon as we shoot him, they're going to know what they're dealing with. Border bandits don't carry M-16s. At least not yet."

"Of course not. Neither do Vietcong."

"Master Sergeant, you're not making any sense, and we don't have time for long-winded explanations right now, so if you've got something constructive to say, get on with it."

"Sir, we picked up two SKS carbines and an AK-47 from that trio we greased back at the river. It won't have escaped your notice, I'm certain, that the clothing worn by our scout on this mission is standard issue to many VC units. One of the men we killed earlier was, in fact, dressed almost identically. Also, since the Vietcong is an equal-opportunity employer, and as a general rule, the U.S. Army isn't, I propose that we give Miss Brouchard the AK-47 and allow her to march Sergeant Kepler and myself up to the tracker and his two security men as though we were her prisoners. They'll hopefully be lulled into a false sense of security by the appearance of an armed Cô Cong with knowledge of this area and native-speaking ability, and by the fact that there are three of them, four counting Miss Brouchard, and only two Americans, who will look very dejected at having been captured. If the plan works, they'll allow us to approach. When we reach them, Sergeant Kepler and I will kill them with our knives.''

"Kepler's already admitted fluffing one kill today. What makes you think he won't fluff another?'' asked Gerber, then to Kepler said, "Sorry, Derek, nothing personal.''

"I have every confidence in Sergeant Kepler's abilities, sir. His timing was a little off earlier, that's all,'' responded Fetterman.

"The odds would still be three to two.''

"The odds *should* be even, sir. I'm counting on Miss Brouchard to at least keep the third man occupied until we can deal with him. If she really has come over to our side, she ought to be able to do at least that much. With a bit of luck we ought to be able to kill all three and slip away before the rest of the squad shows up. If we can do it quickly enough, and quietly, it might even be some time before they realize they're missing their point. It depends on how far out in front the tracker is working and what their contact schedule is.''

"And if the VC get suspicious before you can get close enough to knife them?''

"I'll draw my pistol from beneath my shirt and shoot all three of them. Then we'll run like hell.''

"Suppose you're not fast enough to get all three?''

Fetterman looked offended. "In that unlikely event, Sergeant Tyme will be covering us with one of the SKSs, and he'll shoot as many people as may be necessary.''

Gerber looked at Kepler. "Well, what do you think?''

The intel Sergeant shrugged. "Hell, sir, might as well give it a try. What have we got to lose but our lives.''

"All right,'' said Gerber. "Start putting it together. We're going to go ahead and cross that open area right now, on the double. They're sure to send the point across to scout it first, and we'll take them as soon as they can't be seen from this side. That way, if things do go sour, we'll have a good field of fire to keep them from coming across after us until nightfall. They're apt to be a bit cautious about crossing that open ground if we have to shoot a few of them trying it, and even after it gets good and dark it'll take them a little while to work up to it. By the time they do, and get across, we won't be around to be found any longer."

"I'm not real sure I should feel honored, but thanks for the vote of confidence," Kepler muttered to Fetterman as they hurried back down the trail from the outcropping. "I'd have thought you'd have wanted Krung with you on this one."

"Krung would've been my first choice," Fetterman admitted, "but he'll be busy."

"Doing what?"

"Covering our Kit Carson with the other SKS. He's the only one I could trust not to hesitate. Being a Tai, he's got no use for most Vietnamese, and he hates all Communists. If she betrays us, he'll kill her first."

They linked up with the others and moved immediately through the jungle toward the stream. Gerber briefing them on the situation as they moved. The stream was maybe fifty feet wide, but only three to four feet deep, and after Washington and Tyme had scouted the opposite bank, they forded it without incident.

Perhaps it was inaccurate to say totally without incident. Except for Anderson, who stepped into a hole a couple of feet lower than the streambed but wasn't greatly bothered by it since his head stayed above the water, no one took a dunking. But a small radio transmitter carried by one of the indigenous personnel got too soaked to work anymore. Staff Sergeant Galvin Bocker, the team's radio genius, could have dried it out and fixed it had he known about it at the time and been so inclined, but by the time he discovered the radio he couldn't have fixed it even if he'd wanted to.

The trip across no-man's-land was an altogether different kind of experience. They had emerged dripping wet from the blood-warm water of the stream, scrambled up the bank and double-timed through a couple of hundred meters of jungle to come to the edge of desolation. Fetterman decided he'd been wrong when he'd said the place looked like the end of the world. When he got a good, close look, it was more like a view of an alien planet.

Near the wasteland, green, reasonably healthy-looking trees had been scorched and blackened by the terrific heat, but where the dead zone itself started, there was only a fine, flaky gray ash, with randomly charred tree trunks sticking up out of the stuff. The ash was a good three inches deep and appeared relatively smooth and featureless, except for the occasional ripple pattern of a bomb crater. In fact, the area had been bombed so many times that the craters had tended to wash one another out, obscuring their outlines as they redistributed the ash.

"Christ, Fetterman, what is this place?" Tyme said when the two of them happened to bunch up close together.

"The captain says he thinks the CIA or somebody working with them tested a new kind of defoliant spray here. Looks like they waited until everything died, then dropped napalm and HE on the place. At any rate, something started things burning, and all the dead stuff burned up pretty quick. I guess the fire kind of petered out when it got to the living trees."

"But why burn it if they were testing a defoliant?"

"Who knows? Maybe they were trying to destroy the evidence. Or maybe they were just trying to see how well the stuff would burn."

Fetterman found the whole experience surreal. He was humping probably fifty-five or sixty pounds of equipment, weapons and ammunition through southeastern Cambodia. He was soaking wet from the river crossing, and he was sweating from the heat and exertion, yet the landscape around him was like nothing else quite so much as walking through a new fall of snow. The slightest movement disturbed the powdery ash, which swirled about their feet, and when it settled you could tell that someone or something had come this way, but you couldn't clearly discern the shape of the boot print. Bizarrely he kept expecting to see a skier or a snowman at any moment.

At the far side, where the jungle resumed again, Fetterman stood off to one side and let the others go past him, counting heads to make sure no one had gotten left behind. As the last of the strikers tumbled past, he turned back, and the toe of his boot kicked up something with a familiar shape from beneath the ash. He glanced down and saw that it was a small notebook, similar to the one he had removed from the body of the VC officer earlier. The canvas cover was scorched, and the edges of the pages looked singed. Against his better judgment, he bent over and tried to pick it up, but something seemed to be holding it. Mindful that the book might be attached to a trip wire and a booby trap, Fetterman didn't tug on it. Instead, he reached down and brushed back the ash to reveal the object. Clenched tightly about the book were the charred, baked bones of a human hand.

12

SPECIAL FORCES CAMP
A-555

When she returned from Saigon around ten the next morning, Robin Morrow found Lieutenant Mildebrandt seated in the team house, looking as miserable as ever. He had a cup of tea, a warm Coke, a cold beer and a glass of water, all sitting in front of him next to a barely touched bowl of dry cornflakes. He was sweating profusely and had exchanged his copy of *Playboy* for a book with the improbable title of *Ralph the Action Wonder Dog: #3 Hack Doberman's Return*. Morrow decided immediately that the *Playboy* would have made a much better fan, and probably a more interesting read as well.

"Miss Morrow. Well, hello. I didn't expect to see you back here so soon. Did you find that information you were looking for in Saigon?"

He stood in a show of politeness, but Morrow quickly motioned him to sit back down. He did not look healthy enough this morning to be doing anything as stressful as standing up.

Morrow sank into the chair opposite him and shrugged. "You know how MACV is."

"Uh, no. Actually, ma'am, I don't. I haven't been in-country long enough to know much about how anything is."

"Sorry," said Morrow. "I forgot. MACV is where everyone is very polite, but not very informative. Well, almost everyone is polite," she added, remembering Maxwell. Although to be fair, he had bought her an excellent dinner and hadn't seemed quite so much like an ogre after she quit trying to pump him for information.

"I take it then that you didn't get the answers you were looking for?"

"No, Lieutenant, I didn't. But a few things happened that lead me to believe I'm onto something. I just don't know what it is yet. Say, are you feeling all right? You don't look at all well this morning, if you don't mind my saying so. Maybe you should see the team medic."

"I've already been over to see Phil. He gave me something for my stomach and told me to drink more fluids, remember to take my salt tablets and try not to sweat so much. He says some people have a hard time adjusting to the heat and humidity, and I'm having a harder time than average. He says the condition is complicated by a lack of sleep, but that I'll probably get better in a few days if I don't get a lot worse."

"That's encouraging news." Morrow smiled. "I saw Sergeant Yashimoto outside, and he looked a bit haggard, too. Did you guys have a rough night of it or something?"

"Actually. I slept better last night than I have in weeks. It was the alarm clock this morning that was a little hard to take. I was lying in my bunk when there were all these explosions outside. At first I thought the camp was under attack, maybe being mortared or something like that, but it turned out it was just Sergeant Smith helping Captain Minh deliver an early morning demolitions lecture to some of the troops. They hadn't bothered to mention it to me, they said, because it was only my third night in camp, and they thought I looked tired from all the excitement. They said they figured I'd want to sleep in rather than help out with the lecture so early in the morning."

"Very considerate of them," said Morrow, laughing. "Is there any word from our people in the field?"

"Captain Gerber's patrol, you mean? Not much. They sent the prearranged code message, indicating they had crossed the . . . oops! I think maybe I almost just said too much."

"Crossed the border into Cambodia, you mean? Relax, Glen, I know that much already. I also know it's not for publication. I was just curious as to whether or not they were having any problems. Captain Gerber owes me a night in Saigon, and I'd hate not to be able to collect.''

''I don't know . . .''

''Look, just forget it. You don't have to tell me anything if you don't want to. They wouldn't tell me anything in Saigon. Why should you be any different?''

''Well,'' said Mildebrandt, ''we haven't heard much because they're operating under fairly tight radio security procedures. At one point they did indicate they were being followed by somebody and planned to take care of it. Later, they made no mention of any continuing pursuit. That's really about all I know, and probably more than I should say.''

Morrow's interest was instantly peaked. ''Did they say who was following them? Do they know how they got onto their trail?''

Mildebrandt shook his head. ''I'm sorry. That's really all I know.''

''Well, thanks for letting me know. Like I said, I was just wondering how they were doing. If you'll excuse me, I need to do some thinking. I've got three stories to file before next Friday, and right now I don't have any idea what I'm going to write about. I'll go see what great new ideas I can come up with, and you can get back to your breakfast.''

When Morrow had left, Mildebrandt eyed the cornflakes suspiciously. He poked them experimentally with the tip of his spoon a couple of times. Finally he poured the warm Coke over them and stirred them with the spoon. Cautiously he tasted them deciding they weren't half bad that way. Carefully he scooped out another spoonful and chewed the cornflakes slowly. It was a little like eating caramel-flavored popcorn. When he'd had another five or six bites, he decided not to press his luck. He scooped the remains of the cornflakes into the garbage, added the tea, put the barely sampled beer back in the refrigerator and bravely drank the glass of water. Then he went outside to check on the camp.

He made it as far as the latrine.

WHILE MILDEBRANDT WAS DIVESTING himself of the breakfast he'd worked so hard to get down, Morrow wandered about the camp until she realized she was getting in everybody's way.

She returned to her quarters and dragged out her battered old Brother portable from its equally battered case, propped it up on a folding metal chair, fed a blank sheet of paper into the carriage and tried to think of something to type. When after twenty minutes no words had magically appeared on the page, she gave up, leaned back against the wall and jammed her hands in the pockets of her shorts.

Something was rotten somewhere. She was sure of that. General Crinshaw had been far too pleasant to deal with and had been very free with his uninformative answers. And something was bothering Maxwell, too. It was impossible to know what, but no member of the Saigon press corps had ever seen Jerry Maxwell drink more than one rum and Coke. Never. Until yesterday. A man with that kind of control didn't drink unless something was really bothering him, and it took a lot to bother a man in Maxwell's line of work.

Everybody involved with this big hush-hush mission seemed to be acting a little odd. Mildebrandt with his upset stomach. Emilie Brouchard with her backgroundless personality. Even Gerber had acted strained when she'd bumped into him at Tan Son Nhut. He'd been polite, but not friendly, strangely distant. At the time she'd been annoyed about it, but not overly upset; she'd put it down to the presence of the Brouchard woman and all the attention she was obviously showing Gerber.

Morrow eyed the wall locker containing Kit's belongings. She considered searching it again, but what would be the point? She'd already gone through it once and nothing was there, with the possible exception of that Russian-made knife, which by itself proved nothing. Damn it! How could anyone's personal effects be so utterly devoid of any past? The woman had to be hiding something, but what?

Morrow cast one last look at the typewriter and pushed it aside. It was the first time in her journalistic career that she could ever recall suffering from writer's block. She had notes in her spiral-bound steno books sufficient to write four or five current what's-happening-in-the-war stories and at least three dozen human interest items. She just couldn't bring any of it together. There was no point in forcing it. She might as well do something else for a while.

Morrow unpacked her bags, noting that the skirt and blouse she'd worn to Saigon, as well as the set she'd bought there, still needed a washing. She unwrapped her spare underwear and boot socks from around the bottle of Scotch she'd brought back from Saigon for herself, and the bottle of bourbon she'd brought back for Gerber, putting the Scotch in her locker. When she'd finished unpacking, she strolled over to Gerber's hootch, intending to leave the bottle on his desk as a surprise.

For a moment, Morrow stood in the doorway, which was heavily sandbagged like all the other entrances in the camp except those in the dependents' quarters, and looked at the room. It was at once both familiar and foreign. The folding metal bunk along one wall might have been the same one she remembered. There were still a couple of plastic webbing-covered lawn chairs, although she thought they were a different color than the ones Gerber had had before the camp had burned a few months ago. And the captain's homemade desk, which he'd hammered together out of old ammo crates and scrap plywood, had been replaced by a spindly, unstable-looking folding desk painted an even uglier shade of green than the usual military olive drab. But technology was gradually coming to Camp A-555.

A huge paddle-bladed ceiling fan hung overhead, there was a small radio in the corner plugged into one of the room's two electrical outlets and Gerber had finally consented to a telephone on his desk. True, it was only a field phone and connected only with the tiny switchboard Sergeant Bocker had built in the communications bunker, but through it Gerber could speak to almost any part of the camp. Also, when the land lines were intact, which wasn't often, he could even be patched into the military telephone network and talk to Saigon or Nha Trang, although the calls were frequently routed in a somewhat bizarre manner. It might, for instance, be necessary to go through Cam Tho, Vinh Long, Moc Hoa, Tay Ninh and Bien Hoa to reach Colonel Alan Bates's office at B-team Headquarters in Saigon. That was on a good day.

Morrow looked at the hopelessly cluttered desktop, piled with requisitions, advisories, MACV directives and reports, the bureaucratic paper refuse of running a war, and shook her head in amazement.

"Sort of makes you wonder how they get any fighting done," she muttered.

There was no place to put the bottle.

She looked around for the upended ammo crate Gerber used as a nightstand, but found it covered with science fiction novels and a copy of *A Field Guide to the Fungi of Southeast Asia*. She wasn't sure if the guide was a mushroom hunter's handbook or something designed for the serious mycologist and decided she didn't care.

She considered leaving the bottle on his bunk, but was afraid he might come in and toss something on top of it without noticing it. Soldiers coming in tired from the field frequently weren't the most observant of people once they got inside the safety of the camp's perimeter.

Finally she remembered that Gerber used to keep his spare Beam's in his wall locker. That, of course, was before his hootch had burned with most of the rest of the old camp, but it was possible that old habits hadn't changed. It was worth a try. She walked over to the locker. There was no padlock on the door, so she tried the handle. It swung open easily.

Inside, in contrast to the general chaos of his hootch, Gerber's spare equipment and uniforms were neatly hung on pegs or hangers. She checked the top shelf, but it contained only a helmet, a ranger-type patrol cap and, wrapped in plastic bags, several new green berets with the Fifth Special Forces flash sewn on them.

For a moment, Morrow wondered why Gerber would have so many berets, and then it dawned on her. They wouldn't be Gerber's. At least not exactly. He would have bought them, to be sure, but he was merely holding them in trust. They belonged to people like Bill Schattschneider and Steve Kittredge, Ian McMillan and Sean Cavanaugh and young Miles Clarke and the strange-acting "Vampire" Schmidt. Master Sergeant Fetterman had told her once that Gerber saw to it that a fresh green beret accompanied the bodies of each of them when they were sent home for burial. It was their captain's way of paying his final respects to the men who had fought and died alongside him. The hats on the shelf would be for those who had yet to fall.

Morrow didn't like thinking about the hats. It made her feel uneasy. What if one of them was there to accompany Gerber home? She didn't want to think about that.

She was about to close the door to the locker when she realized she hadn't checked the drawers in the bottom. She bent and pulled one out, but the top drawer contained only underwear, which Gerber, indeed all of the men, never wore on patrol because its only effect in the hot, humid environment of Vietnam was to chafe the wearer something fierce. Morrow couldn't help thinking that at least Gerber owned a change of underwear while Emilie Brouchard apparently did not.

Morrow tried the second drawer and was rewarded for her efforts. Along with all the neatly rolled pairs of socks was an untapped bottle of Beam's Choice and a box of those small cigars Gerber rarely smoked but insisted on having around to chew on when he was immersed in the planning of any new mission. To Morrow they smelled like baby owl feathers. When smoked, they smelled even worse.

Morrow had to move the cigar box slightly to fit the second bottle of Beam's into the drawer. That was how she found the letter.

It might have been anything; it was just a small scrap of white paper sticking out from under a corner of the cigar box. Morrow couldn't say what made her do it. Perhaps it was her journalistic training. Perhaps it was just natural human curiosity. It wasn't as though she intended to go snooping in Gerber's locker. But something made her move the box and look at the envelope, and when she did, the familiar handwriting hit her like a slap in the face.

Stunned, Morrow stared at the light blue ink in the looping slant with the Seattle address she knew so well. With a slowly growing sense of horrified fascination, her eyes moved to the post office cancellation. The date was only a little over two weeks ago.

Morrow knew that it wasn't nice to read other people's mail without their permission, yet it would have been a strong character indeed with the determination to resist under the circumstances. Kneeling before the locker, she carefully placed the bottle of Beam's to one side, then gently lifted out the envelope, as though she were afraid the thing might suddenly bite her.

Morrow removed the two lavender sheets with a studied deliberation, noting with a sinking feeling in the pit of her stomach that they smelled faintly of her sister's favorite brand of perfume. She unfolded them cautiously and glanced at the greeting and signature of the letter, feeling the sinking feeling slowly solidify into a cold, hard mass.

With a mask of grim determination upon her face, Robin Morrow read through her sister Karen's letter to the man that Robin loved. She read it through twice to make sure she hadn't misunderstood anything, but she understood it all with painful clarity. When she had finished with the letter, Morrow knew that, as far as Mack Gerber was concerned, she'd been worried about the wrong woman.

Morrow carefully refolded the letter, placed it back in the envelope and returned the envelope to its spot beneath the cigar box. Gerber's aloofness wasn't at all hard to understand now.

"Damn you, Kari. How could you do this to me?" breathed Morrow softly. "You said he didn't matter to you."

Morrow carefully rearranged the drawer and closed it, stood and examined the entire locker. Satisfied that she had disturbed nothing, she closed the locker door, picked up the bottle of Beam's she had brought as a present and walked out the door of Gerber's hootch and back to her own quarters. Once inside, she sat down on her bunk, put the bottle of Beam's between her legs and leaned her head back against the wall. Only then did she allow the tears to fill her eyes.

CIA OPERATIVE JERRY MAXWELL huddled over a plate of mu shu pork and chicken fried rice in the back upstairs room of a small Chinese restaurant in Saigon's Cholon district, contemplating the end of his seventeen-year-long career in government service, if not his life.

Since he had dropped Robin Morrow off at her hotel around ten last night, Maxwell had been a very busy man. First he had spent nearly two hours bouncing all over Saigon in Lambrettas, in taxis, by bus and on foot, shaking the tail he and Morrow had picked up as they'd left the restaurant after supper. It hadn't been an easy task, but then Maxwell hadn't expected it to be. The man following him was the man who had taught Maxwell how not to be lost when you were spotted tailing someone.

Maxwell hadn't known that because he'd seen the man's face. Jack Jirasek wasn't the kind of man to make *that* kind of mistake. Indeed, Maxwell was having a hard time deciding whether or not his spotting the tail had been a mistake at all. Back in the old days in Berlin there had been a saying that you didn't spot Jack the Ripper unless he wanted you to, and by then it was too late.

So Maxwell had first had to resolve in his own mind the thorny issue of whether or not Jirasek had chosen to expose himself in such a manner as an unorthodox method of establishing contact. Maxwell had considered that carefully while taking Morrow back to her hotel and had decided that it just didn't wash. They were in Saigon, for Christ's sake. It wasn't as though they had to play by Moscow rules. Furthermore, Jirasek hadn't shown his face, which he would have if he'd wanted Maxwell to slip away and make contact. Maxwell had only realized he was being tailed when they'd left the restaurant, not who was tailing him. He hadn't realized who the shadow must be until he'd had such a damned hard time losing him.

He'd finally taken the time to ponder all of it in a crowded smoke-filled bar just off Le Loi Street, once he'd felt reasonably certain he'd lost the tail. It had been a noisy place, full of Vietnamese and off-duty American servicemen and bar girls offering conversation and perhaps something more for the soldier unwary enough to take them up on it. It hadn't been a place that was really what you'd call conducive to clear, rational thought, which might, perhaps, Maxwell told himself now, account for the very paranoid-sounding conclusions he had drawn.

But there was no denying certain facts. It was a fact that Maxwell's boss had been in-country for two days and hadn't tried to contact him. For a station chief's boss to do that was like spitting in Maxwell's face. Among the old eastern school tie crowd that ran the upper echelons of the Company, it was considered to be very bad form.

Maxwell, an outsider who had grown up in public schools in New Jersey and made it into Columbia on the strength of an academic scholarship where he'd majored in languages and East European politics, had no such preconceived notions of effrontery.

A fact which, along with his innate intelligence, had made it easy for him to shift his special field of interest to the Far East when the Orient began to look like a more interesting area to work in.

To Maxwell, Jirasek's behavior simply meant that his superior didn't want Maxwell to know what was going on. That could only mean one of three things. Either Maxwell was being cut out because he had come under suspicion, which was ridiculous because there hadn't been as big a patriot as Maxwell since Nathan Hale, or Jirasek was running some kind of a maverick mission on his own, without the knowledge or official sanction of the home office, or it was a wild card play, an ultrasecret, one-time operation that, because of the political ramifications if it were blown, demanded that the doctrine of plausible deniability be in effect. In other words, an operation that, although endorsed at the highest levels of the Company, demanded that it appear Jirasek was working on his own so that responsibility could be denied if anything went wrong.

The fact that Jirasek had come back into harness to run the operation personally and from the field didn't help greatly to differentiate between the two latter alternatives. If it were a maverick, Jirasek might be limited in the number of people he felt he could trust or might not wish to involve others who would be hurt by the fallout if the play went sour. If it were a wild card, it seemed unlikely that the home office in Langley would want to risk a man of Jirasek's caliber. But if the potential benefits were great enough, the Company was perfectly capable of throwing even bigger managers than Jirasek to the wolves. The potential payoff would have to be pretty awesome for that, though.

So why had Jirasek suddenly decided to shadow Maxwell? Again the possibility that Maxwell was under suspicion had to be rejected. Jirasek would have sent somebody to do the job, not come himself, unless Jirasek himself were under suspicion as well, in which case he wouldn't be shadowing Maxwell in the first place.

The only common denominator in the whole mess was the reporter. Jirasek had gone to see Crinshaw three times. Morrow had gone to see Crinshaw to ask what he knew about Emilie Brouchard. Crinshaw had told her what he knew. Only Crinshaw didn't know shit about Brouchard. Maxwell had seen to that. Still,

Maxwell was beginning to think sending her on the mission had been a mistake. But she had been available and knew the area, and Gerber's team was going to need all the help they could get, if the reports from the LRRPs were any indicator. And then Morrow had come to see Maxwell, and the next thing Maxwell knew it had come full circle and he was being tailed by Jirasek, who had been conducting secret meetings with Crinshaw.

And bingo! Crinshaw was somehow the key to the mystery. He had to be. He was the only person that all the others had been in contact with.

So Maxwell had done the only reasonable thing for a conscientious chief of station in his position. He'd avoided going back to his apartment or office or any other of his well-established hangouts, he'd called on a few friends he'd established outside of the normal networks he'd set up in Vietnam for a little specialized assistance, and he'd begun his own maverick operation.

He had bugged General Crinshaw's office.

And that move, Maxwell knew, was likely to cost him his career.

What he didn't know, what he couldn't find out until tonight when he broke back into Crinshaw's office and recovered the tape, was what that was going to tell him.

13

THE CAMBODIAN JUNGLE

Fetterman killed the tracker.

In the final analysis, it proved a fairly easy thing to do, although it didn't go exactly as planned. Killing all three Vietcong was a much harder proposition.

Following the agreed-upon plan, Fetterman and Kepler, their hands held high over their heads, stepped onto the trail a few meters ahead of the VC and were followed immediately by Kit carrying the AK-47. There three VC were so startled that they almost dropped their guns. Almost, but not quite.

There ensued immediately a rapid, sing-song conversation between Kit and the three Vietcong. Fetterman, who had learned all the Vietnamese he knew during his current tour with Gerber's A-Detachment, could get along fairly well in the language under ordinary circumstances, provided he didn't have to read much of it and the natives spoke slowly. The convoluted machine-gun prose of Kit and the VC quickly left him behind, however, and he looked to Kepler for some sign that things were okay or seriously amiss.

Kepler had learned his Vietnamese from native instructors at the U.S. Army Language School and had spent his tour in Vietnam polishing it until he could pass for a Vietnamese, provided no one saw his face. That had been the biggest drawback he had experienced in developing his own network of local agents in the countryside around Camp A-555. No matter how well he could speak Vietnamese, he still didn't look like one.

But Kepler gave no indication that the conversation was going either way, and Fetterman had to content himself with the knowledge that at least they hadn't started shooting at them yet. He was able to pick out a few bits and pieces of the conversation and gathered that Kit was telling them a story that was uncomfortably close to the truth about their mission and strength, but quickly got lost again when she started telling, with obvious enthusiasm, a complex tale about how she had come to be in the area and had captured Fetterman and Kepler.

After a moment, some sort of argument seemed to develop, accompanied by much animated gesturing, chiefly involving Fetterman and Kepler. It seemed to be a debate over what, exactly, should be done with them. The tracker and the two VC with him obviously wanted to take the prisoners back to the main body of their unit, while Kit apparently was insisting that since she had captured them they were her prisoners and should be taken back to her camp, where there were both a field grade officer and a political cadre who could decide how to dispose of the Yankee pigs.

She also stressed the possibility of capturing, through speedy pursuit, the other soldiers who had been with Fetterman and Kepler and seemed quite convincing in her hatred of all things American, especially Fetterman and Kepler, coming forward to kick and shove the two Green Berets closer to the Vietcong. Fetterman noted that for such a diminutive woman, she packed a vicious kick, and wondered how big the bruise might be later as he mentally gauged the distance to the tracker and calculated how many tenths of a second it would take him to draw the knife, and how long after that to make the kill.

It occurred to Fetterman that the entire procedure might be taking too long and that the rest of the VC unit might, at any minute, decide not to wait any longer and come ahead across the defoliated, burned strip of ground. Anderson and Washington, along with a couple of the Tais, would be positioned to prevent that from happening, but how long they would be able to hold them would depend on the enemy numbers, even with all that open ground to cross. And if the VC turned out to have mortars with them, as VC frequently did, you could just pretty well forget the ball game.

Gradually the distance closed.

Kit suddenly kicked Fetterman in the back of the knee, giving him a shove that forced him to his knees, but did bring him a couple feet closer to his target. It wasn't a good position to launch an attack from, but it would have the advantage of additional surprise, since he looked pretty helpless on his knees. Kit gave Kepler a shove forward as well, practically screaming a stream of very imaginative obscenities at them. Fetterman thought she really was overdoing it a bit. If she got too noisy, the rest of the VC unit, wherever it was, was bound to hear and come running to investigate. Fetterman couldn't help wondering if that was what she had in mind.

They were nearly within range now. A single step would carry Fetterman to within striking distance of his target, although he would have to come up off the ground first to do it. Kepler was perhaps two steps from his man, but was on his feet. The problem was the third VC. While the tracker and the other one seemed quite happy to argue with Kit over the fate of the two Americans, the third VC insisted on remaining back a little to one side. He seemed a bit uncertain, perhaps even wary of the two Americans. He twisted his rifle nervously in his hands and looked back over his shoulder a lot.

It was Kit who finally broke the stalemate. She stepped past the first two and started shouting at the nervous one. Fetterman gathered it was an appeal to the third man to get him to side with Kit in her argument with the other two. The confusion drew the attention of the two men closest to Fetterman and Kepler for a fraction of a second, and when it did, Kit buttstroked the third with her AK-47.

Fetterman came off the ground in a rush, took a quick step forward and launched himself at the man, wrapping his legs around the Vietcong's body and using his weight to throw the man off-balance and disorient him. He grabbed the tracker's nose and mouth with his left hand, drew the knife from under his shirt with his right, reversed his grip and slashed twice, the razor sharpness of the old Case VS-21 severing both carotid arteries and the trachea. His blood sprayed into the air, but like many dying men he refused to recognize the fact. He somehow found Fetterman's knife hand, and with surprising strength gripped the wrist. Fetterman found himself momentarily unable to pull free.

Kepler, meantime, had gone for the quick, certain kill, rather than a clean or quiet one. He'd dashed forward, drawing the Ka-Bar he'd loosely taped to the inside of his forearm, and knocked aside the man's rifle. Kepler held the knife blade up, then drove it into the man's abdomen just over the belt buckle with such force that it penetrated nearly to the spine. Then, seizing the hilt with both hands, he yanked hard, ripping upward, gutting the man like a deer until the blade finally lodged about halfway through the sternum. Transected intestines, liver, stomach and pancreas cascaded onto the ground with a terrible stench as the knife ripped diaphragm muscle, punctured the lower lobe of one lung and cut into the heart tissue itself. For a moment the man hung there on the knife, held up by Kepler's adrenaline-enhanced strength. Then Kepler yanked again, pulling the knife clear and splitting the breastbone, opening the man clear to the throat.

The third VC was much harder to kill. He had spotted the swinging Kalashnikov a split second before Kit had connected it to the side of his face and had managed to roll with it. Otherwise the blow would likely have decapitated him. As it was, it broke both his maxilla and mandible, knocked out three teeth and loosened two others. There was a great sheet of searing, white-hot flame before his eyes, followed at once by a rapidly darkening gray. Yet somehow he managed to hold on to his consciousness.

Not wanting to shoot, Kit stepped forward and spun the assault rifle around to smash the buttstock down onto his larynx.

But the VC got a foot hooked between her legs and pulled her off-balance. As she fell, the VC rolled to one side, snatching the AK-47 and smashing it down across her neck as he rolled on top of her. He drove a knee up into her groin with enough force to completely disinterest a man from continuing the struggle and leaned forward, putting all of his weight behind the assault rifle, trying to force it down below her chin and strangle her with it.

Kit gripped the buttstock and forearm of the rifle and tried to push it away from her throat with all her strength, but the VC was too strong and had the advantage of having all his weight behind him to push downward with. He managed to work it past her chin, and she could feel the heaviness of the receiver at her throat, bearing down on her neck until she was struggling for air, her face purpling from cyanosis. Her arms ached as though they had a thousand pins and needles driven into them, and she could feel her level of consciousness beginning to slip away when at last she saw a hand take the VC by the hair and jerk back his head to expose the neck.

The point of the blade went in just below the mastoid sinus behind the ear, and the edge ripped forward across the throat, pivoting about the point and tearing out the front of the man's neck, taking the right carotid, the right internal and external jugular veins and a good part of the esophagus and windpipe with it.

And then for Kit everything went black.

"Miss Brouchard. Kit. Are you all right? Can you speak?"

She recognized the voice, was a little surprised at the hoarseness of her own. "Yes, thank you, Master Sergeant. But something is wrong. I cannot see."

She heard a ripping sound, felt someone wiping at her face with a rag, then heard Fetterman speak again.

"Try to hold your eyes open."

The stream of water hitting her in the face made her gasp for breath. There was more wiping with the rag, more water and then suddenly she could see again.

Fetterman was leaning over her, his knife and sodden rag, torn from one of the VC's shirts, in one hand, a canteen, and for some inexplicable reason, the two halves of a disassembled ballpoint pen in the other.

"You gave us a bad moment there when you couldn't speak," said Fetterman. "Thought maybe he'd managed to smash your trachea with the rifle. Sorry about all the blood. Are you sure you're okay now?"

Kit nodded, reached for the rag and wiped more of the Vietcong's blood from her face. "I'm fine. See to your friend."

Tyme and Krung had emerged from the bushes and were checking the bodies of the VC. Not to see if they were dead. There was no question of that. It was just the routine search for papers, maps, anything that might prove to be of intelligence value. Normally Kepler would have been conducting the search, but at the moment he was busily bent over at the other side of the trail, decorating the Cambodian landscape with the contents of his stomach.

Fetterman walked over and put a hand on Kepler's shoulder. "You okay, Derek? You did fine. Nothing to be upset over."

Kepler tossed a derisive glance in the direction of the gutted VC and gave a snort of laughter. "Him? No. It's nothing like that. I suppose it was all the excitement. Washington would probably call it adrenaline overload. Whatever strength I had, I used in the few moments it took to do him. I was fine until I saw how you and the girl had made out. But then I just couldn't get the old organism calmed down. Pulse was so fast I could hear it pounding in my head like a jackhammer. Just couldn't get my breathing slowed down. Next thing, I started feeling woozy, and then this. Kind of embarrassing, but not because of the standard Hollywood gambit. Christ, Fetterman, you know me better than that. He's not my first, or even my tenth. Help me up, will you? We got work to do."

Fetterman grinned. "Just checking, Derek. Some guys it doesn't get to the first time. Or the fifth. Or the fifteenth. But it grows on them until one day there's this little voice inside them that says, 'Too much. I just can't do this anymore.' I was just making sure you weren't hearing that little voice."

He put out his hand to help Kepler to his feet.

"Just because I was a little slow yesterday and picked today to have a delicate stomach doesn't mean I've gone soft, you know. I did the guy, didn't I? I did both of them. This one and yesterday's."

"Don't get excited. I said I was just checking. I'm the team sergeant, remember. I'm supposed to worry about all you guys."

"Then why don't you worry about something useful, like where we're going to find a beer out here?"

Fetterman slapped the other man lightly on the back. "I'll buy you two beers when we get back to camp. One for each hand. Right now I'd rather worry about getting out of here."

"Hey, Fetterman, did you ever hear that little voice talking to you?"

"Fetterman, can you come here a minute," called Tyme.

"Coming."

"Sure," Fetterman told Kepler. "I've heard it lots of times. I just learned to ignore it."

When they had finished searching the three VC, Fetterman had them do it one more time, just to make sure they hadn't missed anything. Then they dragged the bodies off the trail into the brush. They didn't bother trying to camouflage them. These men would be missed soon, perhaps already had been, and would be looked for when the rest of their squad worked up the nerve to cross all that dead, open ground out there. A search of any sincerity was sure to turn up the bodies, so there was no point in spending a lot of time trying to hide them. The idea was just to make it not too easy. That way the VC might waste more time looking for the bodies than it had taken to kill and hide them. So Fetterman and Tyme stood in the path and kicked dirt over the bloodstains, then rejoined the others.

Anderson was making a considerable, unnecessary fuss over Kit's condition. She still had a fair amount of blood on her face, which was beginning to dry, but none of it was hers.

Fetterman pulled Washington, the team's senior medical specialist aside, and had a word with him.

"You check out the girl?" asked Fetterman. "One of the VC tried to strangle her with a rifle."

"Already done."

"And?"

"She'll live if she doesn't die."

"What the hell is that supposed to mean?"

"It means she's doing as well as can be expected for somebody who's had the shit choked out of her. The tissues in the pharynx are pretty sensitive. Once they've been traumatized, edema frequently sets in. It can take anywhere from minutes to hours to a couple of days later. With the equipment I've got, which isn't much, she doesn't appear to have any swelling now. There's no telling what it may look like by tomorrow morning. I've given her some antiinflammatories as a precaution. I've no idea whether or not they'll help."

"And if they don't, what can you do for her?"

"Out here?" The big black shrugged. "Same thing you were going to try with your ink pen, *if* the swelling is high enough up. Tell me, you ever do a cricothyrotomy before?"

"Once," said Fetterman. "In Korea. My machine gunner got buttstroked in the neck and bayoneted when the Red Chinese overran us. He was a good man. Saved my ass more than once by knowing what a machine gun was for and how to use it. I could tell the poor bastard was suffocating, and I had to do something for him."

"What happened?"

"He died. But not because of anything I screwed up. Abdominal infection got him six weeks later at the hospital."

"Great," said Washington. "If she needs it, I'll call you. I've never done one before."

"So at this point, there's no way to tell?"

"None at all. One thing about it, though. Either way we don't have to worry about her loyalty anymore. Looks like she's pretty well proved which side she's on."

"Yeah," said Fetterman. "It sure looks that way."

"May I see you a moment, Master Sergeant?" Gerber motioned Fetterman over. "I want you to have Anderson lay a mechanical ambush along the main trail back there fifty meters or so. Tell him not to get too elaborate. We don't want to waste a lot of time on the project. That is if you can pry him away from our scout long enough to string a couple of claymores. All I want is something that will make those guys over on the other side of the dead zone think twice about following us in the dark when they come across. If we move all night, we ought to be able to put a pretty fair amount of distance between them and us by morning."

"Yes, sir. Direct route of march to the objective?"

"Let's not make it too easy on them in case they're persistent. Once we get into the next valley we'll lay a false trail to the south, as though we were going to do an end run and cut back past them." He held out the map. "When we get to this area here, we ought to be able to move onto this rocky ridge line and swing back to the northwest."

"Right, sir. May I have a word with you privately, sir?"

Gerber looked puzzled. "Let's step over here away from the others a moment. It's the best I can do."

They walked a few yards apart.

"Okay, Tony, what's all this about?"

"Sir, is there anything about this mission you're not telling me? I'm not asking you to break any confidences. I'm just asking you to tell me if there's something more going on here than what we've been briefed about."

Now Gerber was genuinely perplexed. "Tony, what are you getting at?"

Fetterman reached into the pocket of his jungle fatigues and removed something. He held it out to Gerber.

"Sergeant Tyme found this in the tracker's knapsack, sir. It looks to me like some kind of electronic tracer, similar to the one we used in Hong Kong."

Gerber examined the small black metal box. It had a simple toggle switch, a short, telescoping antenna and a horizontal line of three lights running across the top of it.

"Does it work?"

"I haven't tried it, sir. It *looks* like a receiver, but I didn't think switching it on would be a real good idea, since I didn't *know* if it's a transmitter."

"Have you shown this to Bocker?"

"Not yet. I haven't had the opportunity to speak to him alone."

"All right. Get Anderson started on the mechanical ambush, then give that thing to Bocker. Tell him I need to know what it is, if it's working and who it's talking or listening to. You think they were using it to follow us," he added suddenly. It wasn't a question.

"That would merely be wild speculation until we have more information, sir."

"But that is what you think, isn't it?"

"Yes, sir. We've been pretty damned careful about covering our tracks, but twice we've picked up shadowers. Once can happen to anybody, but twice, and with a tracker who was probably good enough not to need this dingus the second time—it was in his pack, remember—well, sir, that's the sort of coincidence that begins to stretch a man's credulity."

"It does, indeed, Master Sergeant. It does indeed."

SETTING THE MECHANICAL ambush was a straightforward matter. Anderson noted with distaste that it didn't incorporate the sort of subtle variations that Sully Smith would have insisted upon, but it did have the distinct advantage of simplicity. At a slight bend in the trail, he set a claymore designed to fire directly down the pathway when its trip wire was triggered. That alone would probably have been sufficient for the task, but he couldn't resist the temptation to improve it slightly and tied two white phosphorus grenades into the firing chain, using time-delay detonators, one with a twenty-second fuse, the other with full-minute delay. It would give any survivors of the claymore a little something extra to occupy their minds with.

By the time Anderson had finished with his destructive tendencies, Bocker had completed his analysis of the black box.

"It's a pretty basic model, sir," he told Gerber. "Receiver only. Single crystal, single channel. Frequency Modulation. I'd guess somewhere between 145.5 and 155.9 from the antenna and a general knowledge of the type. Impossible to say positively without test equipment. As you can see, it's robustly built, indicating it was intended for hard field use. I confess, though, I'm a bit puzzled by why they didn't put in a bearing indicator. The additional cost would have been minimal, and it gives you a much better idea of the location of the beeper than these idiot lights."

"Is it operational?" Gerber wanted to know.

"Yes, sir. All you have to do is switch it on and it works. Runs off a standard transistor battery and four penlights. I checked it out, and the unit appears to be functioning normally, although it didn't pick up the beeper."

"Meaning?"

"Either the transmitter isn't operating for some reason, or it's out of range."

"I see." Gerber nodded thoughtfully. "Galvin, what's your best guess on the range of this thing?"

"That would depend on the power of the transmitter, topography of the intervening terrain and atmospheric conditions. Assuming that the transmitter is about a third the size of the receiver and must rely on an internal antenna, which we infer from the obviously clandestine purpose for which such a device is designed, and known properties of the general type, I'd think we're dealing with no more than one to three watts of power. In this particular configuration, that would suggest a maximum range under ideal conditions of perhaps fifteen klicks at the outside. I'd think that under conditions of surrounding terrain, a range of three to five kilometers would be much more reasonable. Go to the short end of that if you want any accuracy of reading, although, as I said, this isn't really set up for accuracy. Pity. It could have been so easily.''

Gerber looked askance at the communications sergeant. ''You'll forgive me, Staff Sergeant, if I fail to share your enthusiasm over the aesthetics of this thing. What is it? Russian or Chinese?''

Now it was Bocker's turn to look askance. ''Neither, sir. I can't speak for the hand that built it, but the components are all American. To be fair, the transistors were probably fabricated in Japan for sale in the United States, but it's U.S. technology all the way. It's not that either country couldn't have built it. As I said, it's a fairly simple unit. But the Russian mind has an absolute fixation for vacuum tubes, and most of the best Chinese work copies Russian equipment. If this were Russian or Chinese, it would be twice the size and only half as durable.''

''So what are a bunch of VC doing with an American-made tracking device?''

''Sorry, sir. I specialize in electronics, not clairvoyance.''

''Thank you for your analysis, Galvin. Keep this under your hat, will you?''

''Of course, sir. And, sir. I don't mean to belabor the obvious, but assuming they were using that to track us, shouldn't we search through everyone's things? What I mean is, well, sir, somebody's got to be carrying the beeper.''

''I know that, Galvin, but there are other factors to consider. First, we don't know that they were using it to track us. Although I'd put my money on that as the most likely possibility, since we seem to keep picking up tails, it could be intended for tracking someone or something else. Second, you pointed out that it's American-made. What would the VC be doing with an American-made homer? Maybe they just found it somewhere and it's got nothing to do with us. Third, you pointed out that although the receiver appears to be working, it isn't receiving anything. Which may mean that the transmitter is no longer operational.

''It could have been damaged in some way, or intentionally shut off or destroyed by whoever is carrying it, which means they already know or suspect we've found this thing, and they've already ditched the beeper so they won't be incriminated. Fourth, if there's another one of these things out there somewhere listening for the beeper to start talking again, I'm not so sure I want to find the transmitter. At least not yet. And fifth, we've spent too damned much time here already. We've got to move. Once we put some distance between us and the rest of that VC unit, we can start thinking about conducting searches.''

"And if the traitor ditches the transmitter in the meantime? It's nearly dark, sir. It would be easy for whoever is carrying it to just let it drop into the brush along the trail somewhere.''

"Which is fine. The VC won't be able to follow us anymore, which is, after all, the main thing we're after.''

"And we'll have lost our chance to identify the traitor.''

"Who would you like to nominate for traitor, Sergeant? One of the team? Or maybe one of the Tais that we've fought alongside for a year and a half? How about the obvious candidate, our scout, the one who got herself half killed helping us kill the three guys who had this thing? Does that make any sense, that she would kill her cover team?''

"I just meant that it was something we should think about, sir.''

"I know, Galvin. I understand you're just trying to help. But let's do our thinking about it on our feet okay? Let's just get the hell out of here.''

MAXWELL THOUGHT THAT what he should do was get the hell out of there and forget about the whole mess. As he slipped the pick into the lock on the door of Crinshaw's outer office, he figured he could hide out in Cholon for a few days until whatever was going on blew over, then surface again once things were nice and quiet.

No, he admonished himself, dismissing the thought. He really couldn't do that. Just think of all the fun he'd be missing. After all, when was the last time he had a chance to break into U.S. military offices in a foreign country and wire the guys who were supposed to be on his side? When was the last time he bugged one of the boss's conversations with a general officer on the MACV staff? When was the last time he risked his job, his career, twenty years in Leavenworth, and maybe his life because some woman reporter thought things just didn't feel right? Jesus!

There was a click from the lock, deafening in the silence of the deserted hallway, and the door popped inward a few millimeters. Maxwell cautiously eased the door open enough to allow himself to squeeze inside, silently cursing the cacophony of creaks and groans emanating from the hinges. He slipped inside, barking his shin on the corner table near the doorway, eased the door back shut behind him, the hinges protesting vigorously, then froze there for a moment in the darkness, listening for any telltale sounds in the passageway outside and trying to remember the exact layout of the room from his earlier visits.

Satisfied that no one had heard the caterwauling of the hinges and come running to investigate, Maxwell breathed a great sigh of relief and slipped a small tube of graphite from the pocket of his jacket. Carefully, working by feel, he dusted each of the door hinges with the powdered lubricant. It wasn't a modification he would have tried had he been breaking into a certain building on Dzerzhinsky Square, where some sharp-eared KGB officer might have noticed a door that suddenly no longer squeaked, but he felt reasonably safe with the modification here. It just might prevent some late-night MP walking his rounds from taking notice at an inopportune time. Even if it didn't, it might prevent Maxwell from having a heart attack the next time the door started squeaking.

Having finished with the door, Maxwell pocketed the graphite, turned around with his back to the door and took a moment reviewing once again the layout of the room. He could have used the small penlight in his pocket—there were no windows in the outer office that might permit someone outside to notice a bit of unusual illumination in what should be a deserted room—but he had an almost pathological fear of even a few photons of light escaping between the door and the jamb and being noticed by a passing guard. When he was ready, he crossed the floor in darkness without incident and found the door to Crinshaw's inner office. It was locked.

For some reason that surprised Maxwell. Doors to offices were supposed to be locked up at night on military installations, particularly those in foreign countries, but somehow that seemed out of character for the brigadier. Crinshaw had a most cavalier attitude toward security. He would keep his notebook, in which he jotted endless trivia, in a folder in a locked drawer of his desk, but leave uncovered the map in his office that marked the location of every major U.S. base and facility in South Vietnam. The map also showed the progress of each significant operation underway, updated daily, so that anyone who happened to enter his office might see the precise disposition of all U.S. commands at any given time. Anyone, including the Vietnamese cleaning woman. Of course, the cleaning woman had been cleared by Military Intelligence. And equally, of course, that meant nothing. Most of the greatest spies in the history of espionage had been cleared by the other side's intelligence service.

So for that reason, if no other, Maxwell had half expected the door to be unlocked. He hadn't tried the door last night, entering instead through a convenient partially open window. It hadn't been too hard to force the window open a little farther, just enough to allow entry, but it had been a bit noisy, and getting it closed exactly the same amount it had been when he'd found it had been a real bear. Those factors, plus the fact that the window was fairly exposed to observation from outside—indeed, when he was ready to leave he'd had to wait twice before it was safe to exit—had persuaded Maxwell to try the inside route this evening.

It took three tries to find the right set of picks, but once he did only a couple of minutes of skillful manipulation was necessary to get the lock to yield. Maxwell smiled. Only two-thirds the time the outer office lock had taken. His old skills, learned so many years ago at the Farm, were coming back to him. He couldn't help marveling at the expertise of all those celluloid agents he'd seen in countless Hollywood spy movies through the years. Those guys could always manage even the most stubborn door locks in fifteen seconds flat, usually with only one pick, and sometimes with nothing more sophisticated than a paper clip or the leading lady's hairpin. In the real shadow world of secret intelligence, things were seldom as easy.

When he finally eased the door open, Maxwell nearly had a heart attack as a breath of frigid air hit him in the face. Crinshaw had left the air conditioners running.

That sudden realization made Maxwell wonder if he had committed a terrible tactical blunder. Last night the air conditioners had been shut off and a window left partially open. It made Maxwell ask himself a lot of questions. Like, did the fact that the air conditioners were running mean Crinshaw was hiding in the darkened room, waiting for the opportunity to pounce upon him like some demented bird of prey? Or, did the fact that he *had* found an open window last night mean that Jirasek had *wanted* him to break into Crinshaw's office? And if so, what was the purpose? Was Jirasek now trying to arrange a meeting in his roundabout fashion, or was it some kind of trap he was baiting? Or perhaps Jirasek wanted him to break in and wire Crinshaw's office so that he would, when he played back the tape, hear exactly the conversation Jirasek wanted him to hear?

When no one sprang upon him screaming from out of the darkness or shot him outright, Maxwell finally decided that the only thing it meant was that Crinshaw had left the air-conditioning on, and that for some reason, when he'd left, his administrative sergeant hadn't been around to shut it off for him. Not wanting to risk the noise of stopping and restarting it, nor knowing exactly what the air conditioners were set at and being unwilling to risk his flashlight to check the knobs, Maxwell tightened his tie, buttoned his suit coat as best he could and got on with the job at hand.

Although the curtains were drawn, they weren't quite closed, and the light passing through the teakwood venetian blinds threw a striped rectangle on the carpeted floor. Maxwell eased the inner office door shut behind him, in case anyone should suddenly decide to enter the outer office, and waited shivering a few minutes for his eyes to adjust to the light level. When it got to the point where he could see the outlines of large objects fairly well, even if they weren't silhouetted against the window, he pulled a pair of white cotton gloves from his pocket and slipped them on, then he got down on his hands and knees and crawled over to the general's gigantic desk. There was no sense risking tripping over something at this stage of the game.

Maxwell felt along the underside of the bottom edge of the front of the desk until he found the ultrasensitive microrecorder he had taped there. Once he had it located, he lay on his back and slid his head and shoulders underneath the desk. Only then did he risk the penlight. Taking it from the inside pocket of his jacket, he switched it on and held it in his mouth while he worked, the piece of red cellophane he'd taped over the end allowing only the slightest of light to come from the penlight. It was enough, barely, to do the job.

Working quickly, he shut off the sound-activated microphone and rewound the magnetic tape. He had to untape the recorder from the tiny space between the front of the desk and the back of one of the lower drawers in order to change the tape spools.

Doing it in the minimal light proved to be a lot more difficult than it would have sounded, had he described the procedure to someone. Maxwell fervently hoped he would never have to explain to anyone how he had bugged a U.S. Army brigadier general's office. That kind of explanation wasn't likely to get him anything but a quick trip to Kansas.

Having switched the spools, Maxwell deposited the used one in his jacket pocket and retaped the recorder into position, using fresh adhesive tape. He then gathered up the mass of used adhesive, put that in his other pocket and slid back out from under the desk.

As he was preparing to leave, it occurred to Maxwell that someone could have been hiding in the closet the entire time, watching him, and that he should have immediately checked the closet upon entering the room for safety's sake. It was the kind of mistake a man of his experience shouldn't have made, but exactly the sort of thing that comes from spending too many recent years managing agents instead of doing the job yourself.

It seemed as if it might be a little late to remedy that kind of error now, but Maxwell crossed silently to the closet and checked it anyway. Inside, however, along with a raincoat and Crinshaw's familiar field jacket, he found only a dress uniform, two sets of khakis and three fatigue outfits, all freshly cleaned and starched with razor-edged creases pressed into the pants. There were also a couple of sets of slightly limp-looking fatigues and one lackluster set of khakis, all of which lacked the plastic bag laundry covers of the fresh ones.

Maxwell had often suspected that Crinshaw changed uniforms several times a day in order to maintain his appearance. The presence of the fresh uniforms and used ones—you couldn't call them dirty—in the general's office tended to confirm the idea.

Otherwise the majority of the items would have been in the general's quarters, not in his office.

Maxwell closed the closet door, switched off the penlight and returned it to his inner jacket pocket. Then he crossed back to the office door and stood there a moment, listening to be sure no one had come into the outer office and was now waiting on the other side of the door.

As he listened, Maxwell slipped off the cloth gloves and returned them to his pocket. His fingerprints in Crinshaw's office by themselves would mean nothing. He had been in the office many times on official business. But he had worn them while changing the magnetic recording tape. His prints on the spools or the recorder, or even the underside of Crinshaw's desk, would have been damning.

Satisfied that there was no one lurking in the outer office, Maxwell opened the door and went out, pausing to make sure the door locked behind him.

He crossed the floor of the outer office without incident, then paused again to listen. He was just about to open the door when he heard the sound of footsteps in the hallway outside.

There was no time to retrace his steps across the room and pick the lock to Crinshaw's inner office again. He slid to the hinge side of the doorway and flattened himself against the wall, bumping up against a coatrack in the process. It didn't fall, and in fact made only a slight scraping sound on the floor, but to Maxwell the noise was deafening. He pressed himself up even tighter against the wall and practiced becoming invisible.

The footsteps outside, however, passed by without stopping, and after many long, heart-pounding seconds, Maxwell exhaled slowly, drew a breath and tried the door again. He listened for perhaps forty-five seconds, in case the hall walker should come back, but when the silence remained unbroken, he unlocked the door and opened it a tiny crack.

Although he could see only up the hall in one direction, it looked clear. He listened again for the footfalls of anyone coming from his blind side, but there were none. Cautiously he opened the door wide, risked a peek in both directions and stepped boldly out into the hallway, closing and locking the door behind him.

Then he strolled nonchalantly down the hall, remembering to unbutton his coat and loosen his tie as he went.

"Good evening, Mr. Maxwell. Working late?" The guard at the desk greeted him.

"If it's not late, it's early," said Maxwell, trying hard not to seem overly friendly, but not unusually brusque either.

"Yes, sir. You boys in the U.S. Information Agency sure do keep odd hours."

"We wouldn't if I could help it. But when the embassy staff wants something, they usually get it, regardless of the hour."

"Yes, sir. It does look like they could get you a nicer office than that little place you've got down in the basement though with all the work you do."

"If you've got any influence with the ambassador or General Westmoreland, I'd appreciate something with a view."

The army private laughed. "I don't even have any influence with my sergeant. Sign here, please, sir."

Maxwell dutifully signed the log and wrote the time in the out column, then trudged out the door as though it had been a very long day. It had.

Outside he walked some distance before hailing a taxi, had the driver drive around Saigon for half an hour with no particular destination in mind, paid off the cab, walked several blocks and hailed another. After three changes, he was satisfied that no one had picked up his tail, and he took another cab to the safe apartment he'd established in Cholon, having the driver let him out a couple of blocks away and walking the remaining distance. Upstairs he paused and listened before unlocking the door.

The room was littered with the refuse of Maxwell's recent occupancy. A variety of empty take-out food containers from diverse Chinese restaurants covered the small tabletop, and there was a row of Coke cans running along one edge. They made a ninety-degree turn at the corner and ran partway along the wall, which the table was pushed up against. Two shirts were draped over the back of the armchair in the living area, one clean, which he had bought this morning along with the shirt he was now wearing, the other dirty. There was both a Chinese and a Vietnamese language newspaper on the rickety coffee table, and a

French language weekly on the floor beside it, all of them this morning's editions.

Maxwell checked the bedroom of the apartment, including the closet and beneath the bed, then went back to the little kitchen area. He took off his jacket and hung it over the back of the unused second chair. He checked the tiny, ancient refrigerator, but found it empty, then searched among the cans on the table until he found one that contained a swallow or two of Coke. He drank that, explored the others, and finding them all empty, opened the tiny cupboard and took down a tape recorder and a portable radio.

Maxwell put both items on the table. He eased the big hard-chromed Swenson .45 Auto Custom with the ambidextrous safeties and slide releases from his Milt Sparks shoulder holster and laid it on the table next to the radio. He switched on the radio and tuned in to AFVN, which was blaring out "Green Onions" by Booker T. and the M.G.s, adjusted the volume to something just short of physically painful and fished the spool of magnetic tape from the recorder in Crinshaw's office out of his jacket pocket. Then he sat down and fed the tape into the recorder.

The microrecorder, identical to the one beneath Crinshaw's desk, was designed to utilize the tape at a very slow rate. Since the microphone was voice-activated, or triggered by any other sound of a significant volume and amount, he had to wade through a lot of one-sided conversations consisting of Crinshaw speaking to people on the telephone or yelling at his administrative sergeant over the field telephone intercom Crinshaw insisted on using because he thought it gave the office a military look.

Eventually Maxwell hit pay dirt. The conversation was far from straightforward, but what was said, and what could be inferred, was far from reassuring.

"Do you think it's a good idea for us to keep meeting here?" Crinshaw's voice asked.

Maxwell recognized the reply as Jirasek's. "What do you want us to do, General, meet in the officer's club? Here is an appropriate place for two people of our rank to be conducting business. If anyone who knows me sees me coming in here, they may wonder what we're talking about, but it won't raise nearly as many questions as it would if we kept 'accidentally' bumping into each other in bars and restaurants and on park benches. That sort of cloak and dagger nonsense only happens in the movies.''

''Yes. I suppose you're right. It's just that so many people come in and out of here that I worry someone might spot you. Maxwell's office is in the basement, you know. What if he should see you coming in the building?''

''I felt it important that we talk, and I don't think Maxwell will be in today.''

''Oh? Why is that?''

''He saw me last night.''

''Oh, my God!''

''Relax, General. He didn't see my face. I'm sure of that. All he knows is that someone was shadowing him, so he'll stay away from his office, his apartment, anyplace he usually goes for a couple of days, on the assumption those places are being watched. It's standard procedure for an agent in the field. Just routine. Nothing to worry about. It might even work to our advantage if this thing blows up and we need to find a scapegoat. He'd have to explain the missing time when nobody saw him, and since he's trying to avoid being seen anyway, that might not be the easiest thing for him to do.''

''You mean, if anything goes wrong, we could shift the blame onto Maxwell?''

''Why not? That Kit Carson we sent with Gerber is one of Maxwell's people. That's already a nice, neat little tie-in to the situation.

''I just can't believe you'd do that so easily. Throw one of your own people to the wolves like that.''

''Listen, Crinshaw, I'd throw you to the wolves if it were necessary to the mission. You're a great one to be talking anyway. Let's not forget who picked Gerber and his boys to go on this little suicide mission, shall we?''

''It's not a suicide mission,'' said Crinshaw uneasily. ''You shouldn't say that. What if someone should hear you call it that?''

''I don't know what else you could call it. We're using them to draw the VC out into the open so we can clobber them with air power. That sounds to me like an awfully good way for Gerber and his boys to get zapped.''

"If anything happens to them in the line of duty, it's an accident of war," snapped Crinshaw. "We can hardly be held responsible for that. They're doing a dangerous job, and if anything untoward should happen to them in the process, well, I mean, after all, they are soldiers."

"Yeah. Soldiers who haven't been told what the job is they're doing, who don't know that they're the guinea pigs in our little experiment. It'll make a nice epitaph. 'They did their job. Too bad they didn't know what it was.'"

"As I told Maxwell, if they do their job right, they might not have any problems at all."

"Come off it, Crinshaw. We're dangling them out there as bait, hoping the VC will come along and take a big bite out of them. And then, as soon as Charlie starts knocking on the front door, we're going to slam the back door shut on them."

"You said it was important that we talk," said Crinshaw. "Why? What is it you want to talk about?"

"I've got a report from my man in the COMSECINT network. He tells me they've lost the signal from that tracer I gave the Brouchard woman."

"Hell! How the fuck did that happen?"

"He doesn't know, you idiot. He's got no direct communications with either Gerber's bunch or the VC search teams in the area. All he knows is that the beeper has stopped sending. At least we're not picking it up on our equipment, and we've got equipment that can pick up a flea fart in a tornado."

"Maybe the Vietcong have got them already. Maybe our plan didn't work."

"It's not your plan, and it's not my plan. The decision was made at the highest levels to try this. We're just implementing it."

"If they're dead, or the VC have captured them already, then we have nothing to implement."

"If you'd stop jabbering and keep your mouth shut for a minute, you might find out things. The VC don't have shit. The tracer may have stopped sending, but Gerber's bunch has made a routine commo check since. There may be a few flies in the ointment, but the plan is still viable and still in operation. My friend at COMSECINT tells me their intercepts indicate that Charlie had three separate units triangulating on Gerber's patrol before the beeper stopped. The VC knew the general area and Gerber's exact last position before the tracer conked out. They can make some educated guesses about where to look for them. All we have to do is be patient. Sooner or later one of the VC search teams will make contact with Gerber's unit and fix their position while they call up the reinforcements. All we have to do is wait for Gerber's evacuation call, and we'll know exactly where to send the B-52s. We could knock out a major VC unit, and maybe even do some substantive damage to the Ho Chi Minh Trail. If we can get Gerber to direct the strikes for us, we'll get even better results."

"How big an area of destruction are we talking about?" asked Crinshaw.

"Big. A B-52 carries around forty-eight 750-pound bombs. A single plane can lay waste an area a hundred yards wide and a quarter of a mile or more long. We can lay on thirty planes, more if we really need them. Once we start hammering them, the only way for Charlie to survive it will be if he grows himself some wings and flies out. Even then I wouldn't give him much of a chance."

Or Emilie and Gerber and his men, thought Maxwell. Crinshaw had made it very plain that there would be no air evac for them if any trouble started. That SOB had signed their death warrants.

Maxwell listened to the rest of the tape, but there was nothing else of significance.

He searched futilely through the Coke cans one more time, looking for something to drink. He scratched at the stubble on his chin and promised himself he'd buy a razor in the morning. He had an answer to at least one of his questions. He now knew that Jirasek was running a wild card operation with official CIA approval. At least he'd *said* it had been approved at the highest levels. The only proper thing for Maxwell to do was just forget he'd ever heard of the thing. To interfere would be interfering with national policy.

But he couldn't just sit back and watch Crinshaw murder Gerber and his men. That was what it really came down to.

Jirasek was perfectly capable of spending a few troops if it was necessary to accomplish the mission. But in this instance it wasn't necessary. Maxwell could see that. Jirasek could use Gerber's patrol to pull the enemy out into the open for the bombers and still evacuate them just before the Arc Light.

Except that Crinshaw had no intention of permitting them to be evacuated. Maxwell had known ever since that business of the trumped-up court-martial attempt that Crinshaw harbored a hatred of Mack Gerber and his men, but he had never actually believed Crinshaw would go this far. Maxwell couldn't let him get away with it. He owed Gerber that much and, of course, there was Emilie to consider. He would have to find some way of keeping Gerber and those with him alive without interfering with the basic goal of the mission that Jirasek had outlined.

There was only one real question he had to answer first.

How?

14

THE CAMBODIAN
JUNGLE

"Kit, may I speak with you a moment?" asked Gerber when they halted for a rest.

"Of course, Mack. How may I help you?"

Gerber looked annoyed at her familiar manner of address. The woman was getting altogether too friendly. It was another problem he didn't need, especially when what he had to talk to her about was very unfriendly. He took the tracer receiver out of his pack and showed it to her.

"I'm afraid I have to ask you if you know what this is," he said.

There was only the slightest hesitation before she looked surprised. "I am sorry, no. Should I?"

She said it just a little too easily. Gerber felt himself growing icily calm.

"You may not know precisely, but I'll bet you can make an educated guess, can't you, Bien Soo?" His carefully chosen use of her Vietnamese name was intended to distance and establish that this was a serious conversation, not a friendly one. Nor was the subtle implication of a threat lost on Kit.

"I have never seen this thing before, Captain."

"That wasn't what I asked. I asked if you knew what it was."

She shrugged almost convincingly. "Some sort of electronic device, I suppose. A radio of some kind, perhaps. I see it has an antenna. Is it important?"

"No," said Gerber levelly, "but the transmitter someone is carrying is, because it's been chirping out our location to the Vietcong. That's how they've been able to follow us so easily. That's why I've ordered Sergeant Bocker to search everyone's packs."

"I see. And who will search Sergeant Bocker's pack?"

"I've already done that. If Bocker doesn't find it in someone's pack, then I'm afraid we'll have to consider a strip search of everyone."

"In that case, I look forward to seeing you with your clothes off, Captain. Who will take off mine, you, or that nice Sergeant Anderson?"

"Damn it, Kit, this is no time to be cute. You know our situation. If we find the beeper, you know what I'll have to do to whoever has been hiding it."

"And you believe I am that person."

"You've got to admit that you're the most promising candidate. I've known all the rest of these people for over a year. I've fought alongside them. You're an outsider."

"I see, Mack. I am sorry you feel that way. I have fought alongside you, too, have I not? Or have you forgotten the three men I helped kill earlier? And I have told you things about my past that I have told to no one else. I had hoped that by now you would think of me as a friend."

"That's part of the problem, Kit. The story of your past seems to keep changing, depending on whom you're talking to. What you told Master Sergeant Fetterman doesn't exactly fit with what you told me, or with what Jerry Maxwell told me about your past. Is there any truth in any of it?"

"A little. Enough. What does it matter?"

"Who are you?" Gerber practically shouted.

"You know who I am. I have told you. I am Brouchard Bien Soo Ta Emilie. I was once a Vietcong. Now I am Kit Carson scout for you."

"And whose side are you on, ours, or the VC?"

"My own, Captain. There is no other side worth being on."

There was a long moment of silence.

"If you find that I am the traitor you believe me to be, you will then have to kill me, yes?"

Gerber said nothing.

"Suppose I were to walk away right now. Just disappear into the bush and never come back?"

"Then I'm afraid *I* would have to kill you right now, ma'am, with much regret of course," said Fetterman, who had come up softly behind her.

"Thank you, Master Sergeant. I trust your professionalism and know that you would make it as quick and painless as possible."

"You may tell your Sergeant Bocker that he can save himself a lot of time, Captain Gerber. He will not find the beeper, as you call it, in my pack. Nor will a strip search be necessary. The transmitter is in Sergeant Krung's pack, at the bottom along the right-hand side."

"Lady, you can't seriously expect me to believe Krung is a traitor."

"Of course not. I put the transmitter there. I am simply telling you where it is, because I've no wish for you to find it necessary to kill an innocent man after you've murdered me."

"Murder would hardly be the word for it," said Gerber.

"I think Jerry Maxwell may feel differently, Captain. I have worked for Mr. Maxwell for over a year now. I am one of his best agents."

"Christ!" said Gerber. "Another lie. Aren't you capable of telling the truth at all?"

Abruptly she turned so that both Gerber and Fetterman could see, dropped her shorts and pulled up her shirt. Even in the pale, poor half-light of predawn, the scars Gerber had noted earlier were clearly visible. There were even more of them than he had imagined. With a sickening feeling, he noted their similarity to another set of scars on another young woman's backside. Robin Morrow's.

"You want truth, Captain? This is truth. Do you think even for one second that I would continue to help the people who did this to me?"

She stood there, bare-assed and silent for a moment, then looked at Fetterman.

"You may kill me now if you like, Master Sergeant. I will make it easy for you." There was something defiant in her voice.

The silence stretched for perhaps a full minute.

"Sir?" said Fetterman at last. "What are your orders?"

Gerber waved him to silence.

"Pull up your pants, for Christ's sake," he told Kit. "Nobody's going to kill anybody tonight. At least not until I find out what this is all about."

"Thank you for believing me, Captain."

"I'm not entirely sure that I do. Now tell me. Why did Maxwell give you the transmitter?"

"Maxwell gave me nothing, except this assignment to act as your guide, and the other assignments I have done for him in the past year. That, and help getting out of the detention center after I *chieu hoi*ed."

"Then where did it come from?"

"From a man who called himself Jack. He claimed to be Maxwell's superior."

"He claimed to be? And you believed him?"

"He knew the right challenges and replies, what you would call passwords, and he carried both the MACV Form 6 and a Special Operations Group ID card. He knew me, although we had never met, and he knew all about Maxwell and how he had helped me and what I had done for him in the past. I had no reason to doubt his authenticity. The area of covert operations in which I work is rarely as cut and dried as your combat assignments, Captain. We seldom have the luxury of well-known superiors and written orders."

"So what did this guy named Jack tell you when he gave you the transmitter?"

"That it was a marker beacon to help them track our progress and pinpoint our location when the time came for us to be extracted. And that it would be necessary to guide the bombers to their target."

"What bombers? What targets?"

"He said that when we reached the Ho Chi Minh Trail, your people would direct air strikes against the enemy."

"That was never a part of the plan. We're supposed to make an intelligence assessment of the traffic on the Trail only. Nobody said anything about directing any air strikes in a neutral country."

"Nevertheless, that is what he told me, and I assumed that was the real purpose for your mission, even though that is not what Maxwell had told me. As I said, in covert operations we rarely have the luxury of written orders or clearly defined mission profiles."

"Did you discuss any of this with Maxwell?"

Kit gave him the sort of look a parent might reserve for a very small child.

"Of course not. Maxwell had briefed me for a reconnaissance mission. When his superior gave me the transmitter and told me it was to be an air strike coordination, I knew without having to ask that Maxwell had been cut out for some reason. The assumption was that there was a leak of some sort in Maxwell's organization, possibly Maxwell himself."

"My God, lady, you do think in devious patterns."

"I think of how I must do my job, Captain. Like you, I am sure, I do not always enjoy it, but it is my job. In this business, being devious is what keeps you alive."

"Well, Captain, what do we do now?" asked Fetterman after a moment.

Gerber took his helmet off and ran a hand through his hair. After a moment he sighed deeply.

"First, have Galvin get that damned beeper out of Krung's pack. Tell him he can look it over first, but then I want him to make sure it's put permanently out of commission." He glanced at Kit. "Then, tell him I want him to continue with the search of everyone's packs. I'm beginning to be just devious enough myself that I'd like to make damned sure our friendly little spy here hasn't hidden another one of those things somewhere else. All packs, webgear, poncho and blanket rolls to be checked. Anything big enough to hide a transmitter." He glanced at Kit again. "I think we can dispense with the body searches. We've already seen the only one we're likely to find anything taped to, I believe."

"Yes, sir. Disposition of the prisoner, sir?"

Gerber looked at the female scout and noted how small and defenseless she seemed, standing there, yet vaguely defiant, too. When he reminded himself that she had acquitted herself well during the ambush of the three VC trackers and at least claimed to have killed the VC officer who had raped her, he reevaluated his opinion of her as helpless. He'd have shot her himself if it hadn't been for those damned scars. They were the one thing that persuaded him that this time, possibly, she was telling the truth, if she was capable of such a thing.

"For the moment there is no prisoner," said Gerber. "However, if at any point during the remainder of the mission Miss Brouchard attempts to leave our company, make contact with the enemy or is found to have any other form of communications or tracking device, you are to shoot her on the spot if I am unable to do so. Is that clear, Master Sergeant?"

"Yes, sir. Our route of march?"

"As planned. We proceed with the mission."

"Sir, you can't be serious," said Fetterman.

"Our orders are to make an assessment of the traffic and troop strength along a specific section of the Ho Chi Minh Trail. Those are written orders, signed by General Westmoreland himself, and I intend to carry them out. Get the men ready to go. If we push it, we can be in position by noon."

"We're going to travel into the operational area in daylight, sir?"

"That's right, Master Sergeant. We've wasted enough time fucking around trying to shake off our tail. You have your orders. Now are you going to carry them out, or do you plan on finishing out your career by questioning my orders?" snapped Gerber.

"Take it easy, Captain. I wasn't questioning your orders, just your judgment," said Fetterman softly.

"Just get them moving. Now."

"Yes, sir."

"Now you," said Gerber, holding up his M-16 and pointing it in Kit's general direction. He had to remind himself not to shout. "You're supposed to know this area. Well, by God, it's time you started earning your pay. It's time to climb down off that fence of yours and decide whose side you're on once and for all. You get us there without being spotted by the VC, or so help me God, I'll use this on you myself. I don't know whose side Maxwell is on, or his boss, or how the hell the VC got hold of a receiver for that damned beeper, but by Christ this time you'd better be straight with me. Do you understand?''

"Of course, Captain," said Kit quietly. "Whether you believe me or not, that is all I have ever wanted."

Gerber glared at her. "Fine. Just so we understand each other. Now get moving."

15

SPECIAL FORCES CAMP
A-555

Mildebrandt was sitting in the team house with a cold, wet wash-cloth on his forehead, cradling a cup of warm tea in his hands. On the table in front of him were bottles of Alka-Seltzer, Pepto-Bismol, Kaopectate and aspirin. He'd spent most of the night in the latrine, holding his helmet between his knees. At the sound of a knock he looked up.

"Jesus, sir, you look terrible." It was the team's heavy weapons sergeant, a serious young man with the improbable name of William Henry Schattschneider IV, or possibly, V. Schattschneider himself claimed not to be entirely sure. He'd joined Gerber's A-Detachment only a month earlier at his own request, replacing a man who had been killed in hostile action. It had made for a few awkward moments. Schattschneider's father had been A-Detachment 555's team sergeant before he himself had been killed in a mortar and rocket attack on the camp a little over a year before.

Mildebrandt slid the washcloth up over one eye so he could peek out from underneath it. "Thanks for the encouragement. Actually, I'm feeling a bit better. About an hour ago I ate a banana, and so far it's stayed down. What do you need?"

"Sergeant Yashimoto says we got a chopper inbound, about five minutes out. Thought you'd want to know."

Mildebrandt mopped his heavily sweating face with the wash-cloth and straightened in the chair. "Thanks. Any idea who it is?"

"Sergeant Yashimoto said the pilot gave his call sign as Black-bird One One, but it's not listed in the SOI, so we've got no idea who it is. You want me or Sergeant Smith to meet the bird, sir? I mean, if you're not feeling well . . ."

"No, that's all right, Sergeant. I'll do it."

Mildebrandt slid back his chair and used both hands to push himself up from the table. The prospect of having something to do actually seemed to have a recuperative effect on him.

"You said the call sign wasn't listed in our SOI? You don't suppose it's some kind of a trick, do you?"

"I wouldn't think so, sir. Charlie doesn't have any choppers. At least we've never seen him have any. Besides, I hardly think he'd call and announce himself beforehand if he were planning to air-assault this place. You sure you wouldn't like me to take care of it, sir? You don't look at all well."

"Thanks for the offer. I'll be fine."

Mildebrandt waved Schattschneider aside, picked up his M-16 from where he'd leaned it against the wall and walked down to the helipad. In the distance he could hear the chopper and wondered who it could be. He stood there waiting for a moment, finally remembered someone should pop smoke, then got a grenade out of the rack Bocker had built near the helipad to hold them. He peeled the tape from around the canister, shook out a colored smoke grenade, pulled the pin and tossed it onto the helipad. A few moments later a Bell UH-1B slick painted a uniform flat black without markings swung into view and settled onto the pad, releasing a single passenger in a white two-piece suit, which looked as though it had seen better days.

"Lieutenant, uh, Mildebrandt, isn't it? Remember me? Jerry Maxwell, USIS."

"Sure. Mr. Maxwell. I thought you were CIA, though. What can we do for you?"

Maxwell gave the young lieutenant a pained look, then forced a smile.

"Actually, I'm looking for Robin Morrow, the reporter who flew out here with you from Saigon. I spoke to her about forty-eight hours ago in Saigon, but I understand she's come back out here. Can you tell me where I can find her?''

"It's kind of early. She's probably still in the temporary quarters we fixed up for her. I'll take you there.''

"Uh, well, Lieutenant, actually I'd kind of prefer you didn't do that.''

"No?"

"No. You see, it's kind of a personal matter.''

"A personal matter? But I thought she and Captain Gerber...uh, that is, sure, I understand,'' said Mildebrandt, not understanding at all. "Will you be joining us for breakfast, sir?''

"No. No. Thanks for the offer, but I've got to get right back. I'm in kind of a hurry.''

"Of course, sir. Perhaps your pilot and crew would care for something while they wait?''

"That won't be necessary. They have orders to stay with the aircraft.''

"Well, okay,'' said Mildebrandt doubtfully. "I just thought maybe we should ask them if they'd like—''

"Do you speak Macedonian, Lieutenant?''

"How's that again, sir?''

"I said, do you speak Macedonian?''

"Uh, no, sir, I don't.''

"Then I'm afraid you won't be able to ask them, because they don't speak English.''

"Don't speak English? Then what do they...oh, I'm beginning to understand.''

"Fine, Lieutenant. Now could you just give me directions to Miss Morrow's quarters, please? As I said, I'm in kind of a hurry.''

Mildebrandt gave him the directions, and Maxwell walked off, leaving the lieutenant standing by the helipad.

"What was that all about, sir?'' said Schattschneider, coming up.

"Well, uh, I don't know. Said he wanted to talk to Miss Morrow.''

"Must be a pretty high-powered press type to rate his own chopper. Who is he?''

"Some guy named Maxwell. I met him in Saigon. Thought he was CIA, but he says he's with the U.S. Information Service."

"That is the CIA," said Schattschneider.

"Nobody tells me anything," lamented Mildebrandt. "Say, Bill, you don't happen to speak any Macedonian, do you?"

"Macedonian? Why, no, sir, I don't. Why do you ask?"

"Never mind. I was just wondering. Thanks, Bill."

"Uh, sir, it's Hank. Actually it's Henry, but I kind of prefer Hank. That's what the men all call me. That's what everybody calls me. Bill was my dad's name."

"Hank. Okay. Thanks." As he walked off, Mildebrandt muttered, "Nobody tells me anything."

MAXWELL FOUND MORROW sitting on her bunk, wearing a pair of combat boots covered in red dust, the familiar fatigue pants cut off into shorts and a khaki shirt that looked as though it had been slept in, and had. Her eyes were red and puffy-looking, and her face looked streaked. Maxwell noted that her bags were packed and sitting out on the dirty plywood floor and that there was a half-empty bottle of Beam's Choice sitting on the floor next to her bunk.

"Must have been a rough night," observed Maxwell, picking up the bottle and sinking down on the other bunk across from her. "You look like hell, lady, if you don't mind my saying so, and even if you do. But it's all right. I think I like you better this way. I always did prefer my women a bit dirty. Must have something to do with this damned business I'm in." He uncorked the bottle and took a long pull. "I *must* be becoming an alcoholic. That was smooth."

"You don't look so shit-hot yourself, Maxwell," Morrow told him. "And drinking at this hour? Mr. One-Rum-and-Coke-a-Day Maxwell? The Russians must be in Washington."

"Not at last report. Saigon, maybe. Besides, I told you I was going to try and change my drinking habits. Anyway, I mistrust a man who doesn't drink. He must be afraid he'll talk too much when he does."

"Did you want something, or did you just come way out here to be obnoxious?"

Maxwell took another drink, then recorked the bottle. "Hmm, very smooth. I came out here to talk to you, young lady. What's the matter, you got some place you got to go to in a hurry?"

"Yeah, Saigon. I've got to get out of this dump for a while."

"Fine. I'll give you a lift back when we're done talking. Got a chopper waiting outside."

"Great. I'm ready. We can leave now."

"Not just yet. I'm not through talking. Are you going to pass up a chance to hear what the Dirty White Clam has to say when he tells you he feels like talking? Yes, I know what you press people call me. There's not a hell of a lot goes on in Saigon I don't know about, Miss Morrow. Now then, where's that famed reporter's natural curiosity? Where's your sense of journalistic endeavor?"

"Where's the point to all this? Just what in the hell are you doing here, Maxwell?"

"Very probably throwing my career away. A lot depends on whether or not you're the kind of person I think you are."

Morrow found herself wondering just what Maxwell was leading up to. In spite of everything, the conversation did seem to be taking an interesting turn.

"Spare me the character analysis, Maxwell. Why would I want to help you?"

"I can't think of a reason in the world," he said, uncorking the bottle and taking a third drink. "But I did think you might be interested in helping your boyfriend, Gerber."

Morrow felt the skin of her cheeks draw tight. "What makes you think I'd want to help him, or that he's my boyfriend, for that matter?"

"Miss Morrow, we're not going to get anywhere if you maintain this attitude. I told you, there's not a hell of a lot goes on in Saigon I don't know about. In fact, there's not much in this whole damned country. That includes you and Gerber. And your sister. Karen's her name if I remember right."

It came as a shock. "Just what is it you think you do know, Maxwell?"

Maxwell waved a hand airily. "I don't think, Miss Morrow. I know. My spies are everywhere, as they say in the movies."

In point of fact, Maxwell didn't know anything, but years of experience at keeping his eyes and ears open and his mouth shut while other people talked had made him pretty good at drawing conclusions from dozens of disjointed scraps of information and rumor.

Maxwell glanced at his Rolex watch, saw that it was a little after 7:30 a.m. and took another drink of the Beam's.

"Here," he said, passing the bottle over. "I think you're going to need this."

Morrow took the bottle but set it down on the floor.

"Do you like stories, Miss Morrow? Of course you do. All reporters love a good story. Well, hold on to your bra and panties, missy, because I'm going to tell you a whopper."

Maxwell leaned back against the wall and scratched his chin. He still needed a shave. For a moment he said nothing, then he began.

"Once upon a time in a far-off exotic land, there were some noblemen who kept the king's secrets for him. And in order to keep the king safe and his kingdom secure, they sent their agents throughout the world to spy on the king's enemies. Some of them went halfway around it."

"Does this story have a point to it?" said Morrow.

"Just bear with me a moment, please. I think you'll find it interesting.

"Now as it happened, one of these agents who was sent halfway around the world was very good at his job. So good in fact that one day he noticed something that he shouldn't have. He noticed that his boss, the nobleman who had sent him halfway around the world to spy on his king's enemies, had shown up in his neighborhood and was acting strangely. In fact, he'd been in town for two days and hadn't dropped in to say hello. But he had stopped in to see somebody else. Several times, in fact. A certain general of the king, whose job it was to make sure all the king's troops in this faraway land had everything they needed to fight the king's war with, but instead kept the best for himself and gave the troops second best.

"Is the story beginning to interest you now, Miss Morrow?"

"It begins to," said Morrow. "Go on."

"Now as it happens," said Maxwell, "this agent who was very good at his work had recently been forced to cooperate with this not very nice general in the planning and implementation of an expedition to a neighboring land to see what the king's enemies were up to there. The expedition was led by a gallant young captain of the king's army, who was also very good at his work, but who wasn't very good at picking girlfriends or playing politics and had run afoul of the nasty old general. In fact, the general disliked him so much that he had intentionally picked the captain for this expedition, which was very dangerous, hoping that something bad would happen to the gallant young captain.

"And then he made sure of it by making sure the enemy knew exactly where the gallant young captain would be."

"Oh, my God, you can't be serious," breathed Morrow. "Not even Crinshaw would do that. Surely you can't mean—"

"It's just a story, Miss Morrow. Would you like me to finish it?"

Morrow nodded for him to continue. She was sitting bolt upright now.

"Oh, this general was evil enough to do such a thing, all right. Especially when it had been made easy for him. You see, the agent who was very good at his work, well, his boss had given the general the perfect opportunity, because he'd asked the general, in the name of the king, to mount an expedition that would draw the enemy out into the open where they could be destroyed by a powerful new secret weapon of the King's, called Arc Light. Have you ever heard the term Arc Light used before Miss Morrow?"

Morrow nodded slightly. "Saturation bombing by B-52s."

"Good. I thought perhaps you would have. It makes the telling of the story easier.

"Now the problem was that this new weapon of the king, this Arc Light, wasn't a very accurate weapon. In fact, when you used it, it destroyed a huge area, which meant it would destroy the expedition led by the gallant young captain, too, unless the men in the expedition could find a way to escape in time. So the evil general made sure they couldn't by seeing to it that when the time came they'd be denied airlift."

Morrow sat stunned for a moment. "How did you find this out?"

"You're jumping to conclusions, Miss Morrow. This is just a story. But the agent who was very good at his job found out about it because a lady friend of the gallant young captain's had convinced him something was rotten somewhere. Not in the way she'd planned, but because the agent discovered his boss had been following the captain's lady friend."

Morrow put her hand to her mouth. "I was followed? From Crinshaw's office?"

"The lady in the story was followed. And when that happened, the agent who was very good at his job decided that it was time to have an ear in the general's office so he could find out exactly what kind of intrigues were going on in his bailiwick."

"You bugged Crinshaw's office," said Morrow, and wondered why that revelation didn't particularly surprise her.

"It's a dirty job, but somebody's got to do it. And, of course, I haven't the slightest idea what you're talking about."

Maxwell took an envelope out of his pocket and laid it on the bunk. "Inside there's a piece of paper with an address on it and a key to an apartment in Cholon. I think I can get your boy and his people out in one piece, but I've got to be careful because it has to be done without jeopardizing the primary mission."

"Why, for Christ's sake?" interrupted Morrow. "Why not just pull them out?"

"Because I'm still one of the king's men, damn it, and the orders for this had to come from high up. And because I am very good at doing my job."

"That's just great. That'll make a terrific headline, Maxwell. 'American Patrol Dies in Cambodia Because Superspook Is Good at His Job.' That's just marvelous."

Maxwell sighed. "And I thought you were a smart lady. You just don't get it, do you, Morrow? I can't pull them out. I don't have the authority. I doubt whether even Crinshaw does, because a plan like this had to be approved at the very highest levels of the executive branch. We're talking about launching a secret bombing war in Cambodia on a hitherto unprecedented scale. Even if I did have the authority and could pull them out, I'd be violating the wishes of the President of the United States. All I can do for Gerber and the rest of them is try to leave open an escape route for them for when the time comes, or to be more accurate, try to make sure Crinshaw doesn't slam it shut in their faces. Now are you with me on this or not?''

''What is it you expect me to do?'' asked Morrow.

''Nothing. At least I hope you don't have to do anything. But I need an insurance policy, and like it or not, you're it.''

''How can I be your insurance policy if I don't know what you want me to do?''

''Easy. All you gotta do is stay alive. Only if you stay here, I'm not so sure that's going to happen.''

''I see,'' said Morrow levelly. ''You think it's as bad as all that, then?''

''Don't you? There are careers at stake here. Not just yours or mine, or even Crinshaw's. I told you, it's a decision to intentionally betray an American patrol to the Vietcong in order to draw the VC out in the open so that they can be annihilated by a mass bombing raid in a neutral country. That kind of decision had to come from the highest levels.''

''I just can't believe the President of the United States would give such an order.''

''That's not the way these things get done. The President mentions to the director that he thinks it would be an awfully good idea if the DCI could come up with some way that the Company could help the military do something about all those supplies that keep getting through on the Ho Chi Minh Trail despite all the air interdiction missions being flown. He makes this comment to the director in the presence of the chairman and maybe just a couple of the joint chiefs of staff and then bops out to the Rose Garden for a spot of lunch with some visiting dignitary. The DCI and the chiefs are bright boys. They correctly interpret the situation to mean that the President wants them to get those VC bastards any way they can, but that he doesn't want to know the details.

''That way, if anything goes wrong, the President can stand there blinking soulfully into the klieg lights and honestly say to the press and the American public that he had no prior knowledge of any such action, because he didn't actually give them any orders or know what was planned. It's what we call the *doctrine of plausible deniability*. A very neat system. And if you're naive enough to believe that sort of thing doesn't go on, you've got no business being a reporter. At least not over here.''

"It's a frightening story, all right," said Morrow, "but I don't scare easily."

"Maybe you should. The man I spotted wasn't following me. At least not at first. If he had known who I was, he'd never have been careless enough to allow me to spot him. He was tailing you and wanted to see who you talked to."

"You sound as if you know him."

"I do. There's none better."

"Except you, right?"

"Wrong. I'm pretty good in the field, but this guy taught me everything I know. He used to be one of the instructors at the Farm. The only reason I spotted him was because I got lucky, and because he was busy making sure you didn't spot him following you. I'd never have seen him if he'd been on me. The only reason I was able to lose him when he switched from you to me is because I already knew he was there."

"You make this guy sound pretty dangerous."

"Very is the word. I've seen him in action. He's a killer."

"I've killed people before, too," said Morrow, remembering the two VC soldiers she'd been forced to shoot a few months earlier when Camp A-555 had been overrun.

Maxwell snorted. "Lady, this guy has killed more people than you've got friends. Next to him, I'm a Boy Scout. You? You wouldn't even make Campfire Girl."

Morrow indicated the envelope. "So why Cholon?"

"It's a safe house. Or at least an apartment. The guy who followed you doesn't know about it. I'm the only one who does. You take a taxi to the address in the envelope, then send the taxi away. When it's gone, you walk back east to the end of the block, go one more block, then north for five. It's in the sixth block, right in the middle. You go through a green doorway and down the hall to the end. Then up the stairs. Apartment 2C."

"Safer than here? The guy is hardly going to walk into a Green Beret camp and shoot me."

"Here Crinshaw can find you. Here they know where you are. They can make the move at any time, and believe me, this guy is too sophisticated to just walk in and shoot you. But if he wants you, the only chance you've got is if he can't find you."

"So how does that make me an insurance policy?"

"Are you with me on this or not?"

After a moment, Morrow nodded.

"In the apartment there's a tape recorder and two spools of tape. One from Crinshaw's office, the other a complete report, detailing everything I know or suspect."

"Jesus. You know, Maxwell, this is quite a story. What's to keep me from just sending it off to my editors?"

"Nothing. If that's all Gerber means to you. You blow the whistle on this thing prematurely and they'll have no choice but to make sure those people never get out of Cambodia alive. They'll have to do what they can to cover their tracks. You'll have a great story and a dead boyfriend."

Morrow wasn't at all sure she still had a live boyfriend. "What's to keep me from using it after you get them out?"

"Again nothing. Except Gerber. You go making waves afterward, and he could wind up finishing his army career in Greenland as a private. That's if he's lucky. They have ways of making it happen. You'd better believe that."

"So what good do the tapes do us at all if we can't use them, as you say."

"There's one thing we can use them for. Revenge. The only chance Gerber and his people have is if I can convince my boss and Crinshaw that if anything happens to him, or us, that we'll drag them down with us."

"That's it?" Morrow asked incredulously. "That's your great plan? You're going to try to bluff them?"

"Miss Morrow, it's only a bluff if you aren't holding the cards. I told you, the man who's in this with Crinshaw, my boss, taught me everything I know. That's what I'm counting on. And one of the most important things he taught me was never bluff. Never make a threat unless you're willing to carry it out. That's what I'm banking on—that he'll remember what he taught me and believe I'll do it."

"So that's how I'm the insurance policy. You want me to hold the tapes."

"Hell, no, I don't want you to hold the tapes. I don't even want you to go near the place. Not unless I call you, or rather, fail to call you at certain times."

"I don't understand. I thought you wanted me to go there so they couldn't find me."

"If I can find you, they can find you. And if they find you with the tapes, you're dead. I'll have my pilot drop you in Bien Hoa. I've arranged for a car for you there. You drive back to Saigon and lose yourself. I don't care where. Just don't go to any of the places you usually go there."

"Then how are you going to call me when you need the tapes?"

"Every two hours, starting at noon, I'll call the Saigon Press Club and leave a message for you. Something simple. 'Jerry called about dinner, please call him back. Jerry called, he can't make it tonight, please call him back,' that sort of thing. The message will change slightly each time, but will always begin with 'Jerry called,' and end with 'please call him back.' If for any reason I fail to call at the appointed time, you wait until the next time to make sure it wasn't some kind of screwup. If I miss two calls, you get the tapes and get them out of the country. Don't try to take them out yourself, because if I don't call, they'll be watching for you to do something. You got all that?"

Morrow nodded. "I think so."

"Good." Maxwell reached into his coat and pulled out another envelope. "There's ten thousand dollars and a phony passport in here. You can use some of the money in Saigon if you need it. The rest is in case you have to run. I got the picture for the passport from your application for press credentials from the South Vietnamese government."

"You've been a busy boy."

"Very. The chopper's waiting. Shall we go?"

For a long moment Morrow considered the possibilities. It was one hell of a story. And she wasn't sure what she was going to do yet about Karen's letter to Gerber, wasn't sure if she should do anything, or could. Finally she stood and picked up the envelopes.

"Sure," she said. "Why the hell not?"

16

THE CAMBODIAN
JUNGLE OVERLOOKING
THE HO CHI MINH TRAIL

While Kepler used the spotting scope to count the truck traffic, Gerber scanned the Trail through binoculars.

It wasn't really accurate to call it a trail; a network would have been more appropriate. In the far distance, Gerber could see two double-lane roads of packed earth, the nearer of which, Kepler reported, appeared as though it had been graveled at some point in the past but was now in disrepair, although still obviously in use. On a far bluff a whole series of foot trails was visible.

The foot trails had been cut into the rock of the cliff face, making them difficult to spot from above. Extensive camouflaging of the roads was evident as well, although it was spotty and by no means perfect. Netting had been hung between trees, but the foliage was beginning to brown. In other spots it appeared that trees had been bent over and tied so that they created a tunnel-like effect. The living trees provided a much more effective camouflage, and even from this angle they screened the road. Those sections of the Trail were completely invisible to Gerber's binoculars, but Kepler's far more powerful spotting scope revealed tantalizing details.

"They've got an antiaircraft gun just off to the left of that short, open stretch of road at about two-fifty degrees," said Kepler quietly. ''I can't be absolutely positive, but it looks like a 57 mm S-60.''

''Can't spot it,'' Gerber told him.

''It's just right at the edge, where the trees start. They've got camouflage netting over the top of it, but you can make out a little bit of the muzzle sticking out at about sixty degrees to the horizon.''

''All I can see is a little lump right at the edge of the trees.''

''That's it,'' Kepler told him. ''You haven't got enough magnification to be able to make out the barrel. Sure wish we could get a little closer. Like to have a better look at what they've got over there. If that's a fifty-seven, they've probably got some twelve-sevens or fourteen-fives with it.''

''Sorry, Derek. That's out. This is as close as we go. We know Charlie's got troops out hunting for us. We're really hanging our asses out in the breeze just doing this.''

''Yes, sir. I sure would like to know what all they've got over there, though. I mean, shit, triple A like that, sir, they must be expecting a visit from our flyboys.''

''More likely they've already had a visit. Not here perhaps, but somewhere nearby. Don't forget that burned-out area we crossed.''

''Christ, who could. That wasn't done by just a couple of T-28s with gun packs and a napalm canister under each wing. That was a heavy, concentrated bombardment. I didn't realize we were dropping anything that intense this side of the border. Air commandos have been flying a few limited surgical strikes ever since the French pulled out, but word from the Pentagon has always been very low profile. Looks bad in the newspapers to drop heavy ordnance in a neutral country. Upsets the man in Washington's breakfast.''

''Maybe the White House is getting a little less sensitive about breakfast.''

''I hope so, sir. That's the third convoy we've seen roll past here in the last hour and a half. Sixty-five trucks in all. And you got to remember that it's broad daylight. The heaviest traffic is probably at night to lessen the possibility of aerial detection.''

''It's a busy road, all right. What bothers me is that the security doesn't seem to be very busy.''

"How's that, sir?"

"You say there's a triple A battery down there. So there's got to be some troops around. Why haven't we spotted any patrols?"

"It doesn't necessarily follow that they'd fortify the entire trail, sir. Probably couldn't. There's just too much of it. More than likely they've got a few individual antiair guns scattered about where there're gaps in their camouflage, like here. Stretches that are fairly well concealed they probably don't bother protecting with triple A unless it's some key passage, like a bridge or a pass through the hills. Things that would probably show up despite the camo and be probable bombardment targets. I doubt they even bother with ground patrols this far inside Cambodia, at least not on a regular basis. Why would they? They know U.S. or South Viet troops aren't going to mount any operations across the border."

"They know we're somewhere in the general area, Derek, and let's not forget what Maxwell said happened to those LRRPs. I think we can safely assume that they're not all that lackadaisical about their patrolling procedures."

"Yes, sir," said Kepler. "There is that."

"Did you ever get a chance to go over the papers we got off those VC?"

"Yes, sir. Both groups. Pretty routine stuff, for the most part. Pay books, ID cards, ration coupons, that sort of thing. The maps we got off the NCO were even worse than ours, with one interesting exception. Nothing marked on them, of course."

"What was the exception?"

"One of them wasn't a normal topographical map. It was an aerial reconnaissance photo. Pretty grainy, medium-altitude stuff. Nothing remarkable in the technology. The remarkable thing was that they had it at all."

"I didn't know the VC had any aerial mapmaking capability."

"As far as I've been briefed, they don't. That's why it's so interesting."

"You think the North Vietnamese took the photos for them?"

"Maybe. My guess is that it was Chinese or Russian military assistance, but the North certainly has the technology, at least from what I can assess of the photo in the field. It could have come from a recon version of the IL-28 Beagle or just from some joker hanging out of an Antonov Colt biplane with a reasonably good 35 mm camera and a wide-angle lens. We haven't had reports of any NVAF jets this far south, but there was an Air America chopper jockey that downed a Colt a couple of months back.''

''How'd he do that?''

''The Colt buzzed him a couple of times and pissed him off, so he stuck the barrel of an AK-47 out the window on the guy's next pass and got lucky.''

''I always knew helicopter pilots were insane.''

''Yes, sir. Crude, but effective, you might say. Anyhow, the guy landed and cut a swatch out of the tail surface to bring back the registration number. Wanted his kill confirmed.''

Gerber chuckled softly at that, feeling some of the tension of the past few days drain away.

''The Air America pilot reported the pilot of the Colt had blond hair,'' continued Kepler. ''That's why I say Russian military assistance. Anyhow, the aerial photo, coupled with the AAA guns Charlie is socking in around here, could suggest a growing interest on the part of the VC and NVA in protecting the Trail from air strikes. The aerial photo might have been part of a survey, sort of a case of the Charlies trying to spot their own trails so they'd know what areas most needed camouflaging to keep our guys from finding them. That would suggest one of two things. Either the Trail is becoming increasingly important to the Communists as a supply route into South Vietnam or our interdiction missions have been making them hurt. It's probably a bit of both.''

''Anything else of interest in the papers the VC had on them?''

''Two small things. One of the guys was NVA, although he was wearing a VC uniform. Not too surprising that. We've had some reports of the Communists mixing troops in the same unit. Probably functioning as an advisor of some kind. It would be nice to know exactly what he was up to, but I don't think we'll likely ever know that now. The other item was more a curiosity. Fetterman found it when we were crossing the burned area. It was a sort of diary. It was pretty badly scorched, but we could make out bits of it. Belonged to an NVA corporal who was apparently a bit of a poet. It also contained an account of his trip south along the Ho Chi Minh Trail, but it was mostly personal impressions, that sort of thing. I don't think we'll get much of military value out of it.

I, uh, I gave it to Kit to see if she could make anything out of it that I'd missed. I hope that was okay, sir."

"I don't know what to make of our Kit Carson scout, Derek. Her having that beeper sure seems pretty damning. On the other hand, she tells an almost believable story about where it came from, and one that does explain why it's of American manufacture, as Bocker says. What it doesn't explain is why the VC had the receiver for it, and why Maxwell's boss, if it was Maxwell's boss, would risk blowing us to the VC with such a stupid stunt. You put it all together and it begins to leave a very bad taste in your mouth."

"Are you saying you think we were intentionally set up, sir?"

"Hell, I'm not sure of anything. It looks that way, but it just doesn't make any sense. If it is the case, it raises more questions than it answers. Who is this guy who claimed to be Maxwell's superior? Does he really exist, or is he just another of our scout's inventive fabrications? Why would he give her the beeper unless he wanted us blown? Why would he want such a thing? Surely Washington wouldn't want the publicity of having U.S. troops captured by the VC in neutral Cambodia, or is there some bizarre reason why Washington would want that? Or be willing to risk it? What were the VC doing with an American-manufactured receiver that was obviously designed to track, after a fashion, the beeper, and where did they get it from? And how much of the truth, if any, is our scout telling us? You figure it out if you can. I can't."

"I hope somebody can, sir."

JERRY MAXWELL HAD.

It was a little past noon when he entered Brigadier General Billy Joe Crinshaw's outer office and inquired of the withered old administrative sergeant whether or not the general was in. Before the sergeant could answer, the door to Crinshaw's inner office burst outward, and the general, resplendent in his freshly changed, razor-creased khakis, blustered out. When he caught sight of Maxwell, he pulled up short.

"Ah, Maxwell. What are you doing here?"

"I came to see you, General. It's about Gerber's patrol."

"Yes, yes, I know. They're in contact with the enemy. I'm just on my way over to the TOC now. Got to keep abreast of the situation, you know. That damned fool Colonel Bates is already hollering to get his boys pulled out of there. No backbone, that man. Doesn't seem to understand that a soldier's job is to fight the enemy, not run away from him."

It came as a shock. Maxwell hadn't known. Bates was right, of course. The team needed to be extracted at once.

"I think we'd better talk in your office, General," said Maxwell, casting a meaningful glance at the sergeant.

"Confound it, man, didn't you hear? I've got to get over there right away. I've got to make certain that pantywaist Bates doesn't pull them out until—"

"Until Jirasek can make sure the B-52s get there from Thailand? Yes, General, I figured they'd have to be based in Thailand for this one. It would take too long from Guam. You couldn't be sure there'd been any VC still around to bomb if you waited too long. You'd just be bombing a hillside full of dead Americans and Tais, and oh, yes, let's not forget our one Vietnamese scout."

The blood drained visibly from Crinshaw's countenance.

"I . . . don't know . . . what on earth you're talking about," Crinshaw sputtered.

"I'm talking about murder, General. Premeditated, cold-blooded murder. Now do you want to go back in your office and talk about it, or do you want to stand here and discuss it in front of your sergeant?"

"Why, you . . . Why, I never heard of such nonsense in all my natural life. Why, you're crazy."

"No, General, I'm not. But I'm beginning to think you may be. What I am is somebody who knows all about your little scheme, and is desperate, because I'm running out of time. And although you don't know it, you are too, because if I don't call Robin Morrow at a certain time with a certain message, there's going to be a set of tapes on their way to the networks, and this whole little show is going to blow right up in your face."

"That damned reporter again," snarled Crinshaw.

"Your office, General. Now."

The sergeant behind the desk looked uncertain. "Do you want me to call security, General?"

"No! No, damn it, I don't want you to call anybody. Take a walk."

"Are you sure, sir?"

"Yes, damn it. Do as I say. Take the afternoon off. I don't care. Just get out of here and don't come back."

"Yes, sir." The sergeant got.

"All right, Mr Maxwell. Now you'd better explain yourself and you'd better do it pretty damned quick before I call the MPs myself and have you thrown out of here on your ass." He reached for the telephone.

Maxwell pulled his jacket aside enough to show the Swenson .45 in the Milt Sparks shoulder rig. "I wouldn't do that if I were you, General Crinshaw. At least not just yet."

Crinshaw turned positively livid. "You're the one who'd better be careful, boy. Am I to take it that you are threatening a general officer?"

Maxwell finally lost his cool. "You can take it any goddamned way you like, you Georgia cracker. But you damned well better listen to what I have to say first. Because if I go down, I'm taking you and Jirasek with me. All the way to the bottom. Now why don't you be a good little general and go have a look at what's taped to the bottom of your desk? Then we'll have our little talk. And while you're at it, shut off those goddamned air conditioners. I'm sick to death of freezing my balls off every time I have to come into this stinking cesspool of an office."

"FETTERMAN! WHAT'S THE SITUATION?" yelled Gerber, ducking as a wild burst of AK-47 fire ripped open the air over his head. He couldn't believe how quickly things had turned to shit. Ten minutes ago he and Kepler had been counting the trucks in another convoy. Now it sounded like the entire NVA army had made today Kill Mack Gerber Day. There was another sustained burst of AK fire, and then Fetterman shouted back.

"We got two of the Tais dead, another hit, and Tyme is hit. Where in the hell did these guys come from?"

"How bad? We gotta move," Gerber yelled back.

"Do you think you can walk, Boom-Boom?" asked Fetterman as he finished tying a pressure dressing around the young man's thigh. He flattened abruptly on top of the light weapons specialist as a long rattle of bullets splattered into the trees next to them.

"Get me to my fucking feet and I can run," snapped Tyme.

Fetterman glanced through the trees at where Krung was huddled with the rest of the Tais. The wiry tribesman shook his head.

"We carry him, Sergeant Tony. No problem."

Fetterman gave him a hard look.

"I know, Sergeant Tony, but he not slow us down. Corporal Bhat my friend long time now. He can make it if we carry him. We no leave our men in the field for VC."

"All right, but you've got to keep up."

Krung nodded.

"Ready to move, sir!" Fetterman shouted back at Gerber. "Just give the word."

"Right. When I give the word, try working around to the left. We'll see if we can't flank these bastards and then break contact."

"Anybody seen our Kit Carson?"

"Over here, Captain," called Kit. She had slid in under the overhanging branches of a medium-sized pine tree. Anderson was stretched out next to her, almost covering her with his huge body, as if to protect her from the bullets knocking pine needles out of the branches over their heads.

"Cat, get your ass down, for Christ's sake! The scout can take care of herself," yelled Gerber, then to Kit, "We're going to need a defensible position, a rocky hilltop, a draw we can keep them from coming up, something like that. One that's got a clear enough area for a chopper to get in and pick us up. You got any ideas where we can find one, you better start thinking about how to get us there."

There was another burst of firing from Fetterman's direction. It was immediately answered by the rattle of M-16s.

"Bocker! Get hold of B-team and get them working on an extraction. We're not going to be able to outrun these guys forever."

"Patched into the relay ship now," came back the reply.

"Is everybody accounted for? Where's T.J.?"

"Over here, Captain," Washington called out.

Gerber glanced at Kepler. "You okay?"

The intel sergeant nodded.

"Right. Fetterman, can you see those guys?"

"I can see some of them. That is, I can see their muzzle-flashes."

"Give 'em two rounds from the M-79. When the second one pops, we'll move."

"Right!" Fetterman snatched up Tyme's M-79, guessed at the range and fired. He flattened as the round hit, blowing up a big geyser of dirt and branches, and used the opportunity to reload. He came back up to where he could see, increased the range slightly and let loose another round. The point of impact was directly on top of one of the muzzle-flashes. Fetterman leaped to his feet, dragging Tyme up with him, and shouted, "Go!"

The air was filled with the rattle of M-16s and the deeper throated hammering of AK-47s. If any of the VC were using rifles or carbines, their individual cracks and pops were drowned out by the din of automatic weapons. Gerber and Kepler were last men out as the patrol collapsed in upon itself and broke to the side. While Kepler sprayed the trees with his M-16, Gerber pulled two HC smoke grenades from his shoulder harness, yanked out the pins and threw them as far toward the enemy positions as he could. They immediately billowed out dense white clouds. Gerber stooped and snatched up his M-16 from where he'd let it drop when he'd pulled the grenades.

"Run!" he yelled at Kepler.

"I DON'T HAVE to be told twice," said Crinshaw irritably. "You want them pulled out. Now I hope you don't have to be told twice. Just give it up, and we'll forget any of this ever happened. It's not too late to stop this madness."

"That, General, is precisely what I'm trying to do," said Maxwell. "Now, then, do you want to make the necessary phone calls, or do you want me to do it for you?"

"You just don't get it, do you, boy? You just don't see the big picture. This isn't just my idea, you know. Big people made the decision on this thing. Important people. They're not gonna appreciate your tryin' to muck it up."

"I'll take my chances on winning friends and influencing people later. Right now I think you'd better be more concerned about how much they're going to appreciate having the full story of this little fiasco smeared all over page one of every newspaper in America, not to mention the six o'clock network news. Now are you going to pick up the phone, or not?''

"It's not that simple. I can't stop the bombers. They've already been scrambled from Udorn by now. This thing has taken months to coordinate. I don't have the authority to stop them. Your boss doesn't either. We're not in control of this. I don't even know who is. We're just the trigger mechanism.''

"I don't expect you to stop the B-52s. I do expect you to give the necessary clearance to allow Army Aviation to go in there and pull Gerber's team out before the bombs start falling. That was the original plan, wasn't it? To pull them out at the last minute and let the B-52s plaster the VC? Wasn't that the plan until you saw the opportunity to get rid of a troublesome officer and his irksome men by making sure that they didn't get pulled out in time?''

"Bah. You're talking nonsense now. You make it sound like I wanted those boys dead.''

"No, not wanted. Want. You'd still like nothing better. And you planned it, all right, Crinshaw. That's why you told me in this very office that there'd be no airlift, that Gerber and his patrol would have to get out on their own.''

"You've got no proof of that.''

"Haven't I, General?'' said Maxwell, nodding significantly at the tape recorder. "I wouldn't be too sure about what I have and haven't got proof of if I were you. Are you willing to gamble a general court-martial on just how long I've had that thing taped to the underside of your desk? I believe the *Uniform Code of Military Justice* still prescribes the death penalty for premeditated murder.''

"You can't prove that! I've done nothing. There's no way that you can prove anything like a murder charge while I'm sitting in Saigon and they're in Cambodia.''

"Perhaps you're right. The trial board might decide it was only negligent homicide. But they'll be looking for a lot of scapegoats after this hits the presses. They'll need somebody fairly important to hang a responsibility tag on. My guess is they'll think a brigadier general is just about important enough to satisfy the blood lust of the media. Oh, I'll probably be given the choice of resigning without pension or being fired, but you, General, you and Jirasek, they'll crucify you. They'll nail your asses to a fucking cross. You want something to think about, you think about that for a while. But don't think about it for too damned long, because if you do, and Gerber's team dies, I just might decide to save you all the embarrassment. I might just show you what a trigger mechanism is really all about.''

To emphasize the point, Maxwell pulled the Swenson .45 from its holster and laid it on the blotter of Crinshaw's desk. He let his hand rest lightly on top of it.

"Now I know you're bluffing," said Crinshaw. "You wouldn't dare."

Maxwell sighed. "God, I get tired of people telling me what I wouldn't do. They usually do it just before they die. It's so depressing."

He picked up the pistol and snapped off the safety. In the quiet of Crinshaw's office, without the air-conditioning running, the sound seemed very loud.

"Crinshaw," said Maxwell heavily, sounding almost sad, "I've killed lots more important people than you."

He picked up the telephone receiver in his left hand and tossed it at the general, who fumbled the catch, but got it on the second try.

"Why don't you give Jirasek a phone call and ask him what he thinks I would and wouldn't do. Just be nice and calm and take your time. Explain the whole situation to him, so he understands about the tapes and Miss Morrow, too. Then, if you're still breathing, you might want to put a call through to the Crusaders at Tay Ninh, and have them go pick up Gerber's patrol. I think they'd be the closest. I'd have Air America do it, but I'm not sure we could get the word to them in time. They have such a limited number of aircraft available to them. Besides, I think it would be so much nicer to have army boys picked up by the army, don't you? A great heroic rescue, and all that. There might even be some medals to hand out afterward. Be a pity if you weren't around to do it. So you just take all the time you need talking to Mr. Jirasek, only remember, time's getting short. For everyone."

"ARE YOU SURE this is the right one?" panted Gerber. He was out of breath and sweating heavily.

Kit nodded vigorously. "This draw runs straight to the top. There is only a narrow trail down the back, and both sides are nearly vertical. Maybe not impossible to climb, but very difficult. The top is a flat oval with big rocks around the edges, but the center is fairly clear and flat. There is room for a helicopter to land, perhaps two, if one of them makes—what do you call it?— a slope landing. With just the one skid touching, like so." She gestured with her hands, holding one palm out flat, with the tips of her fingers touching the back of her other fist.

"An incline landing," said Kepler. "It must be pretty tight up there. You sure this is a good idea, Captain, pulling the wagons into a circle like this? Maybe we ought to break up and try to E&E individually."

"None of this has been a good idea, Derek. Not from the start. I don't see where we've got much choice. Fetterman says there's a bunch of them out in front of us, and we know they've got troops back to the south. If we go east, we've got all that open ground to cross, and then we'll hit the Ho Chi Minh Trail. Right now that doesn't seem like too good an idea. Besides, I'm not figuring on pulling anybody's wagons in a circle unless we have to. If we can make it to the top, we'll have a look around, see what the enemy's disposition is. Maybe we can slip down that narrow trail Kit mentioned and break away to the north, then work our way back east toward the burned area and the river."

As if to punctuate Gerber's statement, the sound of probing fire could be heard in the distance in front of them, back east, between them and the border.

"Yes, sir," said Kepler. He glanced at Kit, and then uneasily at the steep sides of the ravine they would have to move up. "I just hope the VC haven't already used that trail and are up there waiting for us."

"So do I, Sergeant," said Kit icily. "Or have you forgotten what the VC do to scouts who have *chieu hoi*ed?"

"I haven't forgotten. I'm just wondering if there are any of those around."

"That's enough, Derek. We've got better things to do than argue," Gerber interrupted. "Get them moving up the hill, Sergeant."

"Yes, sir," replied Kepler. He still didn't like the idea.

"Cat!" Gerber yelled to Anderson. "Drop off about fifty meters up the ravine and lay something to slow them down if they come our way. T.J., help him out. Let's go."

The climb was more than just grueling. It was brutal. In a state park on a crisp fall day, it would have been a challenging hike, but with each of them carrying between sixty and eighty pounds of gear and ammunition, it was a nightmare. When they finally pushed through the last of the brush and crossed the bare slope leading to the top, Gerber's heart was pounding as if it was trying to escape from his rib cage. Chest heaving, he staggered to the top for a look, with Bocker, bowed beneath the weight of the radio, struggling along beside him. What they saw below was far from encouraging.

"Jesus Christ, sir, will you look at that!" Bocker gasped. "There must be a reinforced company down there."

"And more over there, and over there," wheezed Gerber. "Looks like Kepler was right. Time to circle the wagons. We're not going to be able to get down that way. At least we've taken the high ground. They'll have to come to us."

"Yes, sir. Sort of looks like that's exactly what they plan on doing."

"Any word yet from Bates on getting us out of here?"

"No, sir. There seems to be some kind of snag at his end."

"Well, find yourself a good spot and then call him back and tell him to fix it, or our butts are going to be in a meat grinder. And tell him I said I'm not kidding, either."

"Right, sir."

"Kepler!"

"Over here, Captain."

"Two riflemen and a grenadier to cover the north trail. And pass around the captured weapons and ammo. We're going to need everything we've got."

"Right."

"Sergeant Krung!"

"Right here, Captain Mack," said Krung at his elbow.

"How's your injured man doing?"

"He bleed some, but still okay fight. Sergeant T. J. say be okay fine if we get out of here."

"We'll get out of here," said Gerber without any real enthusiasm. He was beginning to appreciate how Custer must have felt when he stepped into it at Little Big Horn. "Who was it?"

"Corporal Bhat wounded. Privates Krak and Mung dead. I bring their weapons and ammo."

Gerber nodded his approval. "Good thinking. Tell Re and Jai to set up the M-60 to cover the ravine. When they come at us in force, they'll have to come that way."

"Yes, Captain."

As Krung hurried off, Fetterman came bounding up the slope like a deer, skidded to a stop and nearly toppled under the shifting weight of his jungle ruck.

"Report," Gerber told him.

"Sir. A large body of VC to our east and south. Company strength at least, moving our way fast. No way to get past them without getting cut to ribbons. Last casualty count I had, we'd only lost the two Tails. T. J. said Corporal Bhat was doing okay. Just a nick in Tyme. He'll need stitching when we get out of this place, but nothing vital hit. We going down the back slope or going to make a stand here?"

"Here. No choice. Charlie's got about half a battalion down below."

Fetterman glanced around. "Well, we've got the high ground, reasonably good cover, most of the ammo's left. We can probably hold out as long as they don't have mortars. I guess it could be worse."

"Not much. You and Tyme set up with Kepler to cover the north trail. I told him two riflemen and a grenadier, then realized Washington and Anderson are still down the hill. I'll use them to fill in here and cover the ravine."

"Yes, sir. They shouldn't be too far behind."

From below came a short series of shattering explosions.

"I'd guess that would be them coming now, sir."

"Captain Gerber!" It was Bocker. "Some guy on the blower calling himself Linebacker. Says he's about ten minutes out and wants to know why we haven't turned on our marker beacon, whatever the hell that means. Says if we can't do that, they'll have to bomb the whole grid. Either way he says we'd better get the hell out.''

''Find out what he's talking about and then get me Bates. I want to talk to him personally.''

''Yes, sir.''

There was a long burst of firing from below, and Washington and Anderson came into view, cranking out rounds behind them as they ran.

''Get ready,'' Gerber said. ''This is it. They're coming.''

To his horror, he watched helplessly as an RPD opened up somewhere, stitching a long line across the slope of the hill. Anderson was chopped down like a Norwegian pine. Washington ran on for a short distance, realized he was alone, turned and went back for his friend. There was another burst of machine gun fire, and the big black medic went down, too.

''No!'' yelled Gerber.

Kit was on her feet immediately, sprinting down the hill, conspicuous in her black-and-khaki clothing, long dark hair flowing behind her, face terribly contorted. A long, hideous scream issued from her throat like the cry of some wild animal. She ran past Washington and knelt beside Anderson, but only for an instant. She spun away, ran back to Washington and helped him to his feet. With Washington using his rifle like a cane, they hobbled back up the hill, but were both cut down. For a moment, Gerber thought they, too, were dead. Then he could see Kit crawling forward, desperately trying to drag Washington, who weighed more than twice her weight, with her.

''Fetterman! The M-79! Blanket the whole area down there. Give them some help.''

The Tai machine gun crew was already raking the edge of the tree line. Firing rose to a crescendo as the others opened up with their M-16s. For two long minutes the battle raged. Finally they were close enough that Fetterman popped a smoke grenade and ran out to help the scout drag Washington into the safety of the rocks.

''How bad?'' asked Gerber.

''Bad,'' said Fetterman, stripping the cellophane from a pack of cigarettes and flattening it over the hole in Washington's chest before tying a pressure dressing over it to hold it in place. "At least it didn't go all the way through. In this case that's an advantage, I think. Can you hear me, T.J.? Is there anything else I can do?"

"You're doing fine," said Washington weakly.

"Captain, would you get me a morphine styrette out of his kit?"

"No," said Washington, shaking his head. "No morphine. Not yet. Want to stay alert. Don't want those bastards to find me napping."

"Okay. No morphine just yet. You take it easy and save your strength."

"Never have made it without the girl," said Washington.

Both Gerber and Fetterman looked at Kit, who was sitting very still and holding a hand to a blood-covered thigh. She looked very pale and was sweating profusely. She smiled at them weakly.

"Here, let me have a look at that," said Fetterman.

"Now, Captain," she said. "Now perhaps you will finally believe whose side I am on." Then she fainted.

"Captain Gerber," yelled Bocker from behind a pile of rocks. He snapped off three quick rounds at a VC who had been foolish enough to show himself and was apparently trying to get to Anderson's body. "B-team says evac and gunships are on the way. That Linebacker joker is a BUFF. Says they're fixing to plaster the whole area."

"Can you get that damned beeper working again?"

"Negative, sir. I rendered it permanently inop per your orders. If I leave the mike open, though, the B-52s can shoot a bearing on it."

"Do that, and tell them to drop it anywhere but on us. But first call those choppers and tell them they'd better hurry."

"Yes, sir."

The hillside below them was exploding in flame as the last of the Huey slicks lifted off the hilltop.

17

SAIGON RVN

It had been nearly two weeks since the helicopters of the 187th Assault Helicopter Company had pulled them off the hilltop in Cambodia while the B-52s had turned the hill into a gully. Sam "the Cat" Anderson was dead, officially missing in hostile action, his body buried beneath the rubble of a Cambodian hillside, along with the bodies of an undetermined number of Vietcong. T. J. Washington was in a Saigon military hospital recovering from a sucking chest wound. Brouchard Bien Soo Ta Emilie was there as well.

The doctors thought they'd saved her leg, but no one was saying how much use it would be, yet. Corporal Bhat hadn't made it, after all. He'd survived the trip out but had succumbed to infection eight days later. Strikers Mung and Krak were rotting on another Cambodian hillside somewhere. All in all, it seemed to Gerber to be a less than spectacular ending to a mission that had only accomplished the precedent of mass bombing in Cambodia.

Bocker and Kepler had already returned to Camp A-555, and Justin Tyme had been DEROSed back to the States a month early, having picked up his third Purple Heart. Gerber and Fetterman were both still in Saigon, having picked up minor wounds in the last moments of the battle. Gerber now walked with a cane and a slight limp, which was daily getting better. Fetterman's left arm was in a sling, which he insisted was unnecessary.

Fetterman had persuaded Gerber after supper that the biggest recuperative medicine they needed was a good stiff drink, and the two men had slipped out of the hospital complex by hiding in the back of a deuce-and-a-half truck. Now they were sitting in a smoked-filled tavern, drinking whiskey and Ba Muoi Ba and watching a nearly naked half-French, half-Vietnamese dancer who looked painfully like Kit do everything but fuck herself on top of the bar while a stereo somewhere blared out Manfred Mann's "Doo Wah Diddy Diddy."

"Maybe it wasn't such a good idea coming here after all," said Fetterman. "You don't seem to be enjoying yourself much, and while the atmosphere isn't much, you got to admit the scenery is fairly breathtaking."

"Sorry, Tony." Gerber had to practically shout to make himself heard. "Guess I just got a lot to think about, things going bad with the mission and all."

"And with Miss Morrow, sir?"

Gerber felt like asking which one, but just smiled, shook his head and went back to watching the dancer, who was picking money up off the bar in a truly astounding fashion. He felt a bump against his elbow and turned.

"I might have known I'd find you in some sleazoid joint like this," shouted Robin Morrow.

Gerber could see instantly that she was more than a little drunk.

"Robin. Good to see you. I was wondering why you hadn't dropped by the hospital."

"Liar. You probably hoped you'd never see me again. Besides, I was waiting for you to make up your mind."

"About what?"

"About me. About you. About Karen. About everything. I know about the letter, Gerber. Did you write her back and say you were going to come running home to her? She'll fuck you, you know. And I don't mean like I will. She's done it before and she'll do it again, but I guess maybe all you men ever want is sex. You don't care about love, do you? Somebody loves you, goes through hell for you, and you just don't give a shit. All you want is my sister's ass and her kinky little perversions. You want sex? All right, goddamn it, I'll give you sex."

Before Gerber could stop her, Morrow leaped onto the bar and proceeded to rip off her clothes to the thunderous applause of the many GIs crowding around and the considerable consternation of the dancer at being upstaged by a round-eyed girl. She strutted up and down the bar a couple of times, amid much cheering and hooting, then walked over and stuck her behind almost in Gerber's beer.

"You see those marks, Gerber," she shouted at him, pointing at the thin scars covering her posterior. "That's what it's really all about. I go through this because of you, and I still want you. I helped Maxwell get you off that damned hilltop even after I knew about Kari's letter. If it wasn't for me, you'd still be in Cambodia. Forever."

"Robin, please. Not so loud. Come on down off there, will you?"

She ignored him.

"But that's all right, Gerber. Don't think about all the pain and suffering you've caused me. You just go ahead and run back to Seattle and look up my big sister for some fun and games, 'cause that's all you'll ever get from her. That and heartache, because she doesn't know the meaning of the word commitment. And while you're doing that, just you think about what you could have had instead."

Morrow stepped off the bar, stumbled unsteadily and marched out the door, leaving her clothes behind. The GIs gave her a standing ovation.

"Quite a performance, I'd say," observed Fetterman in the silence that followed.

"You can say that again," said Gerber uneasily. He cleared his throat and took a sip of beer.

"Captain," said Fetterman sternly. "You're not going to be a complete jerk and let her go like that, are you? She'll catch her death or the MPs will pick her up. You don't take that lady home, I don't think I'll ever drink with you again, sir."

Gerber smiled and pushed back from the bar. "You know, Master Sergeant, I believe that once again you're right as usual. Dealing with drunks is a dirty job, but somebody's got to do it. Tell the night nurse I won't be in for breakfast, will you? And when you get back to camp, look in my locker. You'll find a letter in the drawer where I usually keep the Beam's.

"Burn it."

"Yes, sir," said Fetterman. "With pleasure, sir."

GLOSSARY

AC—Aircraft Commander. Pilot in charge of an aircraft.

AFVN—Armed Forces radio and television network in Vietnam. Army PFC Pat Sajak was probably the most memorable of AFVN's DJs with his loud and long "Goooooooooooood Morning, Vietnam!"

AK-47—Selective fire assault rifle used by the NVA and the VC. It fired the same ammunition as the SKS carbine, which was used early in the war. The AK-47 replaced it.

AN/PRC-10—Portable radio. Also called Prick-10.

AN/PRC-25—Became the standard infantry radio used in Vietnam. Sometimes called Prick-25.

AO—Area of Operation.

AP ROUNDS—Armor-piercing ammunition.

ARVN-Army of the Republic of Vietnam. South Vietnamese soldier. Also known as Marvin Arvin.

ASH AND TRASH—Single ship flights by helicopters taking care of a variety of missions, such as flying cargo, supplies, mail and people among the various small camps in Vietnam, for anyone who needed aviation support.

BAR—.30-caliber Browning Automatic Rifle.

BEAUCOUP—Many.

BISCUIT—C-rations. Combat rations.

BLOWER—See *Horn*.

BODY COUNT—Number of enemy killed, wounded or captured during an operation. Used by Saigon and Washington as a means of measuring the progress of the war.

BOOM-BOOM—Term used by Vietnamese prostitutes to sell their product.

BOONDOGGLE—Any military operation that hasn't been completely thought out. An operation that is ridiculous.

BOONIE HATS—Soft cap worn by the grunts in the field when not wearing a steel pot.

BUSHMASTER—Jungle warfare expert or soldier highly skilled in jungle navigation and combat. Also a large deadly snake not common to Vietnam but mighty tasty.

C AND C—Command and Control aircraft that circled overhead to direct the combined air and ground operations.

CARIBOU—Twin-engine cargo transport plane; C-123.

CHINOOK—Army Aviation twin-engine helicopter. CH-47. Shit hook.

CHURCH KEY—Beer can opener used in the days before pop tops.

CLAYMORE—Antipersonnel mine that fires 750 steel balls with a lethal range of 50 meters.

CLOSE AIR SUPPORT—Use of airplanes and helicopters to fire on enemy units near friendly troops.

CMH—Congressional Medal of Honor.

CO CONG—Female Vietcong soldier.

COMSEC—Communications Security. The term refers to the need to be careful with useful information when using the radio so that the enemy doesn't get it.

DAI UY—Vietnamese Army rank equivalent to U.S. Army Captain.

DCI—Director, Central Intelligence. Director of the CIA.

DEROS—Date of Estimated Return From Overseas Service.

DONG—Unit of North Vietnamese money about equal to an American penny.

FIIGMO—Fuck It, I've Got My Orders.

FIVE—Radio call sign for the Executive Officer of a unit.

FNG—Fucking New Guy.

FRENCH FORT—Distinctive, triangular structure built by the hundreds throughout Vietnam by the French.

FUBAR—Fucked Up Beyond All Recognition.

GARAND—M-1 rifle, which was replaced by the M-14. Issued to the Vietnamese early in the war.

GO-TO-HELL RAG—Towel or any large cloth worn around the neck by grunts to absorb perspiration, clean their weapons and dry their hands.

GRUNT—Infantryman.

GUARD THE RADIO—To stand by in the communications bunker and listen for incoming messages.

GUNSHIP—Armed helicopter or cargo plane that carries weapons instead of cargo.

HE—High-explosive ammunition.

HOOTCH—Almost any shelter, from temporary to long-term.

HORN—Specific radio communications network in Vietnam that used satellites to rebroadcast messages.

HORSE—See *Biscuit*.

HOTEL THREE—Helicopter landing area at Saigon's Tan Son Nhut Air Force Base.

HUEY—Bell Helicopter. Slick. Called a Huey because its original designation was HU, but it was later changed to UH.

IN-COUNTRY—American troops operating in South Vietnam were all in-country.

INTELLIGENCE—Any information about enemy operations, including troop movements, weapons capabilities, biographies of enemy commanders and general information about terrain features. It is any information that could be useful in planning a mission. Also refers to the branch of the military that specifically deals with the gathering of such information.

KA-BAR—Military combat knife.

KIA—Killed In Action. Since the U.S. was not engaged in a declared war, the use of KIA was not authorized. KIA came to mean enemy dead. Americans were KHA or Killed in Hostile Action.

KLICK—One thousand meters. Kilometer.

LEGS—Derogatory term for regular infantry used by airborne qualified troops.

LIMA LIMA—Land line. Telephone communications between two points on the ground.

LLDB—Luc Luong Dac Biet. South Vietnamese Special Forces. Sometimes referred to as the Look Long, Duck Back.

LP—Listening Post. Position outside the perimeter manned by a couple of soldiers to warn of enemy activity.

LRRP—Long Range Reconnaissance Patrol. A small group that slipped into the jungle to search for the enemy. They stayed out for weeks at a time.

LZ—Landing Zone.

M-14—Standard rifle of the U.S. Army, eventually replaced by the M-16. It fires the standard NATO 7.62 mm round.

M-16—Became the standard infantry weapon of the Vietnam War. It fires 5.56 mm ammunition.

M-79—Short-barreled, shoulder-fired weapon that fires a 40 mm grenade, which can be high-explosive, white phosphorus or canister.

MACV—Military Assistance Command, Vietnam. Replaced MAAG—the Military Assistance Advisory Group—in 1964.

MEDEVAC—Medical Evacuation. Dustoff. Helicopter used to take wounded to medical facilities.

MIA—Missing In Action.

MOST RICKY TICK—At once. Immediately.

NCO—Noncommission Officer. Noncom. Sergeant.

NCOIC—NCO In Charge. Senior NCO in a unit. detachment or a patrol.

NEXT—The man who said he was the next to be rotated home. See *Short-timer*.

NINETEEN—Average age of the combat soldier in Vietnam, in contrast to age twenty-six in the Second World War.

NOUC-MAM—Foul smelling fermented fish sauce used by the Vietnamese as a condiment.

NVA—North Vietnamese Army. Also used to designate a soldier from North Vietnam.

OD—Olive Drab, the standard military color.

P-38—Military designation for the small one-piece can opener supplied with C-rations.

PETA-PRIME—Black tarlike substance that melted in the heat of the day to become a sticky black nightmare that clung to boots, clothes and equipment. It was used to hold down the dust during the dry season.

PETER PILOT—Copilot of a helicopter.

POW—Prisoner Of War.

POGUES—Derogatory term describing fat, lazy people who inhabited rear areas, taking all the best supplies for themselves and leaving the rest for the men in the field.

PSP—Perforated Steel Plate used instead of pavement for runways and roadways.

PULL PITCH—Term used by helicopter pilots that means they are going to take off.

PUNJI STAKE—Sharpened bamboo stake hidden to penetrate the foot, sometimes dipped in feces to increase the likelihood of infection.

QT—Quick Time. It came to mean talking to someone quietly on the side rather than operating in official channels.

R AND R—Rest and Relaxation. The term came to mean a trip outside Vietnam where the soldier could forget about the war.

RF STRIKERS—Local military forces recruited and employed inside a province. Known as Regional Forces.

RINGKNOCKER—Graduate of a military academy. The term refers to the ring worn by all graduates.

RPD—7.62 mm Soviet light machine gun.

RTO—Radiotelephone operator. Radio man of a unit.

RULE OF ENGAGEMENT—Rules telling American troops when they could fire. Full Suppression meant they could fire all the way in on a landing. Normal Rules meant they could return fire for fire received. Negative Suppression meant they weren't to shoot back.

SAPPER—Enemy soldier trained in use of demolitions. Used explosives during attacks.

SHIT HOOK—Name applied by troops to the Chinook helicopter because of all the ''shit'' stirred up by the massive rotors.

SHORT—Term used by a GI in Vietnam to tell all who would listen that his tour was almost over.

SHORT-TIMER—GI who had been in Vietnam for nearly a year and who would be rotated back to the World soon. When the Deros (Date of Estimated Return From Overseas Service) was the shortest in the unit, the person was said to be *Next.*

SIX—Radio call sign for the Unit Commander.

SKS—Simonov 7.62 mm semiautomatic carbine.

SMG—Submachine gun.

SOI—Signal Operating Instructions. The booklet that contained the call signs and radio frequencies of the units in Vietnam.

SOP—Standard Operating Procedure.

STEEL POT—Standard U.S. Army helmet. It consisted of a fiber helmet liner with an outer steel cover.

STORMY WEATHER—Code name for the Cambodian border.

TAI—Vietnamese ethnic group living in the mountainous regions.

TEAM UNIFORM—UHF radio frequency on which the team communicates. Frequencies were changed periodically in an attempt to confuse the enemy.

THREE—Radio call sign of the Operations Officer.

THREE CORPS—Military area around Saigon. Vietnam was divided into four corps areas.

TOC—Tactical Operations Center.

TO&E—Table of Organization and Equipment. This is the plan used to determine the equipment and the personnel for a unit. Everything, down to the last rifle bullet, was in the TO&E.

TOT—Time Over Target. Refers to the time the aircraft are supposed to be over the drop zone with the parachutists, or the target if the planes are bombers.

TRIPLE A—Or AAA refers to antiaircraft artillery. This is actually anything used to shoot at airplanes and helicopters, although it usually refers to weapons designed to shoot at aircraft.

TWO—Radio call sign of the Intelligence Officer.

TWO-OH-ONE (201) FILE—Military records file that listed all a soldier's qualifications, training, experience and abilities. It was passed from unit to unit so that the new commander would have some idea of the incoming soldier's capabilities.

VC—Vietcong. Also Victor Charlie (phonetic alphabet) or Charlie.

VIETCONG—Contraction of Vietnam Cong San (Vietnamese Communist Party, established in 1956.)

WIA—Wounded in Action.

WILLIE PETE—WP. White Phosphorus. Smoke Rounds. Also used as antipersonnel weapons.

WORLD—United States. Always referred to as "the World."

XO—Executive Officer of a unit.

ZIPPO—A flamethrower.

SuperBolan #8

ROGUE FORCE

AN EAGLE FOR THE KILLING

A covert clique within the U.S. military is set to launch an all-out war in Central America. This secret cabal of generals believes the American people are being betrayed by a soft U.S. government. Their idea is to stage another "Vietnam." But this time on America's doorstep.

There's only one way that Washington can neutralize these superpatriots: pit it's supersoldier against the very men who trained him!

SB8-R

FACT OR FICTION?
THE INCREDIBLE ACCOUNT
OF THE RAID THAT NEVER WAS.

CHINA MAZE

LAWRENCE GARDELLA

In the spring of 1952, six American Marines embarked on the most incredible covert military offensive of the bloody Korean conflict. The mission: to infiltrate and destroy a heavily guarded underground atomic laboratory complex located deep in the heart of Red China.

They were expendable soldiers on a suicide run, abandoned by their own government in a deadly Communist hell.

"If It Is Authentic, It Is Quite A Tale; If Not, Gardella's Imagination Is At Least As Good As Alistair MacLean's."

—*Publishers Weekly*

CM-R

GOLD EAGLE

Take
4 explosive books
plus a
mystery bonus

FREE

Mail to Gold Eagle Reader Service

In the U.S.
P.O. Box 1396
Buffalo, N.Y. 14240-1396

In Canada
P.O. Box 609
Fort Erie, Ont. L2A 5X3

YEAH! Rush me 4 free Gold Eagle novels and my free mystery
bonus. Then send me 6 brand-new novels every other month as
they come off the presses. Bill me at the low price of just $14.95*—
a 12% saving off the retail price. There is no minimum number of
books I must buy. I can always return a shipment and cancel at any
time. Even if I never buy another book from Gold Eagle, the 4 free
novels and the mystery bonus are mine to keep forever. 166 BPM BP7S

*Plus 69¢ postage and handling per shipment in Canada.

Name _____ (PLEASE PRINT)

Address _____ Apt. No. _____

City _____ State/Prov. _____ Zip/Postal Code _____

Signature (If under 18, parent or guardian must sign)

This offer is limited to one order per household and not valid to
present subscribers. Price is subject to change.

4E-SUB-1B